Acts of Vengeance

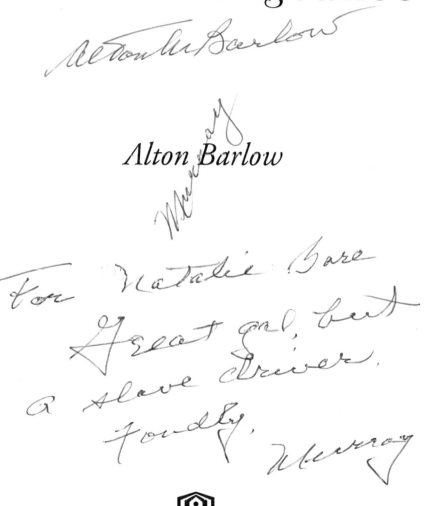

Alton Barlow

Bloomington, IN   authorHOUSE®   Milton Keynes, UK

AuthorHouse™
1663 Liberty Drive, Suite 200
Bloomington, IN 47403
www.authorhouse.com
Phone: 1-800-839-8640

AuthorHouse™ UK Ltd.
500 Avebury Boulevard
Central Milton Keynes, MK9 2BE
www.authorhouse.co.uk
Phone: 08001974150

First published by AuthorHouse 4/9/2007

ISBN: 978-1-4259-8242-3 (sc)

Library of Congress Control Number: 2006910504

Printed in the United States of America
Bloomington, Indiana

This book is printed on acid-free paper.

DEDICATION

This book is dedicated to the two most important and influential women in my adult life: my first wife, Carrie Grace Condon "Caddie" Barlow, (1922-1987), who, through High School and College, and active naval service that encompassed WW2 and the Korean War, blessed me with her unwavering encouragement and support of my ambitions while sacrificing her own as a talented pianist to raise our son and three daughters. After her death, I and the book were for ten years dormant.

And again I was blessed when I found that England had given up one of her daughters to Uncle Sam and I hastened to the claim. Since 1996 Joan Waters Gordner Barlow has been the light and cattle-prod along the path to getting this novel published.

I am grateful to God for blessing me with two such uniquely gifted and patient ladies in my life.

EPILOGUE

The want for vengeance
Springs from darkness in the mind
And grows as fungus, causing logic to go blind;
It's best that one not ever feel the need,
But if Vengeance is desired,
Pause until the heat's expired;
For every blow in fury cast
Becomes a wound upon oneself...at last.

Alton Barlow

PROLOGUE

In 1861 the coastal lands of southwestern Oregon were sparsely settled. Following several years of Indian hostilities with settlers and the U.S. Army, there existed a technical peace established in 1858 by vague treaties in an attempt to put the Indians on reservations. However, because of failed government policies and unfulfilled promises, numerous bands of renegade Indians left the reservations and roamed the area raiding settlers' farms, stealing raping and murdering. Many of the renegade groups included or were led by white outlaws, some of whom were deserters from the U.S. Army, an Army being committed eastward to a war between the states. Forts were being reduced to maintenance status, or abandoned; Civil law enforcement was almost non-existent. Few small towns could afford a sheriff and U.S. Marshals were generally located in the more populated areas around established cities. Civilians who had volunteered to serve without pay with the Army in Oregon, during numerous hostilities with the Indians, were granted land for homesteads as compensation for their service. Settlers, hoping for a peaceful and productive life in the Pacific Northwest frontier, found their biggest challenge to be survival.

CHAPTER ONE

Except for a shallow fog that hugged the shoreline, the first June morning of 1861 dawned bright and calm, a welcome change from the overcast that had accompanied stormy weather off Oregon's coast. Even before daylight, Robin heard the chirping of birds and knew it would be a sunlit day. She smiled as she lay watching the silver pre-dawn light fill her bedroom, then turn amber as the sun rose to do its magic.

Tossing aside her cover, Robin stood and stretched as she looked out the window to the ocean and along the sandy beach just below and a few hundred feet from the house. Although the fog along the shore obscured the pinnacle and haystack rocks that dotted the coastline, she thought she saw something move along the sand in that veil of mist, and stepped closer to the window, squinting, in an effort to sharpen the image of whatever it was that caught her eye. Her gaze revealed nothing. "I just imagined." she whispered, and turned away. Dressing quickly, she went to her parent's bedroom and rapped lightly on the door. "I'm up, Mama," she said, and went into the kitchen area to start the coffee brewing.

Lillie awoke and nudged her snoring husband. "Wake up, Adam. Coffee ready soon and there is much work to do."

Adam MacLean rolled toward his wife and flung his arm over her waist. "Ah, Lillie, it's still the wee of the mornin', and what work are you talkin' about?"

"The wagon, Adam Mac. You bring wagon home with supplies last night, but you drunk. Wagon need unloading. Please get up now," she added.

Adam half rose, then fell back grasping his head. "Oh Lord," he moaned, "Musta hit my head!"

He started to rise again, but was restrained by Lillie's hand on his chest. "Lay back," she told him, I'll get cold cloth." She took a brightly colored, pancho-like garment from a wall peg and put it on as she went to the kitchen. The coffee was brewing and Robin had gone to feed the animals. She soaked a towel in a basin of water, wrung it nearly dry and returned to Adam. Placing the towel across his forehead, she settled alongside him. "Rest for little while," she said. "Get up when coffee ready."

"All right," he muttered. "When coffee's ready."

"You promise?"

"I promise."

With her head on Adam's shoulder, Lillie ran her fingers through his mat of chest hair, graying now on his fifty year old body. She looked at the silver gray hair at his temple, and to his beard which, like the rest of the hair on his head, was only streaked with a few gray strands coursing through the black.

As he lay with his eyes closed, she ran her finger down the bridge of his nose to his chin. He kissed her finger as it brushed across his lips. Lillie was happy with her man, for she knew that he needed her. She knew that she was more to him than just "his squaw", for he was always gentle to her and always there for her when he was needed.

Closing her eyes, she thought of the four years they had been married. This burly, thick chested Canadian Scot was a trapper friend of Charlie Burns, her first husband and Robin's father. A little more than four years before, Charlie had left their cabin before dawn to tend his traps. Later that morning Adam, returning downstream from his trap line, found Charlie's body, face down in the stream with two arrows in his back, his horse, pack animal and weapons gone.

Left in the wilderness of northeast Oregon with a young child, her situation was grave. Adam immediately assumed care of her and little Robin, and began moving them back to the territory of her Nez Perce people. Never married, and at age forty-six, Adam Angus MacLean told her he had suddenly become aware of the lack of real purpose to his lonely existence and found that he liked having their company in his life.

Upon reaching The Dalles, on the Columbia River, Adam asked, rather, he *insisted,* that Lillie marry him. She had known him as Charlie's friend, and knew he was a good man. She recognized that he needed someone, and she was grateful for his protection. He became a dependable husband, a loving mate, and a caring step-father to Robin.

The image of Robin's father suddenly flickered into her mind; as suddenly, tears welled in her large, brown eyes. Abruptly, she got off the bed, brushed at her tears, and went to the kitchen.

At the wood-stove, she opened the fire-box and added a small log, then poured a cup of coffee from the brewing pot. From an urn she poured water into a small bucket. With coffee in one hand and the bucket in the other, she elbowed the door to their bedroom and set the cup on the bedside table. Adam, his eyes covered by the towel, lay quietly. "Coffee ready, Adam Mac, you get up now."

"Umm," he murmered, but was motionless.

"Adam, you not get up like you promised!"

"Umm. In a minute, Lil, in just another minute."

Lillie pulled the towel from across his eyes and, with both hands, held the bucket above his head. Adam looked up, wide-eyed, as Lillie slowly tipped the bucket. "Be-Jesus, Lil, I'm up, I'm up. Don't do it woman, I'm up!"

A smile made the only wrinkles in her round and gentle face, and beamed the love she felt for this boyish man she liked to tease. "Coffee here on table," she said. Putting the bucket aside she took a

3

brush to her hair.

Adam groaned as he stood up, "My head hurts, Lil. I think I musta bumped it good."

"Too much whiskey, Adam, you get drunk!"

"Ah, Arch and me just tippled a wee bit O' the dew."

As Robin approached the house, her chores completed, she stopped and looked carefully along the beach still cloaked in fog. The air was still and she could hear the lapping of waves and smell salt air mixed with the fragrance of the pine and cedar sentinels on their land. Seagulls circled aimlessly above the shore. Now and then one landed, pecked at something on the sand and fluttered off again to join its screeching friends. A crow, perched atop a nearby pine, cawed as though in disapproval of her presence. Robin strained her eyes to pierce the fog, saw nothing and went into the house, still uncertain, but thinking that if something strange did linger there, the warming sun would reveal it within the morning hours.

Nearly seventeen, Robin was a taller image of her Indian mother: lithe, athletic, abundantly female. Her hair, a long, dark-chocolate spill, framed a harmony of contrast with her dark blue eyes, bold and elegant as sapphires against her golden skin. She had her mother's practical sense, the wit of her Scottish sire, with the patience and endurance of her Nez Perce Indian heritage.

The stoutness of her breeding was reflected early by the ferocity of her will: When barely fifteen she escaped being raped by an overzealous Rogue River Indian who found her off her horse picking blackberries. The fact that the knife she wielded didn't permanently compromise his manhood was a stroke of luck for him.

In the kitchen, Robin looped an arm around her stepfather's neck as he sat. She filled his coffee cup, then kissed the bald spot atop his head. "Papa Mac's head is growing through his hair a little more each day," she said, then laughed. It was more a girlish giggle than a laugh, but it had a quality that touched one's ribs and tickled. Lillie laughed aloud, but Adam pouted, as though hurt by Robin's comedy.

"Now see here, lassie," he wimpered, "Be kind an' show a wee bit o' pity; I canna help what nature's done."

Robin hugged him again, and kissed his bearded cheek. "Oh now, Papa Mac", don't cry. Robin loves you anyway."

Laughing, Adam pulled her into his lap. "You know, Lil, you've brought me great happiness in our marriage, and this daughter of yours is a grand bonus. I think we should let her stay."

As their laughter faded, Adam scowled at his bowl of corn mush and the platter of biscuits and bacon. "Sure now, Lil, you're not meanin' this wee bit to be all we are to eat, this mornin'?"

"Work better if belly not full. Sun already up long time; supplies wait outside."

Adam took a deep breath and sighed. "Starvation is an awful way to die," he said.

Lillie fought back a smile as her daughter laughed. She wanted to joke with her family, but the morning was getting ahead of her and she wanted to get the wagon unloaded. "Please say blessing Adam. Food get cold."

Clearing his throat, Adam bowed his head. "Lord, bless our home and us, thy children. We thank thee for grantin' us this food, meager as it is for a man still growin' through his hair. Amen"

Lillie gasped as Adam grinned and Robin giggled. Her stern look of disapproval at each of them choked their amusement. "Adam Mac," she said, "I think it bad you make joke in prayer. Indians say Great Father hear only words from heart; joke come from head."

Her unwitting pun did not go unnoticed by Robin, who looked down at her at her plate and covered her mouth. It was no use. A muffled "hawff" escaped and Adam's laugh joined in.

Lillie shook her head in defeat. Her infrequent attempt to be stern had failed. She smiled. "I have blas... blasphem... ," Lillie struggled, "blas-phem-us, yes, blasphemus husband and silly child. I hope God not mad with us."

"Aw, Lil honey, I wasn't blasphemin' and God knows when a man jokes, right, Robin?"

Robin put a hand on her mother's arm. "I think Papa's right, Mama. Don't worry."

Lillie patted her daughter's reassuring hand. "All right, eat now. Much work to do."

But Lillie was troubled and ate in silence. She could not argue against Christian beliefs, and would not, even if she could. Although she attended Mission school for a year, and was married before to a white Christian, she found their beliefs confusing and often contradictory. She could read and write some english, but she could not understand much of what she tried to read from the Bible. Nor could she understand the Bible reading she had been exposed to at Mission School, and, on occasion, by Robin's father. Charlie, like Adam, was not seriously religious. But Lillie could not cast aside the fears and superstitions that were products of her Nez Perce upbringing, and often wondered if Charlie had not met his untimely and violent death because he had angered the Great Spirit. He, like Adam, was brave and adventurous but careless about giving thanks to God for his successes.

Lil-ah-he-Tupso was seldom afraid for herself. She was tall for an Indian woman, lean and strong. When just Robin's age she fought marauding Paiutes in a skirmish along the Snake River that took the life of the young brave to whom she was betrothed. She killed two Paiutes that awful morning, with knife and tomahawk before she was dropped by an arrow in her back and left for dead. The fact that she hadn't been scalped, or didn't die from her wound, was due in part to the raiders being more interested in taking horses than scalps, and due--even more perhaps--to the arrival of Charlie Burns at the scene.

He, with seven other trappers, including Adam MacLean, drove the remaining Paiutes away. The Nez Perce, under Chief Joseph, had always been friendly with the whites; in that instance their friendship was well rewarded. Charlie's skills at treating wounds saved Lillie's life. As she recovered, the bond between them grew into love, and they married. When their daughter was born, they named her Robin. Charlie had hoped for a son to call Robert, after the Scottish poet he claimed a kinsman, but he delighted in calling his daughter "Robbie Burns". The name was a difficult one for Lillie because R did not exist in her native language, and for a long time she called her baby "Lobbie".

It was dark when Adam returned with the wagon and supplies from Port Orford the previous evening, and he was in no condition to unload the wagon, or even to unhitch the horses, when he arrived. It was a hurried trip he'd made on the fringe of a storm, with his friend and neighbor, Archie Beeman, a grizzled old trapper, ex-cavalryman, and ex-marshal. Archie and his wife, Carilla, raised sheep on eighty acres south of the little town of Gold Beach, and about two miles north of MacLean's. At Beeman's ranch on the return trip, they had unloaded Archie's supplies then "popped a cork and tippled a wee one or two", as Adam put it. Fortunately, the horses knew the way home.

Adam would plan one or two more supply runs before October rains would make the roads unfit for a heavily loaded wagon. The trips were usually timed with the Hudson's Bay Company deliveries into Coos Bay to the north, and with the subsequent movement of goods to Port Orford outlets.

Adam was always well armed when he traveled, and Archie Beeman, an expert with guns, always accompanied him on the two day trip. Even so, Lillie worried about them being ambushed by "bad people". Only a few months had passed since Judd Wiggins and his pregnant wife were murdered on their farm just two miles from the MacLean's, and all their livestock taken. Renegades were suspected, but none had been caught.

After breakfast, Adam, Lillie and Robin began unloading the wagon. It was parked alongside the veranda that spanned the front of their house facing the sea, With a sack of flour under each arm, Adam stood shaking his head. "Damned if this stuff ain't gone up again since my last trip. Mind you, ladies, don't spill a drop; it's danged nigh dear as gold dust."

When Robin disappeared into the house with a load, Lillie took Adam's arm and whispered, "You find Chilkat blanket for Robin, like I asked?"

"Now Lil, I been meanin' to talk to you about that. Have you any mind as to how scarce them are these days, and how much they cost?"

"Did you *find one?*" Lillie wasn't interested in details. The blanket was to be a present for Robin on her seventeenth birthday, only a month away.

"Well now, after two hours of lookin' an' askin', I ran across this Vancouver man who once lived up north in that Alaska Territory around them Tlingits and he--"

"Did you *get* blanket, Adam Mac?"

"Sure, Lillie, I got it." He gave her a quick glance then picked up a sack of flour. "It's in the wagon, under the seat."

Lillie saw the scowl on his face and knew he was disappointed that she wouldn't hear him out. Like little boy, she thought, who can't find listener for exciting story. Smiling, she went to him and kissed his cheek. "You good man, Adam Mac. Want to hear story later."

"That cost me two dollars… two dollars *gold!*" He shouted back as he walked to the house.

Lillie climbed up and lifted the seat board. There it was, an elaborate, shawl-like, fringed blanket, woven of yarn spun from the wool of the mountain goat by Tlingit Indians, neighbors of the Eskimos. She was sure her daughter would like it, and closed the lid quickly as Robin came out from the house.

"What were you looking for under the seat, Mama?"

"Look for whiskey," she lied, "Sometime Adam have bottle there."

Robin was curious. She had overheard her mother and Papa Mac talking about bringing something back for her birthday gift, and she had never known her stepfather to keep whiskey in the wagon. She moved slowly, hoping her parents would go into the house with more supplies so she could get a peek under the wagon seat. But her mother was watching her.

"Come, Robin, you waste time," called Lillie.

She looked at her mother. "All right, Mama," she answered, and shifted her eyes to the beach. It was clearing fast as the fog was losing its battle with the sun. There was no wind. The sea was calm; the tide slack. The surf, thrashing and angry two days before, was now subdued and gentle. Swells, little more than a foot high, rolled tamely to the shore, spread themselves in a thin layer and disappeared into the sand. Robin, eager to delay leaving the wagon, slowly scanned the beach, hoping she might see whatever it was she thought she saw earlier that morning. Ah, suddenly there it was! Then, just as quickly her excitement faded. "Oh, it's only a log," she said aloud, "Just driftwood."

From the wagon bed, Robin picked up a sack and looked toward the house; her parents were inside. Slowly she raised the wagon seat, then heard her mother's angry call and the heavy lid fell with a slam. Robin, her eyes as big as a startled owl's, turned from her mother's scornful stare and looked at the sea. What she saw was not mere flotsom, but a boat, offshore about fifty yards. Excited now, she shouted: "Mama, Papa Mac, look! There's a little boat out there!"

Adam jumped onto the wagon. "Where is it, girl? I don't see it."

Robin pointed and shook her finger. "Look, Papa, to the right of

9

Tunnel Rock!"

"Yeah, I see it now," Adam shouted. "It looks empty. It might be hung up on that sand bar out there." He turned to Lillie. "See it Lil? Maybe I can get it."

"Wait 'til wagon unloaded, Adam. Boat still be there."

"No, Lil, tide might take it back out. Robin, fetch the horses and saddle ol' Magic while I get rope from the storeroom."

"Why you need horses, Adam?" asked Lillie.

"Cuz if she's fast on that bar I might need 'em to pull her off. You stay here, Lillie. Me an' Robbie can handle it."

Looking along the beach, Lillie saw movement from what at first appeared to be a driftwood log. For a moment she froze, fascinated, as the "log" took the form of a human lying on its side. Then slowly, a leg pulled up, an arm stretched out; a push and pull together moved it a foot or so along the sand. Her heart pounded like drumbeats in her ears. "Adam, hurry quick," she called. "There's a *man* on beach. I think he is hurt!"

CHAPTER TWO

Lillie's excited call brought Adam to her side. She took his arm and pointed to the beach. "Down there, You see? He not moving now. Looks like log!"

"Yeah, I see. You sure it moved?"

"Yes, I am sure, but not move now. Maybe he died."

"Maybe, Lil honey. Maybe he's off that boat out there. Maybe he's hurt, but maybe it's a trick to get us down there so his friends can ambush us and raid this place." Thirty years of living and trapping in the hostile western frontiers made caution second nature to Adam, and he thought of the Wiggins' murder. "Maybe it's no trick," he muttered, as though to convince himself, "but I'm takin' no chances."

"Lil, keep an eye on him. I'm goin' back in for the rope an' my rifle. When Robin gets here with the horses, have her tie 'em to the hitchrail and get in the house. Bar the doors and set up to repel raiders. Then keep an eye on me from out the window. When I get to that feller, if he's genuine hurt, or dead, I'll wave so you'll know it's no trick. If somethin' goes wrong, or if someone tries to get in the house, blow up that dead tree I got rigged as a distress signal to Archie."

In the house, Adam strapped on his pistol and Bowie knife, picked up his rifle, powder, percussion caps and a pouch of 54 calibre lead balls, got a coil of rope from the storeroom and went outside.

Robin was standing with the horses at the hitchrail.

"We're ready to go, Papa Mac."

Adam stuffed his rifle in the saddle scabbard and mounted his horse, a big Appaloosa he called Magic.

"Honeygirl, go on inside with your mother."

"What about the boat?"

"First things first, Robbie. We'll fetch it later, if she's still there."

"Quick, inside now, Robin!" Lillie called, and Adam rode off down the path to the beach.

Thirty feet from the motionless figure he stopped the horse and cocked his rifle. "If you can hear me, move a leg, slow like. There's a rifle pointin' at yuh, an' I'll right sure use it if I don't like what yuh do."

The body was on its side, legs outstretched, arms pulled in; it didn't move. The gray shirt and pants it wore were covered with sand and looked damp. Reddish blond hair covered the head in matted, sandy streaks.

"Once more I'm askin', move somethin' a wee bit, now."

An arm twitched. Adam figured it was an involuntary movement.

"Now, try movin' a leg."

The body did not move. Adam watched for a moment, then rode slowly closer and circled it once. The eyes were closed on what appeared to be a young man's face. Watching the eyes for movement, he dismounted, dropped Magic's reins, lowered the hammer on the rifle, and drew his pistol. With the rifle barrel he prodded the man's hip. There was no response. Putting the muzzle at the shoulder, he pushed, as though to roll the body onto its back. He saw no signs of tension: the neck was limber; the face moved only slightly off the sand. There were no weapons visible, but as a precaution, Adam ran the rifle's barrel over the clothes, from shoulder to naked foot, and he probed around the shirt and trousers near the waist.

Nearly convinced now, that the man wasn't faking, Adam returned his rifle to its saddle scabbard. Pistol in hand, he knelt at the head and pressed the fingers of his free hand to the man's neck. The flesh was cool, but a slow, shallow pulse told him that life remained. He raised the shirt and ran his hands along the ribs and back in search of wounds, and there were none.

Rolling the body onto its back, Adam brushed sand from the mouth, nostrils and eyes. With his thumb he raised an eyelid and saw the pupil contract in the light. He unbuttoned the shirt and checked the chest and the other side for wounds; again, he found none, just an empty knife sheath on the belt. From the youthful, lightly whisked face, well muscled chest and body size, Adam judged him to be eighteen to twenty, about six foot, lean, maybe one-hundred fifty pounds, no more.

Adam looked back toward the house and waved. "The poor lad's prob'ly near dead from thirst," he said aloud, and pulled the body into a sitting position. He manoeuvered the youth's head and one arm onto his shoulder and, with a grunt, stood up. With the limp body upright, he slipped his arm under the knees, lifted and carried the boy to his horse. "Either you're over one fifty, or I'm gettin' weak," he blurted out as he boosted the body up and placed him belly down across the saddle.

"Easy now, Magic, ol'boy. We've got ourselves a passenger so I'll be doublin' on yuh goin' back." With that, he swung himself up behind the saddle and put the big Appy into a fast walk back to the ranchhouse.

Lillie and Robin were on the porch, rifles in hand, when Adam returned shouting orders as he approached:

"Bring water, an' a cot, an' a blanket , too."

"He not dead, then, Papa Mac?" Robin's remark was more of a statement than a question.

"Well, if he didn't die on the ride up here, he might in a wee moment if he don't get some water!"

Robin turned and hurriedly followed Lillie into the house.

Adam lifted the unconscious man from the horse and sat him at the top step of the porch, legs outstretched down the steps, then sat beside him to give support. The youth's head flopped limply, chin to chest. Robin came with the water in a bucket and handed Adam a cup.

"Hold his head up, please, Robbie."

Kneeling at the man's back, Robin held his head between her hands. Adam poured some water over the face to wash away the sand and hoped the cool water would start the revival process. It did. There was slight movement of the mouth and a twitch of the eyelids. Adam poured another cup of water over the head and down the back. Facial muscles wakened in a display of flickering smiles and grimaces. Brows twitched, the nose wrinkled, the body shuddered. An arm raised slightly, then fell. Eyelids snapped open and shut, then lifted slowly, as though straining against weights.

Adam held the cup to young man's lips and spoke softly. "You're safe now, lad, you're safe here." Adam felt tension in the back muscles. "If you understand me, just relax now. I'm gonna tip a wee bit o' water to your mouth. Don't try to drink it, just spit it out."

Hazel eyes, full open now, first startled wide, then relaxed as Adam tipped the cup and let a spoonful of water trickle through parched lips.

"Don't swallow, lad, just swish it 'round then spit. There's plenty for drinkin'." He tipped him forward a bit. "Spit now, m'lad."

"Obediently, water oozed through the lips and dribbled down the chin.

"Good lad. Same now, once more, then yuh can take a bit for yourself."

The cup tipped against slightly parted lips; a light swish followed, then the spit, slightly stronger now, as the water cleared the chin. The lad's eyes swung to Adam.

"You may have been to hell, laddie," said Adam, "but you're back now, an' that's what matters. Here's another draught o' the water, an' this one you can drink."

After three swallows, Adam pulled the cup away. "That's enough for now, lad; you can have more again soon. Meantime, I'm gonna put yuh on a cot nearby. Just relax an' I'll carry yuh there."

With fatherly gentleness, Adam carried him to the cot Lillie had prepared on the shady veranda. "Just rest here now," he said, "and in a bit yuh can have more water. But just a wee bit at a time, mind yuh lad, so's not to make yuh sick. And then some food. By Jesus, yuh look half starved, yuh do."

The young man's eyes shifted to Robin, who now stood at Adam's side, looking down, an expression of concern on her face. His lips parted, and moved as though forming words he could not utter.

"Don't talk now," said Adam, "there'll be time for that later." A shaky hand lifted from the cot, then fell back. "If it's more water you're wantin', laddie, you'll have to wait a few more minutes, or yuh won't be keepin' it down."

Perhaps it was the way Adam said 'down'--it sounded like 'doon'-- that brought the lad's eyes wide open and caused a weak, but definite smile to stretch the parched lips. It was one of the few words and phrases that Adam used that revealed his Scottish heritage. When his eyes closed again it seemed as though all tenseness left the young man, and his head sank farther into the pillow. Adam was sure he heard a sigh.

"I think he understood everything you said to him, Papa Mac, don't you?"

Adam pulled at his beard and gazed for a moment at the figure on the cot before answering. "Aye, Robin, that he did, that he did. And I'm thinkin'--" He was about to go on with what he was thinking, when Lillie spoke.

"I will fix lamb and barley broth," she said, "and he maybe can eat something, yes?"

"That's good, Lil. I'm thinkin' that next to the pipes, a scotch broth will be the best thing for him."

"What about the boat, Papa Mac?"

"Bonnie Jesus! I plumb forgot to see if it's still there. My mind's been on the lad."

"Boat same place, Adam."

"Lil, if you'll mind the lad, here, me an' Robbie will try to fetch the boat. It just might be the lad's." Robin, fetch me that rope layin' on the storeroom floor."

"Be careful, husband. Many rocks in surf. Boat not worth you get hurt."

"Hell, Lillie, surf's so calm I'll take the canoe out to the boat."

Catching her arm as she started into the house, Adam turned Lillie around. He saw concern in her large, expressive eyes. She feared the ocean, he knew that. Drawing her gently to him, he kissed her, then held her by her shoulders at arm's length. "Be sure, now, I'll be careful. You're the best reason I've ever had to be careful. Understand?"

"*Kumtux, nika man.*" she answered, in the Chinook jargon. Smiling, she ran a caressing hand over his beard. He turned his head into her hand and kissed her palm.

"You're such a beauty, Lil-Ah-He-Tupso," he said, looking into her eyes. "I thank the Lord every day that you're with me." His emotion embarrassed him, and he gave a little cough and started to turn away.

Lillie threw her arms around his waist and laid her head against his chest. "I love you, Adam Mac, forever."

Her forehead was cool to his lips.

It was Robin that broke up their moment of affection, noisily clearing her throat. "I have the rope, Papa." Her face beamed a smile as they turned to her.

"Good girl. And it's time we get movin', too." He took the heavy coil of rope that Robin held. "Mount up, Honeygirl. Let's go salvage a boat!"

CHAPTER THREE

As they took the path leading to the beach, Robin rode alongside Adam. "What did you mean, Papa Mac, when you said 'next to the pipes, the broth would be the best thing for him'? you didn't mean pipes for smoking, did you?"

"No, I meant the bagpipes, girl. The world's most glorious instrument of music is the bagpipe, to an Irishman or a Scot."

"I don't think I've ever heard one," she said.

"I reckon not, in this part of the world. Exceptin' the Scotch and the Irish, most folks think of 'em as instruments of torture." He looked over at Robin and laughed. "My mother wouldn't let my father play his bagpipe at home; he could only play it on his fishin' boat. That worked out all right 'cuz it kept the other fishermen from crowdin' him."

"I'd like to hear one," she said.

"Aye, me too. That's 'cuz we're both Scotch, to a half."

"Then you must think that the young man is Scotch or Irish?"

"Aye, somehow I have the feelin' he's a Scot."

"Aye, me too," she said.

Adam grinned as he looked over at Robin. She rode looking straight ahead, her lips pursed as though fighting back a grin of her own.

At the bottom of the path, he stopped his horse and dismounted. Throwing aside two large pine boughs, he uncovered a buffalo-hide canoe, stowed bottom up. He turned it over, picked up the two paddles that lay underneath and put them inside along with the coil of rope.

With the bow line in hand, he mounted his horse and towed the canoe across the sand to a point at the water's edge, directly opposite the stranded boat. Dismounting, he took one end of the rope and fastened it to the saddle horn. He then tightened the cinch on Magic, checked the breast-strap and turned the horse around to face away from the water.

"How can I help, Papa Mac?"

"Well now, what I'm aimin' to do is take this rope out to that boat. I reckon it'll reach her, and then some. Then I'll make the line fast to the boat. When I wave my arm, lead Magic forward till the slack's outa the line, then stand aside, clear of them forelegs. Hang onta them reins, girl, but give 'em slack so's not to start him turnin'. Then just holler *Go* at him an' he'll do the rest. When she comes free of the bar, if she does, trot him on up the beach to the base of the hill, there. If she ain't beached by then, you can start haulin' on that line. In no time I should be on the beach to help. If anything goes wrong, cut the line."

"What if Magic can't pull it off?"

Adam wiped the sweat already beaded on his brow. "Then we'll just have to hitch up Feather to help. If that won't do it, we'll wait for the tide to rise a bit and lift 'er off. That might be the easy way, but we gotta worry about 'er broaching in the waves that'll be rollin' in with the tide. It's slack now and there ain't much movement. Ready girl?"

"I'm ready Papa. Be careful of the rocks out there."

He looked at his stepdaughter and smiled. "Danged if you ain't just like your Ma."

"Well," she paused and smiled back, "I love you, too." Adam pushed the canoe into the surf and stepped aboard. With an expertise gained in thirty years of trapping on wild rivers and streams, he moved the canoe with strong, sure strokes through the surf and over the small swells that curled into timid breakers near the beach.

In less than a minute he approached the bow of the stranded boat. As he grabbed the bow ring his nostrils filled with the sticky, gut-twisting smell of death warmed in the sun.

His stomach spasmed in dry wretching. He held his breath and swallowed hard against rising vomit. From his kneeling position in the canoe he could not see over the bow of the boat, raised as it was on the sand bar. Easing the canoe along the boat's port side, he secured his bow line to the oar lock and stood, hands on the boat's gunwale to steady himself against the rise and fall of the swells rolling toward the shore.

She was a double ender; a whale boat type. Sixteen to eighteen feet long, he guessed. There were no oars in the boat. What remained of the mast was a splintered stub. The jibsail lay in a heap at the bow, still attached to a ringbolt on the stem. Adam was familiar with the rig and figured it to be from a British merchantman. It was the kind the officers came ashore in from anchored ships and were pulled by oarsmen when not under sail.

His eyes watered and his stomach heaved in dry nausea as he stepped into the boat, ankle deep in water. A small, oaken water cask floated against his leg. He picked it up; it was empty.

He stepped over a thwart and moved toward the bow. Picking up an edge of the jibsail he flung it back revealing a stout chest, of medium size, secured with a heavy padlock. The terrible stench was stronger here. Slowly, he lifted the canvas sail. The putrid odor that escaped was more than he could stand. Lurching to the starboard gunwale, he vomited over the side.

"Holy Jesus!" he shouted. Taking a deep breath, he wiped his mouth and turned again to the canvas. Taking folds in both hands, he threw it aside. A single body lay on its side. A navy blue coat, with four tarnished gold bands encircling each sleeve, was spread across the torso. A red-bearded face, blue grey in death, stared with sunken eyes. Under the head, as a pillow, lay the Captain's hat.

As he pulled the canvas back over the body, his thoughts returned to the lad he'd found on the beach. "Sure does appear there's been a ship go down," he muttered, "I wonder where."

Returning to his canoe, he cast off and paddled around the boat, assessing her position on the bar. She rested on the sand in about a foot of water from the bow to midship. From that point the bar steepened sharply into deeper water. It was as though she rested with her bow on a sand fulcrum. The stranding was almost in the middle of the sand bar that stretched for about a half mile, parallel to the beach and fifty to sixty yards offshore. Rocks, jutting above the surface of the water, abounded at each end and beyond. No getting her around the bar, he judged. He'd have to pull her over as originally planned.

"Well," he murmured, "it's gonna take one helluva lot a tuggin'." He wondered if maybe he should have hitched up Feather, too. "Well, hell, without a saddle on 'er she'd get rope burned for sure," he decided, and waved his arm at Robin.

He watched as Robin led the big Appy forward until the rope came taut at the saddle horn, then he heard her command: "Go, Magic, *go*! Come on boy, *pull*!"

Obediently, the horse strained against the rope. The boat moved a foot or so, then stopped.

"Hold a minute," Adam yelled, "maybe I can help!" He tied a loop at the end of the canoe's bow line and slipped it over his left arm. Removing his boots, he eased himself out of the canoe and onto the sand bar, alongside the boat. "All right now, *go!*" he shouted, waving an arm. "Move him out!"

In short, lunging, rabbit-like jumps, Magic threw his twelve-hundred pounds against the tow-line. Taking hold of the gunwale, Adam tugged and rocked the boat to break suction on the bottom. Slowly, the craft moved again, inching its way up the sandy obstruction until, finally, the bow tilted downward into deeper water. He heard the water in the boat rush forward, easing the weight in the stern.

Magic was gaining ground with each lunge. As the next swell rolled by, the stern was lifted and the boat slid off the edge of the bar.

"She's free!" Adam shouted. "She's free and floating, Robin. Haul 'er in smartly!"

His canoe, with its bow line still attached to his arm, had drifted beachward to the end of its eight foot tether. As he pulled the craft toward him he felt the sand slip away under his feet and took a step back for firmer footing. When he put his foot down it was swallowed to his ankle by the sand.

Pulling his foot out took more effort than he'd expected. As his foot came free, the surface suddenly gave way under his other foot and his leg quickly sank above the ankle. His heart pounded as he tried to get on firmer ground, only to have it give way. Quicksand! At first he refused to believe it, but he could no longer ignore the reality.

Jerking on the bow line, he made a frantic grab for the canoe as it glided toward him. Grabbing it by the bow he worked it along to midships, then hooked both elbows over the gunwale.

The sand was at mid-calf on both legs and he felt himself inching down. Fighting panic, he let the canoe support part of his weight as he pulled his right leg free. The canoe tipped dangerously and Adam brought the gunwale to his armpit and pressed his hand against the bottom to keep the craft from capsizing.

The water was almost to his hips as he began to lift his left leg from the sand, giving more of his weight to the canoe. Slowly, the sand released its sucking grip and as it did he searched gingerly with his other foot for a firmer area. He knew that the canoe, tipped as it was, could bear no more of his weight without capsizing.

"Dear God," he muttered, "If you're jokin', I've enough of it."

A swell raised the canoe, but his left leg, still shin deep in the sand, anchored his body and the canoe began to overturn with the increased weight. Reaching upward, he caught the gunwale directly overhead.

With a downward thrust of his free right foot against the bottom, he made a jumping motion. The swell passed; the water, shallowing behind the swell, gave him more leverage. As he pushed the gunwale down, he slid his hand to the canoe bottom and returned the craft to an angle of tilt that again supported part of his weight.

He felt both feet being drawn deeper again and fought against a growing sense of panic. He knew that he was in extreme danger of drowning and felt a rising sense of hopelessness. "Stay calm," he told himself, "you've beaten bad odds before."

With renewed determination, he jerked up the ankle-deep right foot, quickly put it down again and pulled the left leg free. As his foot came out of the sand he gave a hop, at the same time twisting his body and pulling the canoe under him. The craft righted as he rolled onto his back. "Thank you, God!" he said, breathing hard through clenched teeth and looking at the sky. "I thought for awhile you weren't jokin'." The whole event had taken less than a minute, he guessed, but he felt very tired.

He sat up and found that he was facing seaward. One paddle was still in the canoe, but his boots were gone. Grasping the paddle, he swung the canoe around and paddled toward the boat now resting on the shore.

Adam beached the canoe and towed it to the dry sand where Robin stood with the sweating Magic. She had already removed the rope from his saddle and held it in a coil on her arm. From her puzzled look, he figured she knew something went wrong out there.

"Good job, Honeygirl. You 'n old Magic here did just fine."

"Thank you, Papa Mac" she answered, "YOU did fine too." But the expression on her face did not change. "What happened out there? And what's that awful smell?"

"Nothin' much happened, Robin honey, I just had a wee bit a trouble gettin' back into that ornery canoe. Gettin' clumsy in my old age, I reckon. As for the smell, well now, I'm hopin' it ain't me."

"Oh no, I mean..." She looked at the boat.

"Ah, I know what you mean, girl. I'm sorry to say there's a dead man in there. I'd guess he's been dead two, maybe three days."

"How'd he die, Papa?"

"Dunno." Adam turned and looked at the boat. "Exposure, maybe. Driftin' around, no food, no water. Musta been a shipwreck somewhwere near. Boat's been in heavy weather, mast busted an' all."

"What're you going to do?"

He didn't answer right away. His brow furrowed as he looked at the boat and thought of what a nasty job it was going to be, handling the decaying corpse. But he'd done it before, and visions of other burials crept into his mind. When finally he answered, his voice was soft--hardly more than a whisper--and there was a sadness in it. "Bury him, I reckon."

Squinting, he glanced quickly at the sun. "Must be high on to noon. We'll be needin' food an' I'll be needin' a shovel, so let's be gettin' back now. Things'll keep here for awhile; leastwise, I doubt they'll get worse."

CHAPTER FOUR

Arms loaded with supplies from the wagon, Lillie was on the porch steps when she heard the horses coming up the path from the beach. Robin was first to appear at the crest of the hill and she loped her horse to the wagon. Lillie sensed her daughter's excitement and expected a flood of words as Feather slid to a stop.

"Mama, there's a dead man in the boat! The smell is awful."

"That is not happy news," was all Lillie said. She watched intently as Adam rode up, dismounted and tied Magic to the hitching rail. From the porch she had seen Adam reach the stranded boat in his canoe, and looked on anxiously as he stood on the sandbar helping to free the boat. After that, she busied herself cooking, bringing supplies in from the wagon and tending to their patient. It bothered her to see him in the ocean. She did not like the sea and feared its changing moods. She was happy now that he had returned but wondered why he wasn't wearing his boots.

"Well, we got the boat ashore all right, Lillie honey. She was a mite fast on that bar, but ol' Magic here, an' Robin too, did fine; you shoulda seen 'em."

"My heart is glad you are back, Adam Mac. Robin told me of the dead man. Was he young or old? How did he die?"

"Well, middle age, I guess… 'bout like me. Prob'ly died a thirst, starvation or exposure… all three, maybe. Might be that the lad can tell us when he comes 'round. How's he doin'?"

"He breaths stronger now; sleeps plenty." She looked at Adam's bare feet. "Where are boots, *Nika man*?" she asked, mixing in the Chinook

25

jargon they often used when joking with each other. She didn't want her question to sound nagging, but she was curious. It was not like Adam to be barefooted outside of his bed or bath.

"Lost 'em, in the water; old ones anyway." He answered without looking at her, busying himself instead with the unsaddling of Magic. Lillie had the feeling that his thoughts turned black over the boots, so she would ask no more questions about them--not of him, anyway.

"Come inside and change clothes, Adam. Robin will care for horses."

"Just let me get this old devil unsaddled, Lil honey. Smells like you got bread bakin'. I'm dang close to starved after that wee breakfast this mornin'." He looked at her and grinned. As he put the saddle and blanket on the porch rail he turned to Robin. "HOW 'bout you, Honeygal, hungry?"

Robin stood at Feather's head, stroking the mare's neck and looking toward the cot on the porch. Seconds passed, as though she hadn't heard, before she answered. "No, papa, just thirsty. You go eat. I'll take the horses to the corral." She turned to Lillie. "Did you talk to him, Mama? Did he say who he is, or anything?"

"I not ask question of sick man. He try to speak when I gave him broth. I tell him stay quiet, talk later." Lillie moved to the door. "Come now, husband, change clothes. Robin, hurry with horses. I will put food on table now."

"Spare a minute," Adam whispered, "and I'll just have a look at the lad."

Lillie watched as Adam knelt beside the cot and studied the boy's face. He pressed a finger under the lad's jaw, then palmed his forehead. After a moment he returned to where Lillie stood. Taking her by the arm, he led her inside. "Pulse is stronger now," he said quietly. "Color's better, too. And no fever that I can tell. I'll change now and have somethin' to eat. Then I've got to bury the poor devil that's in the boat."

Finished with his meal, Adam rose and put on his hat. "That was mighty good, Lil. Now I'm off to be grave digger. Damn, it's a chore I'd rather be without."

Robin, feeling a duty to ask, but hoping the answer would be 'no', summoned her courage as Adam reached the door. "Will you need me to help, Papa Adam?"

He turned and smiled. "You're a good trooper to ask, Honeygirl, and thank you kindly. But I can handle it myself. You'd best be stayin' here to help your Ma put the supplies in."

"Where will you make grave?" asked Lillie.

"I'll find a place on dry land above the beach. I think that bein' a sailorman like he was, he might like a view of the sea, even though it's prob'ly what killed him."

"What about prayers for him, shouldn't there be prayers at the grave?" Robin was surprised at herself that she thought of it. "He might be Christian," she added.

"Right you are, lass. But, Christian or not, we'll give him a respectable send-off. We'll do it tomorrow; 'twill be the Sabbath and a proper day for it."

"I think it's supposed to be done when he's put in the ground, Papa Mac."

Adam looked at the floor and shook his head. In the few seconds of silence that followed, Robin worried that she had said too much. "I'm sorry, Papa, I wasn't trying ... I was just..." She was glad when he interrupted.

"Oh no, you're right, Robin. But, considerin' his condition, I think the Almighty, and all the livin' creatures hereabout, will forgive me fer coverin' him up before the service. Then too, by the morrow the young lad may be strong enough to join in." He put his arm around Robin and kissed her cheek. "I'll be gettin' my shovel an' things now."

As she watched Adam leave, Robin's thoughts swung to the young man on the cot. Curiosity excited her and nibbled at her patience. "Mama", she said, rising from the table, "maybe he's awake now and can tell us something. I'll go see."

"Wait, Robin," said Lillie, "let boy rest and get stronger. He was near death only few hours ago and may still be in its path."

"I won't wake him, Mama. I was just going to see if he's awake." Robin rose from the table.

"If he is awake, tell me; he will need more broth. If he sleeps, bring in supplies from wagon. I have much to do here."

Robin's moccasined feet moved her quietly to the cot. She listened to his deep and even breathing. He seemed more relaxed now, she thought. And though his cheeks cupped in too much and gave his face a hungry look, she judged him handsome, strong and good. On his left cheekbone she noticed now a scar, vee shaped, two purple lines beneath his whiskers, pointing like an arrowhead at his nose. It was an old scar, that she could tell. It seemed to add a bit of mystery to his face. There must be a story there to tell, she thought, and wondered how he got it. On sudden impulse she clasped the silver cross that hung from her neck on a strand of obsidian beads, and whispered: "Please, Holy Father, he is so young and nice looking, do not let him die. Make him well and strong again, soon." Certain that her prayer would be answered, Robin went to the wagon to bring in the remaining supplies.

Looking first toward the porch to be sure her mother wasn't watching, Robin raised the wagon seat. Rusty hinges squealed and she lowered it quickly, after a hurried peek revealed nothing of interest. The colorful something she'd caught a glimpse of that morning, was gone.

She heard the bray of a mule and smiled. "Mama," she called, "It's Uncle Archie! He's riding up the canyon road." She covered her mouth as she remembered their patient and hoped she hadn't wakened him. Looking toward the cot she saw no movement. Satisfied, she jumped off the wagon and ran to where the spur from the canyon road met the MacLean property, about a hundred yards east of the house. She would meet Archie there, as she had many times in the past four years. He would give her a ride on Toad, "the best egg-suckin' mule the Army ever had," as Archie would say.

She hoped Archie's wife, Carilla, wasn't along. She liked 'Rilla Beeman, but if she was with Archie then Toad would be harnessed to their buck-wagon, and riding on the back of the wagon wasn't as much fun as riding behind Archie on the mule. She liked to practice the rescue mount and then, when Archie slowed the mule to a walk, she'd slide back on Toad's rump and he'd buck a little as he walked along. It would make her and Archie laugh, and folks who saw it always laughed and said it looked funny.

Her excitement peaked as Archie came into view a quarter mile down the tree lined path. He was riding Toad and spurred the big mule to an easy lope as he returned Robin's wave. Hiking her cotton skirt to mid-thigh, she raised her left arm. As Archie rode by they locked left arms and, in a single motion,

Robin swung upward and took a seat behind him. Reining the mule to a walk, Archie spoke over his shoulder: "Well now, Robbie, that was just about the slickest mount I ever seed you do."

Grinning, Robin slipped her arms around Archie's chest and gave him a tight hug that seemed to squeeze up the odor of tobacco and mule sweat. She knew she'd made a smooth mount but a compliment from Archie was a rare gift. "Thanks, Uncle Archie, but you always make it easy with the lift you give me." And she meant it. Archie admitted to being fifty-three; in Robin's eyes that was terribly old to have the strength and abilities Archie Beeman had.

"What's been goin' on at your place, Robbie? Yer Pa got all them supplies tucked away yet?"

Robin gave him a rapid account of the day's events. Even before she'd finished, Archie had Toad in a gallop.

"Well, by golly, that's sure the dangdest, ain't it? You slip off at the house, Robbie. I'm goin' on down to see if I can give Adam a hand. My respects to your Ma. Tell her I'll be back with Adam when the buryin's done. Rilla wants to borry a beadin' needle or two."

Taking a sack of flax seed from the wagon, Robin carried it to the porch. The sound of a throat being cleared was more than enough to divert her from her chore. Quickly, she put down the sack and went to the cot. His eyes, the whites still bloodshot, looked up at her; his hand moved shakily across his mouth, then rested on his chest. "Where... where am I?"

The strength of his voice surprised her and it was a few seconds before she could answer. "You're at MacLean's... our ranch... near Gold Beach. Who are you? What happened?" Her hand went to her mouth. She was angry at herself for letting those questions slide from thought to tongue; she felt awkward and childish. "I mean, how are you... how are you feeling?" It seemed now that he was studying her and she thought he smiled slightly. She felt her cheeks redden and a faint buzz sounded in her ear as she grew self conscious under his gaze. She looked at the doorway to the house. "Mama, he's awake. Come quick!"

At the sound of his voice she turned back to him, her eyes wide with interest.

"I am... Franklin Ross," he said, sounding as though he pushed the words out with the air from his lungs. "Who are you?"

"I... I'm Robin. May... maybe you shouldn't talk. You need to... to rest, to get..." Her heart was pounding and her thoughts were stumbling over words. "... strong again. My mother will... ," she paused, looking at the door, hoping her mother heard her call and would come soon.

"Please, I want... to talk." His hand raised off his chest and he stretched out his arm as though to reach for her. "Where... where is this?"

"You are in America; Oregon, America." Suddenly, Robin felt tension at her eyelids and realized she must have been staring at him, wide-eyed, the whole time. She felt foolish and let her brows relax.

"You... have... bonnie eyes," he said.

Heat surged to her neck and cheeks as his eyes moved downward, then to the top of her head before returning to her face. She'd heard 'bonnie' used before by her father and Adam. She smiled and wished that her heart would quit pounding so.

"Are you... Indian?" His eyebrows raised as he asked.

The question surprised her. The smile left her face and for a moment she couldn't gather her thoughts nor hear above her pulse, drumming in her ears. The words of a teacher at the mission school in Walla Walla flooded her mind: "Why, you're neither Indian nor white, little girl, you're 'sitkum siwash', a half-breed!"

She looked away with unfocused eyes, not really seeing. "Sitkum siwash," she said, her voice barely above a whisper, "Sitkum siwash." She felt like she was far away from her body.

"I... I don't understand."

His voice jarred her to reality. Briefly, she looked into his eyes, then beyond them, her mind still detached from her body. "Half Indian," she said. Her voice sounded far away to her. Lifting her head abruptly, she looked away, breaking the trance, and took a step back from the cot. She was shaky inside, almost sick. She felt no anger, yet his question bothered her. Why? she wondered. When she looked down at him again he was smiling. It's a nice smile, she thought, and it warmed her. The shakiness left her as he spoke again:

"The man... the one who brought me here, is he your father?"

Robin heard his voice waver a bit and knew he was weakening. Not wanting to give answers which might need further explanation, she gave a simple "yes" as Lillie approached with a bowl of broth. "And here is my mother," she added, "with more food for you. We can talk more later." Turning to Lillie, she blurted "Mama, his name is Franklin... ah... Rose, I think." She was embarassed by her uncertainty and gave him a quick glance.

"Ross it is, Frank Ross." he smiled again, that nice smile, and his voice seemed stronger. "Please," he said, extending an arm to Robin, "would you mind... to help me sit?"

Hesitating, Robin looked at her mother.

"Help him," Lillie said, nodding her head. "Make better way for him to eat. But keep hold, he is not strong yet."

Robin took his hand and helped him rise. As he swung his feet over the side of the cot, she sat beside him and braced him with her arm around his shoulders. They were broader than she expected and he smelled to her like sea weed that had washed ashore.

Lillie knelt and placed a spoonful of broth to his lips. Robin watched and studied the profile of his face. A good face, she thought. Gentle mouth, strong chin, straight nose--a bit too large, perhaps. Thin face--too thin--that's what made his nose look large, she decided. His eyebrows were thick and reddish brown, darker than his head of red-blond hair still matted with salt and sand. Once he turned and caught her gaze, and when he turned away again to take the broth, she found that she had held her breath. It was his eyes, she guessed. Never had she seen the like--gray as polished steel, with inlaid slivers of brown and green. They held her so it took strong will to break away.

After the last spoonful, Lillie rose from her knees and, with a small cloth, wiped his mouth and chin. "How you feel now?"

"Better, Ma'am." He looked for a second at Robin--she was sure that his mouth quivered--then at Lillie. "I canna..." his voice faltered and he cleared his throat. "I cannot thank you enough. I..." Lillie put a finger gently to his lips.

"No more talk now. Talk plenty later. You rest now."

As Robin eased his back to the cot, Lillie lifted his feet then covered him with the blanket.

"Wait," he said as they were leaving him, "there was a boat, aground off-shore. Do you know of it?"

Robin looked at her mother, wondering if she would answer. A slight nod from Lillie was her approval to speak. "My father got the boat onto the beach. There was a…" She looked again at her mother, wondering if she should mention the dead man. she was relieved as Lillie spoke for her: "There was dead man in boat. Adam, my husband, is making grave for him now."

"That… that is good," he said, and closed his eyes. His body seemed to relax as though suddenly at ease.

"Was he a friend?" asked Robin.

"Aye, that he was. He was my father."

CHAPTER FIVE

Adam's weary footsteps drummed heavily on the stairs to the veranda. At the top he turned and looked back at Archie. "C'mon in Arch. Sure a wee tipple o' the sauce is well deserved by us both, wouldn't yuh say?"

Leaning against the wagon, Archie mopped his head and face with a large kerchief. "Well, I reckon. Yuh know, I been tryin' ta think what it was I come here fer in the first place. Somethin' Rilla wanted." Halfway up the stairs he paused. "Well, if'n the whiskey'll loosen my brain like it loosens my tongue, mebbe it'll come ta me." He turned, and in rapid sequence, spat a stream of brown juice then ejected a wad of tobacco that traveled twenty feet before it hit the ground. "Can't stay long, though, still got some chorin' t'do."

"Shhhaaw!" whispered Adam, "Forgot the lad on the cot there." He tip-toed to the cot and Archie came quietly to his side. Adam listened for a moment to the steady, deep breathing, before going into the house.

At the table, he poured whiskey then raised his glass. "To the Captain, whoever he was. May God rest his soul."

"To the Captain," responded Archie.

Lillie entered the kitchen as Adam refilled the glasses. "Hello, Archie. It is good you help Adam make grave." She put an arm around his shoulders and laid a small package on the table. "Here are needles for Rilla."

Archie slapped his hand on the table. "That's it! That's what I couldn't remember ta git--a danged beadin' needle! How'd you know that, Lillie?"

She smiled. "You tell Robin on ride in. She tell me."

"Well now, I plumb fergot that, too." He took a sip of whiskey. "Yuh know, that Robbie's a gal that's sure gonna turn heads. Too bad there ain't more folks her age aroun' these parts. Heard tell a family with a couple boys been hagglin' wi' the bank about the Wiggins' place. Mebbe they'll be of an age." He downed his whiskey. "By the way, ain't seen her since we come back from diggin'. Where might she be?"

"Feeding animals," answered Lillie. "You find good place for grave?"

"Oh, I think he'd like it, right above where we hauled in the boat. Archie here said some nice words over him." Adam turned to Archie. "They were right nice words, Arch, considerin' not knowin' him, an' all--not even his name."

"Boy say dead man his father, Adam."

Archie sucked air through his teeth. "Gee Hosaphat! That's a right hard ride fer the boy now, ain't it?"

"Might explain why he kept the body in the boat 'stead a pitchin' it overboard," said Adam. "Hopin' to give his pa a decent burial."

"Where'd that chest come from that's down by the wagon?" asked Robin as she walked in and took a chair at the table. "And what's in it?"

"Drug it up here from the boat, Honeygirl," said Adam, "It's locked tighter 'n a clam. Reckon now we should wait to see what the lad's got to say of it a'fore we break it open."

"You not find key on Captain?"

"No, and I don't think the lad's got one on him, or I'd a' noticed it when I went over him for weapons down on the beach. A key to the lock on *that* chest, would be of good size."

"Is it heavy?" asked Robin.

"Oh, it be middlin' heavy," said Archie, "but not like it were full a' gold, or silver, --or a pirate's treasure," he added with a chuckle. Rising, he picked up the package. "I'll be goin' now, folks. What time tomorrow will yuh be takin' the lad to see where we planted his pa?"

Adam looked at Lillie. "About noon?"

She nodded. "I think noon good time."

"Then Rilla 'n me'll be there ta pay respects an' mebbe moan a Christian hymn or two along with yuh, how's that?"

"That's mighty fine, Arch. But if you're gonna sing aroun' Toad, yuh'd best plug his ears, or he'll dang sure head for the high country."

Archie stopped at the door, turned, and furrowed his brow. "Now that just ain't a'tall likely, Adam. That mule's done learnt me all he knows about singin', an' yuh should hear the purty du-ets we do. Why, they'll bring tears to yer eyes."

Minutes later, the bray of a mule was heard in the distance, followed by a loud sing-song *Amen!*

Frank awoke to their laughing and smiled. He tried for a moment to remember when he'd last heard such merry laughter, and he couldn't. He felt better and his spirits rose just by hearing it. The laughter of sailors over pranks and coarse jokes was not the same, somehow. There is no love in it, he decided, and shut the sea from his mind.

He wanted now to go to them. "I must get up," he whispered, and pulled the blanket away. He rolled to his side, and in one motion swung his legs over the cot and raised his torso upright. He swayed in a surge of dizziness and his head bobbled for a moment like an infant's. Gripping the edge of the cot, he stiffened his arms to steady himself, and took a deep breath. Rising unsteadily, he stood, rigid, swaying. "I can do it," he said aloud. He felt light-headed, and there was a leaden feeling in his legs. "I can do it," he repeated, and put his foot forward. But he had no control of his knees, and as they collapsed he fell forward on his belly. "Bloody hell," he shouted, slamming his fist against the floor.

He lay flat and took a deep breath, listening, as the footsteps grew louder. Within a few seconds a pair of moccasined feet appeared. He raised his head a bit, but it seemed heavy, so he let it rest on his cheek again. He felt hands on his shoulder and back, and a man spoke: "I'll turn the lad over, Lillie, then you take his feet an' we'll put him back on the cot."

Frank looked up at a bearded face. He couldn't tell whether it smiled or scowled at him. He was embarrassed. "I'm sorry to be this… this trouble, sir." he said, and his neck muscles strained to raise his head off the floor. Maybe I can…"

"Relax, laddie, it's no trouble a'tall. Up yuh go now."

The face with the beard and soft brown eyes smiled as it peered down, while someone put the blanket on him again.

"It's good that you're feelin' well enough to try your legs, lad, but don't try it alone again, and surely not 'til tomorrow."

"Aye, sir."

"It's Adam, lad, Adam MacLean. And you're Franklin Ross, I'm told, a Scotchman like myself, though Canada's my birthplace."

"Aye," he said, his spirits livened to the point a grin stretched his mouth and he felt his parched lips crack. "It's glad I am, and grateful to be here, Mister MacLean."

"Adam, it is."

"Aye, and my father called me Frank."

"Then Frank it is." And in a quieter voice, he said, "Speaking of your father, we buried the Captain this afternoon in a shady spot above the beach. He'll rest there peaceful-like, I'm sure. Tomorrow you'll be stronger an' we'll all go up there and hold a proper service for him."

On a sudden emotional impulse, Frank pulled his arm from under the blanket and thrust his hand toward Adam, who took it firm in both of his and held on while a smile moved across his face. Frank felt the flow of friendship as it coursed through his heart and added strength and meaning to his life again. He wanted to say "Thank you" but knew he could not hold the welling sobs in check if he unclenched his teeth or loosened his tightly pursed lips.

"There is no need to talk now lad, just rest. We'll soon be bringin' yuh inside for supper." He gave Frank's hand a pat before releasing it. "And if Lillie's cookin' don't put the meat back on your bones, there ain't nothin' that will."

He closed his eyes and swallowed hard as Adam moved away. He sniffed; the smells of cooking food rushed in and his hunger ripened. Suddenly, he was aware of the chirping of birds, then the swish of something close. He turned his head and felt the breeze stirred by her skirt. A few steps past, she turned and looked at him. Smiles were exchanged, and as Robin glided silently into the house, Frank closed his eyes to preserve the image of her. He knew she was the prettiest girl he'd ever seen.

The mound of freshly turned dirt had a makeshift cross at one end. From his seat in the buggy, Frank watched as Robin cast a handful of seeds over the grave and put a bouquet of wildflowers on it. The day was warm, yet a slight chill passed through his body and he felt Lillie's arm firm its grip around him. There primarily to steady him, her arm had now conveyed her concern and he felt a bit embarrassed by her motherliness--something he had not experienced since his mother died.

His thoughts dwelled on his mother; of how he'd been cheated by her death when he was ten. He had loved her and now he loved the memory of her. She was an attentive, affectionate mother and was everything to him during the long absences of his seagoing father. How strange, he thought, and how wonderful that these people, into whose lives he had by chance intruded, could show such care for one about whom they knew so little. He turned to Lillie. "Thank you," he said, "thank you very much indeed."

The service had ended. Simple though it was, he knew it would be to his father's liking. "Somehow I canna take to bein' buried in the sea," he'd confided to Frank. "Be assured I ken to the simple tidiness of it, but mind you, I dinna like to have my backside wet." Frank half-smiled at the memory.

The Beemans were getting into their buggy. Archie had read from the Bible and led the prayers. His wife, Carilla, sang a solo hymn, then they all sang "Rock of Ages." He smiled again as he thought of how the mule, hitched to Archie's buggy, had joined in on the last few bars. Now it was over and he was thinking of what he might say to thank them, when Adam's voice broke through his thoughts.

"The cross there," he said, pausing as he got in the buggy, "the cross is just temporary. I'll be makin' a proper marker the next day or so," Frank felt Adam's hand on his shoulder. "I'll need the Captain's full name, date an' place of birth too, laddie, if yuh know all that."

"Aye, I know, and I'd like to help."

"Oh, you're welcome to do that, and I should've known yuh'd want to. We'll get at it just as soon as you're able." Removing his hand from Frank's shoulder, Adam took the reins. "Well, I see Robin's gotten in with Archie an' Rilla, so we'll get on back home for some nourishment."

"We will have tea and cookies," Lillie said. He'd heard his mother say it a hundred times or more: "We'll have tea and cookies." He closed his eyes and imagined the scent of tea as it steeped, and the aroma of freshly baked cookies.

He wasn't prepared for his mother's death, but what child of ten ever is? It wasn't as though she'd been sick. He'd come home from school that cold February afternoon and, after flinging books and macinaw onto the kitchen table, he felt a chill instead of the familiar warmth, and there were none of the pleasant smells that usually greeted him and made the kitchen his favorite room. The cook-stove was cold to his touch, and only a few tiny embers glowed in the corner fireplace.

"Mum, are you upstairs?" he called, as he opened the door to the pantry. A few cookies would take the edge off his appetite until supper. She lay there, staring at the ceiling, her mouth open a little, like she was surprised. She looked blue around the mouth. He had never been close to a dead person before, but he knew his mother was dead even before he knelt beside her and felt her cold cheek.

He tried not to cry at her funeral, but he did. It bothered him that his father wasn't there. He was away at sea and his not being there seemed unfair to his mother. When he got home, months later, the Captain wept as they stood at her graveside. Frank then realized his mother was the one who had suffered least by her death. He felt closer to his father after that. Maybe his parents were together again, since the Captain wasn't at sea any more.

The buggy jolted, ending his day-dream. He looked up and saw a ranch house come into view. He hadn't seen the MacLean house except from inside, since his back was to it as he was driven to the grave-site. He was impressed by its sturdy, friendly look and the way it blended with the wooded area around it. "That is your house, isn't it?" he asked.

"Aye, lad, that's it."

"It's mighty impressive. Did you build it yourself?"

"Every foot of it. Of course I had a wee bit of help from Lillie, and a wee bit from Robin, too." Adam laughed. "In truth, I couldn't have done it without them, and wouldn't have wanted to."

"How long did it take, and where did you live while…"

"Oh, in about a month we were under its roof. The finishin' took much longer. Mind you now, while I was buildin' we lived in a place that Lillie herself built."

Frank turned and looked at her, amazed. "You built a *house*?"

She smiled at him, "I build tepee."

Her dark eyes sparkled in the sunlight, and in them he saw her pride and gentle strength. In him a sudden fondness spawned for Lillie, and he placed his hand on hers. "My mother would have liked you," he said, "and my father would have, too."

Lillie looked down for a few seconds then back into his eyes. "I am proud you say that." Her voice sounded husky and she cleared her throat. "You must tell of yourself and family when you are stronger."

"Aye, that I will," he said, and the buggy stopped. They were at the house.

CHAPTER SIX

With Adam and Archie supporting him, Frank climbed the stairs to the veranda, halting on each step while deciding which foot to lift to the next one. What before he had done without thinking, now, in his feebleness, required conscious decision and effort. He was exasperated at his frailty. "Let me go it alone, here to the cot," he said, upon reaching the top of the stairs.

Adam protested: "I don't think you're quite--"

"Please," interrupted Frank, "Let me try."

"All right, laddie, but me 'n Arch--we'll stay alongside in case yuh need to grab on to somethin'."

They removed their support. He swayed a bit until his leg and back muscles adjusted to being on their own. Coming up the steps, his knees seemed cooperative enough. Still, he was cautious as he shifted weight to one leg and slid the other foot forward. He looked at his feet, dressed in a pair of Adam's moccasins which were a bit short, and repeated the process, each time with more confidence. The last few feet he made with a normal stride.

Smiling at his success, he stood facing the cot at its edge. His legs were shaking. He was tired and didn't think he could turn around without losing his balance. He put his hands on the shoulders of the two men. Turning his head toward Adam, he saw Robin come out of the door and onto the veranda. Suddenly, he wasn't tired anymore. "Could I please have a chair to sit in? I would rather sit now, than lie down." He watched Robin as she grabbed a porch-chair and brought it to where he stood. As he was lowered gently into the chair, their eyes met and held a long gaze. He wanted to reach out for her--to touch her face, to stroke her hair. He had never known that feeling before.

Lillie brought his tea in a heavy mug. "Easy to hold," she explained, as though she knew his hands would tremble. And tremble they did, as they enclosed the mug. Wisely, she had filled the mug only half full, so he managed to sip from it without spilling. The cookie was good; not like he remembered his mother's, but far better than the hardtack served aboard ship.

He noticed the quiet and looked around as he took the cup from his lips. Adam, Lillie, Archie, Mrs. Beeman and Robin--all seated now--were watching him, and smiling. The scene brought a smile from him, embarrassed as he was at the attention, and he felt his cheeks warming.

"It's surprisin' how well it is you're doin' Frank, considerin' the condition you were in yesterday," said Adam. "I'm doin' just fine, thanks to all in this house." "What happened?" blurted Robin, "Did your ship sink?" "Now, wait a minute," cautioned Adam, holding his palm up toward Robin, "We're all anxious to hear how yuh happened to our shore, laddie, but we can wait 'til yuh feel strong enough to tell us."

He wanted to talk. The tea warmed his belly and he basked now in the warmth of the day and these people. "It's really all right, Mr. MacLean--Adam. I feel very much like talking." Smiling, he looked at Robin. She seemed to be staring, wide-eyed, at him. "I think if I might have another spot of tea, and a cookie, please, I could last the while," he said.

"Oh! Oh, yes. There's plenty," said Robin, getting quickly to her feet. She took his mug and moved briskly to the table where Lillie had put the refreshments.

"Not too full, for him," cautioned Lillie.

As she handed him the mug, he took it in both hands again. She

44

put the cookie on the arm of his chair and their eyes met for an instant. He was sure he saw a blush of crimson on her cheeks before she turned away. The scent of jasmine lingered. How truly beautiful she is, he thought, and found it difficult to clear his mind of her.

It was Mrs. Beeman's patter with Lillie that reminded him of his commitment to tell his story. He took a bite of the cookie and sipped the tea as he waited for them to finish.

"Clam up now, Rilla honey," said Archie, "Frank here's ready ta fill us in." He turned to Frank. "Go on, young feller. If yuh wait fer them two ta stop talkin', you'll never get a word in."

Robin hoped Frank didn't notice her staring. He looked so good now, in spite of Papa Mac's clothes that were a little short and much too loose. His hair, washed that morning by her mother, wasn't red-blond like his whiskers, but tan--buckskin, that was it--long, swept back and held in a queue by a rawhide thong.

Robin listened attentively as Frank told them briefly of his background and of the shipwreck that brought him to Oregon. She watched his lips and liked the way they moved. The sound of his voice -- its soft, pleasant tone--was young, yet firm and manly. She hadn't heard a young voice in six months, not since Mary and Judd Wiggins were murdered. His accent--slight though it was--drew attention to his words; she wished she had one like it.

He said he was twenty, born in Scotland. She was glad he wasn't older--or much younger. His mother died when he was ten. His father, a ship's officer in the British mercantile trade, took him to Boston where he lived with his mother's sister 'til he was fifteen. He then began a career at sea as Cabin Boy and seaman apprentice aboard the Brig "Charlotte", a merchantman out of Glasgow commanded by his father. Now, five years later, with a load of Peruvian copper ore bound for British Columbia, the heavily laden vessel broke up in a storm off the Oregon coast. He and his father were the last to leave the sinking

45

ship and Captain Ross was sorely injured in the process.

Frank paused, and Robin saw his lips purse tightly as the gray eyes drifted downward with their gaze. The furrowed brow, the flexing muscles of his lightly bearded jaw told Robin of his pain and her heart joined in his sorrow. His voice wavered when he continued.

After numerous days adrift in stormy seas, the water and meager provisions of the boat were spent. The injured Captain died two days before the boat stranded on the sandbar. Frank, desperate for water, made it to the beach before he collapsed from hunger, thirst and exhaustion.

The fate of those crewmembers who survived the breakup of the ship and got away in lifeboats, seemed of great concern to him. He spoke of making a report of the disaster to authorities in the nearest port as soon as possible.

"Where might the nearest port be," he asked, "where I can make such a report. And where might shipwrecked sailormen go to look for passage home?"

"I'd say Port Orford's a more likely place than Crescent City, wouldn't you Archie?"

"Yup, I reckon so. They's about the same distance. Oh, Crescent City be a tad closer, mebbe, but it's mostly fishin' boats there. Orford be where the merchantmen come in, bringin' goods n' takin' lumber."

"How far is Port Orford?"

"A days ride north along the coast trail," answered Adam. "About thirty-five miles."

"Is there a place--a livery--where I might arrange for transport?"

"Aye, there's a stage coach line that runs the coast. It stops at Gold Beach every few days, going one way or the other. Now, Gold Beach is only four miles from here. We can get you there when you're able to travel."

Robin hoped that wouldn't be soon.

Frank took the last of the cookie and washed it down with the tea, cold now, but welcome. His mouth was dry from talking; his saliva, sticky. But his hands no longer trembled and he felt as though his strength surged back with each swallow. "I should be able to travel tomorrow," he said.

Lillie fairly sprang to her feet. "No, too soon for travel." It was almost a shout. Obviously embarrassed by Frank's startled look, she sat down. "Tomorrow too soon," she repeated in her usual calm. "You need more food and rest. Strength come back slow, you will see."

Carilla nodded so emphatically the large comb supporting her black lace mantilla dislodged and the mantilla enveloped her head like a curtain. Frank looked down in polite attempt to hide a smile, and was forced to grit his teeth when Archie hee hee'd like he was being tickled. "Heeee heee... I jist knew that was gonna happen," he chided, "the way that there comb was a bobbin' to an' fro."

Seeming unperturbed, Carilla removed the head cover from her face. While reinserting the huge comb in the back of her thick, black hair, and adjusting the mantilla, she said, "Lillie is right, young man. You men always think you're well before you really are, then you're right back down again, usually worse off." She glanced at Lillie, then smiled in a friendly way at Frank. "Lillie does good medicine. You listen to her. Mind what she says and you'll soon be fit again." She turned to her husband. "You know, Archibald, you are beginning to sound more like that mule of yours, every day."

"Well now, Missus Beeman, I'm plumb tickled ta hear that, 'cuz ol' Toad's a danged high class mule, an' smart too. Ain't that right, Robbie?"

"Well now, he sure is," agreed Robin, grinning.

"Well now," mimicked Carilla, "if he be so danged smart, get him to teach you some manners, *Mister* Beeman. His are a danged site better than yours!"

47

Archie laughed along with the rest. "By thunder!" he said, slapping his thigh, "Witness the fac' Rilla finally said somethin' nice 'bout ol' Toad."

Lillie was right. He was weak and tired at sundown. It had been a long day of opposing emotions. Now, his belly full of food, he lay on the cot, alone with his thoughts. Had any of the others survived? It was a miracle *he* survived, for twice his boat nearly capsized in the long and violent storm. A boat more heavily laden with people might easily have swamped.

He had to get word to the shipowners in Glasgow. Perhaps a letter might get there before he would. That was it--tomorrow he would write them a letter with a duplicate to their agent in Boston. The Hudson's Bay Company -- they were represented in Vancouver, B. C. , maybe in Port Orford as well. He would prepare a letter for them too, for they have ways and means with British matters. Surely, in a day or two he would be strong enough to leave.

Scotland seemed far away in time as well as miles. Perhaps he should try first to get to Boston. His aunt--he must let her know. Another letter to write. Good backup for the others. The trunk--its contents, how did they fare? He would need some of the money in it for clothes and travel. The wages due him would be enough for clothes and he could earn his passage. He and Adam would open it tomorrow.

He felt better now, having formed a plan, and was ready to give in to sleep that tugged at his eyelids. He looked out at the ocean and closed his eyes as the trailing edge of a sunset-purple curtain drew below the horizon.

It is pleasant here--the weather, the people. Primitive, but friendly. Even the Indians are civilized and speak English. The Indian women are handsome; much more-so than the illustrations in books. Especially the girl, Robin. Eyes, blue as a reef lagoon. Strange for an Indian, even a half-breed--hate that term--unless her father's are blue. Are Adam's brown or blue? Brown, I think. Maybe his father's or mother's... blue. Robin is so... yes... is beautiful. Speaks well. Sweet... forward, perhaps. Young--how old? Eighteen? Nineteen? Beautiful. She's... bonniest... ever I...

Two days later he rode with Adam in the buckboard to Gold Beach and posted the letters with the stage agent. Had he been fit, he could have been on his way to Port Orford that afternoon. But, as Lillie predicted, his strength seemed to ebb and flow like tides. Short walks with Robin the day before, between letters, confirmed his frailty; buying clothes in Gold Beach emphasized it. In three days there would be another northbound stage. He was determined to be ready.

The walks with Robin lengthened, as did their talks. Within a few days he and Robin had exchanged their personal histories.

Uncomfortable at first with her outgoing manner--he recalled Boston girls as being reserved, stuffy--he considered her too bold, almost tartish. He'd seen the overly friendly type before, frequenting streets and dock areas of port cities. But he was soon convinced he'd misjudged. Hers, he decided--after learning she was a month from being seventeen--was simply innocent naivety and unsophisticated enthusiasm over him as an oddity. A lonely girl, with no one of an age nearby. He knew the feeling well since going to sea. "If I had a sister," he told Lillie, "I'd want her to be like Robin."

The morning of his departure was gray, in keeping with his own dismal feelings. He regretted the day had come for he truly began to savor the warmth of the MacLean's and the Beeman's, and the brief, but memorable, companionship of Adam and Robin. Nor was he happy to forego Lillie's cooking--the best he'd eaten in five years. And he would miss her motherly attention.

Among the guns, books and payroll money, the trunk had produced a Scottish treasure--a set of bagpipes. These, Frank gave to Adam who promised he wouldn't make a sound with them until Frank was far from Lillie's reach. The trunk, its heavy lock shot open (for want of the key) was also a present to Adam, to provide safe haven for the pipes, when properly padlocked again, of course.

To Lillie, Frank gave one of a matched pair of his father's guns: a small, elegantly engraved, .45 calibre percussion pistol made by Henry Deringer of Philadelphia. "Keep it ever close, for your protection," he told her, "It could not possibly be put to better use." The other Deringer, and a .36 calibre Colt Navy revolver, he kept for himself at Adam's insistance.

To Robin he gave what was there of his father's favorite books, recommending several he, himself, had read. "I'm afraid my father's attempts to polish me were wasted tribute to my mother's memory. But with you, such a gem as already you are, whatever they do for you, be it give knowledge or pleasure, will merely add to their value for having served you." Shyness deserted him as he embraced her and kissed her forehead as it met his lips. He felt her arms encircle him, and before he was aware of doing so, he stroked her hair then kissed her forehead once again. He knew his gift was offered with the most words he'd spoken successively since he'd been there; surely, it was the books and his compliment that brought forth her tears and sent her running to her room.

Lillie, too, wept as she hugged and bid him well. "You are strong enough to leave, I think, if bonds here cannot hold you."

"If I stayed longer, I'm sure I couldn't find the strength to leave," he answered.

The ride to Gold Beach intensified his mixed emotions. "It has been a king's holiday, the week I've spent with you and your family, Adam. I owe my life to you."

"You owe nothin', laddie. We've had the privilege of helpin' yuh get back on your feet again." Adam looked at him. "You are in our hearts, now, an' we're gonna miss you. In a way, we're all sorry yuh made such a bloomin' fast recovery."

"In a way, I am too."

"Well, I suppose you're eager to get back to ships and the sea, again. Will you try to get a berth with-- --"

"I hate the sea."

Adam brought the buggy to a halt, turned in his seat and looked full face at Frank. "Then why don't yuh stay with us? Your letters will reach the authorities. I can use the help, lad, truly I can. I'll teach yuh ranchin', give room n' board, an' pay a decent wage. If you don't like it, well… there'll be no tether on yuh lad. Give it a try." Adam's eyebrows were raised in obvious optimism as he awaited Frank's reply.

"I'm sorely tempted to accept, but I have the feeling that I must return, if not to Scotland then to Boston where I have an aunt. And there's the matter of the payroll money. I must see that it's returned to the ship's owners." Frank was saddened as disappointment registered on Adam's face. "It's not that I don't *want* to stay, it's only that I feel I can't. I'm flattered by your invitation, and grateful for it."

Adam's brow creased and he shook his head slowly. "You're an honest man, Franklin Edward Ross--a good Scotchman--an' it's proud I am that I know yuh. Too many would say the money went down with the ship." He ordered Magic on at a trot, then, looking straight ahead, he said, "My offer will stand 'til hell freezes over, in case yuh ever change your mind."

Frank looked over at Adam. Was it the cool wind in his face that stripped tears from the corners of his rugged friend's eyes? It had to be the wind, he decided, for it was doing the same to him.

CHAPTER SEVEN

Lillie held her close as Robin's body shook with sobs, and remembered well how her own grief had tortured her. She knew there were no words that could ease the pain, "There are others who will want you; you are young, you will have another son." Those words, heard in the grief of her youth, never eased the pain of her losses. Frank was gone; to Robin it would be as though he had died, maybe worse, for death is final. For her daughter, the grief would turn to wonder and uncertainty, and the torture would go on. She had watched Robin fall in love, helpless to prevent what she believed would end in disappointment. Now she watched her suffer through her nightmare of broken dreams. "Oh, Mama, I hurt so bad."

"We must learn not to want what we cannot have." "I tried not to feel this way for him, but I couldn't help it, Mama, I couldn't help it." Lifting her head, she smeared the tear streams with her hand and looked in her mother's eyes. "At first I felt the difference between us was too... I mean, I could never... he wouldn't..." Tears spilled onto her cheeks. "Then, the last two days, he... the way he looked at me, things he said. I was... I was so sure... I thought he felt the same for me."

Lillie's heart ached. She had not seen Robin this unhappy since she was told of her father's death. The emotion of her agony now seemed even more intense. Comforting words? Should she try? She could not help herself. "He was happy with you. First happy days for him in many years. He told me, 'If I had sister, I want her to be like Robin'. That is how much he like you."

"I didn't want to be his sister" She sobbed.

"I think he mean you are... special to him. That he feel for you in very special way."

"I *loved* him, Mama. I wanted him to love me."

She pulled her daughter close to her again. "Love sometimes grow slow, bloom slow--like flower."

"Too slow," Robin whispered. "He's gone."

The next morning Robin was awake before dawn. She had not slept well, and there had been tears. Several times she decided there would be no more. That part of her life was over, she told herself. She must look upon it as a pleasant experience, not something to cry over. Still, thoughts of the pleasant experience produced tears, and morning found her with red, puffy eyes. She wanted now to get her mind on other things.

Diverting her thoughts from Frank produced a curious energy that surprised her. Before there'd been an hour's sun, she'd fed the animals and prepared the family's special Sunday breakfast.

After the meal they moved out to the veranda and Papa Mac read from the Bible. The cot upon which Frank had slept was gone. Her eyes moistened when she noticed.

"I want to take a ride," she announced, "I'll check pasture fences, then I'd like to go to the Beeman's for awhile. Is it all right?"

Her mother looked to Adam, then to her and smiled. "All right," she said. "Be careful."

"Yeah, Honeygirl, but take the coast road. I don't want yuh ridin' the east trail alone. An' please, don't stop to pick blackberries."

Riding fence was boring. Feather, not ridden for a week, was eager and hard to hold to the required pace. There was a gate at the east property line. When Robin had checked all but the north fence, she was as ready as her horse for release from the tedious restraint. The east trail was right there and she hadn't been on it for a long time. "I'll be riding fast," she thought, "and I won't stop to pick blackberries." She planned to check the north fence on the return ride. Feather needed no urging. Given her head, she was off at a gallop.

Beeman's ranch was two miles north. The east trail route was shorter than along the beach road, because the house sat on the high ground east of the ocean-front pastures.

She rode across Frog Creek and up onto the ridge of Caves Canyon. Below, small caverns lined the canyon walls and gave shelter to creatures of all levels. Hawks circled above and a putrid waft of carcass-fouled air jarred her senses. Robin shuddered as she thought of snake dens, and of bats that blackened the sky at dusk as they squeeked and fluttered crazily among the hordes of flying bugs.

Farther on--a half-mile or so the canyon shallowed out and broadened. There, she crossed and took a wagon road that ran along the west fence-line of what had been the Wiggins' spread. No cattle grazed there now; no sheep. A doe, with two spring fawns, stood motionless and watched as Robin brought her horse to a walk and looked upon the three. She thought about the joys of babies and motherhood, and smiled, thrilled at the beauty of the sights of mind and eye. Then, almost angrily, she put a heel to Feather's ribs and rode full gallop another quarter-mile, then halted where the road turned eastward to the Wiggins' former home. She hadn't been near there in the six months since their murder. To the west, across the shallow canyon, was the trail to Beeman's.

Shall I cross here now, she questioned, and go on to Archie's, or stretch the ride a bit and wander by the Wiggins' place to see what shape it's in? In an unusual, intimate test of impulsiveness versus good judgement, she gave in to rashness. Reining Feather with unnecessary severity, she turned her toward the Wiggins'.

As she passed a row of pines, she saw a plow resting at the end of a furrow of freshly turned soil. Archie had mentioned that someone was trying to buy the farm; she guessed they had.

Approaching the barn she noticed the rear door was open and heard voices inside. She rode slowly past, looked back and saw no one. A pair of bedsheets hung near the house and moved gently in a light breeze. Mary's beautiful curtains with crocheted edges, still were in the windows. Sadness engulfed her as she thought of Mary, and tears quickly surfaced. She rode on a short distance, clearing her eyes and her thoughts. When she turned around, she nudged Feather into a slow canter.

Two people stood at the side of the road near the barn. As she approached, they moved into her path. The tall one, a thin, young man, carried a rifle. The smaller, younger one, stood slightly behind the other. The tall one held up the rifle in one hand and shouted, "Whoa, there, Injun gal. Pull up for a minute."

She considered putting heels to Feather and skirting them, but his voice didn't sound menacing. The sight of the rifle frightened her. She had visions of a bullet in her back, or in her horse, if she ran. As she reined Feather in, the young man smiled. Well, it was a sort of smile, she guessed. One corner of his mouth went up and his upper lip raised, showing large, uneven front teeth.

The younger boy--about fifteen, she figured--reached for the hackamore, but the distrusting mare raised her head and laid back her ears. The boy quickly withdrew his hand. "That's a mean horse," he said.

"She doesn't like strangers, and she *will* bite," advised Robin. "And stay on the near side, or she might turn and kick before I can stop her." She wondered if she should have told him that, for her own safety. But then, it wasn't the younger boy that concerned her.

"We don't have to be strangers, now do we?" said the tall one. I'm Carl Hogan, and this here's my little brother Billy."

"My name's Robin Burns."

"Well, gol-lee damn, a Christian name! Or is it Rob an' Burn like you Injun folk is always doin' to us whites?" His mouth pinched closed and his eyes squinted.

She was frightened, now, but tried to be calm. "I am a Christian. And all Indians don't rob and burn. White men do it just as much, maybe more." She knew that was the wrong thing to say.

Carl's eyebrows raised as though offended. "Did ya hear that, Billy, she say's we rob and burn more'n the Injuns do. That's a goddamn lyin' insult, that is."

"I didn't say that *you* did, I said... well, you know what I said."

"Yeah, Carl, she didn't say we..."

"Shut up, Billy. You stay outta this, hear?" He looked up at Robin, that smile on his face. "Yer a half-breed, ain't cha?"

There was no strange feeling this time. "I'm half Indian. My father was Scotch--a trapper. My mother is Nez Perce. I am *proud* to be what I am." She felt defiant now, and less frightened.

"Ya say yer pa was Scotch. Wha'd he do, die, er just shack up with yer ma then run off after knockin' her up? An' what 'n hell are ya doin' 'round here?"

She was trembling with anger. She didn't know if it would do any good, but she was going to put Carl Hogan straight about who she was. "My father died when I was eleven. My mother married another fine white man, and we live on a ranch about a mile and a half from here. My step-father's name is Mac..." The name trailed off as Carl took a step toward her.

"Well, ain't that grand. Ya hear that, Billy? We got this here pretty squaw fer a neighbor. Well, now we just *gotta* be friends, wouldn't yuh say?" He took another step toward her and put his hand on her knee. "Them's mighty nice buckskin pants and shirt, there girl. How's about gettin' off that horse an' givin' us a better look, eh?" He grabbed a handful of leather. Feather skittered sideways enough that he lost his grip. He handed the rifle to Billy. "Here, take this, while I help this 'lil whore off her horse." He lunged and got her foot with his left hand.

Feather spun away, but he hung on. "Come down offa there, and we'll have a look at what's under them buckskins." He was laughing. His right hand grabbed her pants above the knee and he shouted in a sing-song manner, "Injun's comin' off her horse an' her pants is comin' down."

Her right leg clamped against Feather's side and she tried to kick loose from his grasp. It was useless. She tried to get her horse to turn the other way, to bump Carl, but the frightened animal kept spinning away from him. She felt herself loosing her seat. The knife! She remembered the knife. Her hand dashed to her right hip. In an instant the blade flashed as she transferred the Bowie to her left hand, letting the reins fall across Feather's neck.

More angry now than scared, she slashed back with the knife and caught his right arm. He yelled and let go of her.

"Oh, Jesus Christ! Jesus Christ! Oh, God, Billy, I'm stabbed. I'm hurt, Billy. Cut bad. Help me, help me!"

Startled by the screams, the horse lunged. Billy, his attention drawn to his fallen brother, was struck firmly and parted company with the rifle as he hit the ground.

Over the pounding of Feather's hooves, Robin heard the wailing Carl cry out: "Help me, Billy, for Christ sake, help me stop the blood! Oh, my arm, I'm bleedin' ta death." As she rode at a run to the Beeman's, she hoped he would.

CHAPTER EIGHT

The two men rode in silence for the first quarter mile or so. Busy with thoughts of what he wanted to say to the Hogan's, Adam felt the heat of anger clouding his reason. He wanted to give Robin's tormentors a lasting punishment, and thought of how Indians might punish a white man who molested one of their young women. The treatment in some tribes would be to let the women have the culprit. They'd beat him senseless with sticks, then crush his testicles, maybe more. Perhaps an Indian haircut. In many tribes it would be death by flaying.

"I'm not a savage," he assured himself, "I'm a reasonable man. I'll just pound teeth down the throat of the older boy and kick the younger lad's ass up between his ears. And if their Pa ain't agreeable to it I'll add to *his* physical problems too."

The thought of such actions made Adam smile. It had been more than two years since he'd been in a fight. That was when a busy Port Orford shop keeper told Lillie and Robin to get their "dirty heathen bodies" out of his store because he was too busy with Christian customers to pay heed to the likes of Indians. That cost Adam five dollars doctor's fees for sewing up the storekeeper's face; fifty cents for a chin sling to hold shut the man's broken jaw; four dollars for damages to the display counter, and a night in jail. Lillie would never go with him to Port Orford after that.

"Those were damn satisfyin' punches," he said aloud, "worth every penny, they were."

"Whatever you mumblin' about?" asked Archie.

"Oh, just how satisfyin' it is to whup nasty bastards with your own hands."

"You ain't thinkin' a beatin' on those boys, are yuh?" I know yer mad but... well, the one's jist a boy."

"The older one, he's about twenty, you say?"

"Well, that's right. But dang it, Adam, they's both jist boys, really, jist farm boys."

"Tell me what you think about 'em, Arch."

Archie lifted his hat and scratched his head. "Well, now Carl, the elder boy, he be tall and skinny like his paw. And horse-faced like him, too. But he shore ain't no man yet, jist a derned big kid. Not too smart, either, I'd say. I kinda peg him as a sneak-bully type. Know what I mean?"

Adam nodded.

"Now, the young'un, Billy, I favor him, of the two. Kinda shy, small fer his age I reckon. More like his ma I'd say, in looks and manners."

"Well," said Adam, "maybe a good ass kickin' is all the young lad needs, and I'd be satisfied if his pa would do it. The older one though, I ain't sure, Arch. Hafta ponder it some more. It's just I feel he's got to be taught a lesson he'll remember, don't you agree?"

Adam watched his friend draw a plug of tobacco from his shirt pocket and bite off a chew. He could smell it, even taste it--tobacco soaked in rum and molasses--above the odor of animal sweat and saddle leather. Finally, Archie maneuvered the wad into the back of one cheek, spit a stream of brown juice, patted Toad on the neck and looked over at Adam.

"Ya gotta remember, my friend, them boys bin taught ta hate injuns mosta their natural lives. Cyrus Hogan ain't likely to agree ta punish his boys for what they do ta no injun, female or otherwise."

"That's what bothers me, Arch. If they get off light on this, they're sure to do somethin' again. And next time... well, I don't want there to be no 'next time'."

"I hear yuh, Adam; I hear yuh."

As they passed the row of windbreak connifers on the west border of Hogan's farm, the barn loomed at Adam and memories erupted. He had, along with Archie and other friends and neighbors, helped raise that barn for young Judd and Mary Wiggins about two years before. Then, just six months ago, he and Archie, along with the others, helped bury Judd and his pregnant wife, beaten to death in their bed, their horses stolen, their milk-cow killed and her calf taken. Everyone figured it was the work of renegades, but no one had been caught or accused. Pity, thought Adam, nice young folks with a fine farm. Mary was only a year older than Robin. The reflection punched his gut and angry thoughts burst through his mouth: "Bastards," he said aloud, "Bloody, rotten bastards!"

"Now, simmer down some, Adam."

"Ah, I was thinkin' about the Wiggins' and my blood boiled a little."

"Me too," said Archie. "Never could figger why it was them kids that was raided like that. Shucks, they didn't have no money and dang little else worth stealin' or a-killin' fer." Archie took off his hat, ran his arm over his sweating head, then pointed with his hat toward the house. "Well," he said, "there be Esther ta home, anyway."

Esther Hogan gave a small rug a few shakes. After a brief look in the direction of the approaching men, she went back into the house.

"The missus seems a nice sort, Adam. She don't say much but she and Rilla seemed ta get on right good the times we swapped calls on one another."

As they turned off the road and headed for the house, Adam noticed faces in a window, the glass reflecting bronze in the afternoon sun. Cyrus Hogan came out of the door as they stopped their mounts at the boardwalk to the house.

"Well howdy, Mr. Beeman," greeted Hogan as he stepped off the porch. "I shore hope that feller with yuh is a law man a some sort."

"No, this here's Adam MacLean, my friend an' neighbor. His spread's a couple miles south a here."

Adam tensed as the tall, thin man moved toward him, smiling, one hand shielding his eyes from the sun.

"Howdy, I'm Cyrus Hogan," said the man, offering his hand.

Maybe it was Hogan's outstretched arm, or maybe it was Adam's tenseness being sensed by his horse; whatever it was caused Magic to toss his head up and back away.

"Easy boy, steady now," coaxed Adam as he calmed the animal. "Glad to meet you, Mr. Hogan." Adam heard his own voice as flat and unfriendly.

Hogan, the smile leaving his face, had stopped his advance and lowered his hand to his side when the horse shied. Adam was glad. The horse's action seemed to override the need to shake hands.

"Likewise, glad ta meet yuh, Mister MacLean. That's a right pretty horse yuh got there. One a them the Injuns 'round here seem to like. Appaloosy, right?"

"That's right."

The smile reappeared on Hogan's face. Not a pleasant smile, Adam judged. The way Hogan's lip raised it looked as if he were about to pick his front teeth.

"Now, Mister Hogan," said Adam, "I rode over here to say--"

"S'cuze me fer interrupting Adam, but lemme ask Cyrus here why he was hopin' you was a lawman, before yuh gets on with yer business, if yuh don't mind."

Cyrus spit and moved a wad of tobacco from one cheek to the other, then turned his head and shouted over his shoulder, "Esther, send the boys out here straightaway." Turning back to Adam and Archie, he lowered his voice. "We, the boys that is, had a run-in with a Injun squaw this morning whilst me an' the missus was ta church over in Gold Beach. I aim ta report it to the law, but was hopin' I wouldn't have ta go on in ta Gold Beach ta do it. Esther's kinda scared a havin' me ride up there now that she knows there's some unfriendly savages hereabout."

Adam's anger overran his patience. "Unfriendly savages?" he blurted, then felt the hand of Archie on his arm.

"Jist hold on an bit, Adam," he said quietly. "Now jist what in thunder happened, Cyrus?"

Cyrus glanced behind him as a door slammed and the two boys appeared on the porch. The tall one had his arm heavily bandaged, held in a narrow sling. He was a head taller than the other boy. "Here they come now," Hogan announced. I wish yuh could see what that damn squaw did ta my boy with that knife. And Billy, notice him limpin'? That's from gettin' trampled. Coulda been killed."

"Whatcha want, Pa?" asked Billy.

"This here's Mister MacLean; he's a neighbor, kinda. Got a spread 'bout two miles south a here. Right, Mr. MacLean?" He looked up at Adam, then went on with the introduction. "The tall one's Carl, MacLean. The other one's Billy. Best not ta walk up ta that horse, boys, he's a might skittish."

Adam gave a nod, glad not to have to go through the formality of shaking their hands. The boys gave their howdies in a polite way. Billy smiled, but Carl looked sullen and squinted up at Adam in the same manner as his father.

"I was just tellin' these gentlemen what happend to you boys here this mornin'," said Cyrus. "Somethin' everyone in these parts oughta know about, I reckon." He paused and spit a long stream of juice.

Adam fixed his eyes on Carl and hoped the cut Robin gave him was deep and painful. Now he wanted to punch Cyrus just because of his attitude.

Cyrus wiped his mouth and went on. "Anyways, as I was sayin', here comes this Injun squaw a ridin' up ta the barn where she musta seed my boys doin' chores. They figures she's wantin' ta beg a chicken, or somethin'. Now, Carl here, he steps up an' starts ta palaver with her, sayin' somethin' nice about the buckskin's she's wearin', an' as he reaches ta touch 'em, danged if she don't lash out with a knife and cut 'im. Now, he's cut deep, I tell yuh, from the inside a his forearm clear inta the palm a his hand. Took a hour ta get the bleedin' stopped an' a bandage wrapped. Won't be no good at chores fer weeks, and that's if'n it don't mortify none. No tellin' where that dirty slut's had her knife."

Adam's face flushed and his jaw tendons twitched. He could hold his tongue in check no more. His voice strained as he tried not to shout. "Now-just-you-hold-right-there, Hogan. I'm here to tell you that was my *daughter* that was waylaid and abused by your sons. They scairt the *hell* outa her, and when that big one tried to pull her off her horse, she defended herself like she had a right to do." Adam lowered his voice. "An' she ain't no dirty slut, Hogan," he warned.

Cyrus Hogan gave his chaw a grind, spat, and squinted at Adam, one eye closed against the sun-bright sky. "The way I sees it, she had no right pullin' knife agin' a unarmed kid, an' him only wantin' ta feel that fancy buckskin she was wearin'. After all, she stopped a-purpose ta jaw friendly-like with the boys, or so they thought. That's right, ain't it boys? Squaw like that ain't oughta be off the reservation." Cyrus continued to look up at Adam and the squint became a sneer.

Adam's anger had grown with every word Cyrus delivered in his sarcastic, sing-song manner. He felt his chest heaving against tense muscles, and his nostrils flared with every breath. Slowly, so as to keep himself under control, he got off his horse and handed his pistol up to Archie. Then he stepped up to Cyrus Hogan. "Apologize", he said.

"For what?"

"For insulting my daughter, yuh son-of-a-piss-ant. You figured I wouldn't move on yuh, yuh bein' unarmed, a game leg, an' all. But you figured me wrong. You'll not be gettin' away with those insults, so long as I got a fist. Now, put up yours, Hogan."

Cyrus's mouth twitched. His eyes widened for just a second, then his weathered face took on a squinting sneer that seemed permanently formed by the deep lines around his mouth and eyes. "Any white shackin' with Injuns is askin' fer insults, an' beatin' on me ain't gonna change that none fer most folks."

Adam's left arm swung from low across his belt line. The back of his large hand caught Hogan flush on the left side of his sneering face. The sound was like the splat of a beaver's tail against wet mud. Hogan's head snapped right; his body twisted and his right foot stuttered sideways before the knee buckled and he fell.

"Now," said Adam, "get up and fight, yuh filthy, no 'count bastard."

Cyrus sat up, shook his head and spit. "Yuh'll be sorry yuh done that, I'll see to it, yuh... yuh squaw's ass."

Adam's anger soared. "Get on your feet 'afore I kick your damn ugly face in."

Cyrus sat motionless, tobacco juice running from the corner of his mouth.

"Christ, Pa, get up! You can take him." It was Carl shouting, moving behind his sitting father. "Get up, Pa!"

"I'm gonna get up, but I ain't fixin' ta fist fight 'cuz a this bum leg. But yuh'll get fought, mister, Yes sir, one way or 'nother, yuh'll get fought."

"You're a skunk, Hogan--worse'n a skunk. You piss on a man with words then hide behind a gimpy leg. The law of most camps is, if you've got guts enough to insult a man, you'd best have the guts to stand to him, face on, with your fists or your gun ready. Now, if you get up, you'd best come up swingin'.'"

"'Tain't fair. Pa's got a bad leg!" shouted Billy standing, fists clenched, at his father's side.

Adam saw a grinning sneer move over Cyrus Hogan's face, obviously pleased at his young son's defensive gesture. But Cyrus made no attempt to get up.

"Since you've a mind for fairness, lad, do yuh think you and your brother were bein' fair to my daughter, this mornin'?"

Billy Hogan looked away from Adam and glanced first at his brother, then down to his father, back at Adam, then stared at the ground, hands still at his sides, clenching, unclenching. Without raising his head, he spoke: "Well, we weren't aimin' to do no…"

"Shut up, Billy!" Cyrus commanded. "Yuh don't hafta answer none a his questions. They never was a damn heathen Injun what knowed the meanin' a 'fair', an' no breed squaw, neither."

Enraged, Adam lunged for the man on the ground. He heard Archie shout "Adam, no!" but, like a provoked bull, he continued his charge.

As Cyrus rolled from his attacker, Adam went to his knees and slid into Hogan's back. The impact drew a loud grunt from Cyrus and jarred his head back. In an instant Adam jammed his forearm against Hogan's throat and had him in a choke-hold. Standing, Adam dragged the struggling man nearly upright. Then, with a step backward, he dropped to one knee and slammed Hogan's back against his other. Legs and arms flailing, eyes bulging, his face turning purple, Cyrus suddenly went limp. Adam, aware now that Billy's arms were tight around his neck, responded to Archie's call:

"Adam, leggo a him, for Christ's sake! Don't kill him! Adam, leggo, I say!"

As Adam stood, Hogan's body rolled, face down, onto the dirt. Billy let go of Adam and dropped to his knees at his father's side, screaming "He's dead! Pa's dead!"

Adam stepped back feeling a bit sorry that he'd done this in front of young Billy.

Archie rolled Cyrus over as Esther Hogan walked up. Her calmness, as she looked down at her husband, shocked Adam from his sense of guilt.

"He's daid, ain't he?" She looked first to Adam, then at Archie.

"No ma'am, he ain't dead, jist sorta passed out. He's breathin' good. He'll come around most any second now, I reckon."

Adam never thought he'd killed Hogan. He really hadn't tried to do him in. He only wanted to avenge the insults with a good beating. Still, he was relieved by Archie's words, for he'd lost his temper and accidentally might have strangled the man, or broken his neck or back. He'd killed that way before, but only when fighting for his own life.

Esther clutched Billy's hand and knelt at her husband's side. She looked up at Adam and he noticed how slowly, wearily, her eyelids moved when she blinked, as though she was fighting sleep. "Reckon y'all best go now," she said. "Me an' the boys'll take care a him."

Adam, his anger nearly spent, mounted his horse. "I'm sorry ma'am, that this had to happen." He looked at Carl standing at his father's feet and saw he wore the same sneer that Cyrus had. "As for you, young fella, don't come near my daughter again. If you ever abuse her, or even *touch* her again, *I'll* kill yuh if *she* doesn't."

Carl stood silent, the contemptuous sneer on his face, and stared at Adam.

A groan came from Cyrus as he twitched, then opened his eyes. He reached for his wife and she took his arm and pulled him to a sitting position.

"Ooww, my back," he yelped, and gasped for breath. "Feels like some ribs is broke. Hurts ta breath." His voice was coarse and unsteady. "I'll getcha fer this, MacLean. Yuh must feel right proud, beatin' on a cripple."

"Your brain's what's crippled most, Hogan. I've seen men that's maimed worse'n you that hunted and fought damn well, an' made no excuses. But they were *men*, Hogan, an' you're somethin' less--an' a coward ta boot. Now, you an' your boys keep a distance from me and my family an' there'll be no more trouble. Otherwise, I'll kill any Hogan that makes a harmful move our way."

Adam spun Magic around and headed toward the road. "C'mon Arch," he said, "I need a change a scenery, an' a drink."

"You puttin' yerself on his side, Beeman?" asked Cyrus.

"Yup, reckon I am, Hogan. I've know'd that young lass fer four years, an' there ain't a finer one, of any blood, anywhere's. Yer a bigot an' yer sons are liars 'n bigots too--leastwise Carl there is--an' yer a flamin' fool fer 'couragin' 'em ta be that-a way. I'll not treat with yuh 'less yuh 'fess up ta bein' wrong, which I reckon ain't likely." Archie tipped his hat. "My regrets ta yuh, Missus Hogan, an' good day."

Hogan struggled to his feet, aided by his wife. "Go ta hell, both a yuh! Yuh'll see who's the fool, dammit, yuh'll see."

As Archie caught up to Adam he handed him back his pistol. "C'mon ta the house, Adam, an' we'll have that drink."

"Thanks, Arch, I'd like that. Yuh know, I don't reckon I've wanted to kill someone that much for a long, long time. I was wishin' he'd been carryin' a gun. I'da called him out an' killed him, or died tryin'. Wheeoow, he sure got my blood up!"

"I don't think yuh could've made 'im draw to yuh, 'cuz, like yuh said, I'm thinkin' he's a natural born coward--a back shooter."

"Well, I'm glad now I didn't kill him. There'd be trouble, a trial maybe. And there's his family."

"His family, huh?" Archie spit. "I'm now thinkin' they'd be best off without 'im, Adam. An' I hate ta say it, but I got a feelin' that we're both gonna wish yuh'd a killed 'im, back there."

"What makes yuh think that?"

"Jist a gut feelin' I got. You put 'im down hard, 'an I told 'im off so's he ain't apt ta favor me none, either. An' knowin' a little a how hard he hates, an' how little stand-up, face-ta-face guts he's got, I figures him fer a bushwacker, an' ta try ta git even, somehow, sometime."

Adam's eyes narrowed. "Aye, the same thoughts are mine, Archie. But I've a feelin' he's the kind to have someone else do his bushwackin' for him."

From there they rode in silence to Archie's ranch.

CHAPTER NINE

It was mid-afternoon when the stage pulled up to The Peter Ruffner Hotel in Port Orford. Frank was hungry. The fish chowder he'd eaten at the waystation could hardly be classified as a meal in itself. And the crackers... tasty, but dainty; not like sea biscuits that could soak the liquid from a bowl of soup and leave the stock high and dry. Lillie's hearty meals had spoiled him for lesser fare. Ah, Lillie, Adam, and Robin. For only brief moments in the six hours since leaving Gold Beach, had his thoughts not been of them. Over and over he'd weighed the pros and cons of his decision. He convinced himself he'd made the right decision, simply because he didn't feel good about it. He likened it to taking medicine: if it was good for what ailed you, it tasted bad.

Through a thicket of masts and rigging, he recognized the house flag of Shaw, Maxton and Company, a British shipping firm. It fluttered from the mainmast of a vessel he could but partially see. Handed his carpetbag by the stage driver, he stood gazing about trying to decide which first to satisfy--his hunger or his curiosity.

Curiosity won. Shaw, Maxton and Company were competitors of Brophy and Dunlop, owners of ill-fated "Charlotte", and he wondered which of their fleet of ships was in, and about its schedule, if it had one. His father had sailed for them in years past and had sustained friendship with several of the officers with whom he'd been shipmates.

As he headed downhill toward the small harbor, the schooner with the Shaw/Maxton house flag came fully into view. She was at the only wharf. Other ships, anchored in the quiet roadstead, were taking on lumber by high-line from the nearby mill. It was an operation he'd

71

heard of, for the Orford cedar was a much favored wood for weather-exposed construction. He watched in awe as cut lumber, bound in rope slings, moved rapidly along lines from shore to ship.

She was moored starboard side to the dock. A wooden skid-ramp was draped over her stern and joined to a lumber chute extending to the wharf from the mill on high ground above the port. With an ear-tingling whistle--almost a screech--a large piece of lumber came down the chute. Slowed to a stop as it reached the ship, by a man operating a braking device, it was then maneuvered onto the stack of lumber by men with piked poles. Facinated by this operation, Frank watched for several minutes before crossing under the elevated ramp and proceeding to the ship.

Approaching from astern, he was pleased to see "Persevere" in bold letters across her transom. If he had the same Master as when last he'd seen her in Sydney, a year before, then he was in luck, for it would be Captain Thomas Evert, for whom his father had once been First Mate.

After a knock on the door to his cabin, there was no doubt in Frank's mind as to the Captain's identity, as the unforgettable bass voice of Thomas Evert, coarse and throaty from years of bellowing commands over gale winds, bid him enter.

"Come in, if you've business wi' the Master of this vessel; otherwise, see the First." It was as though the words originated at the bottom of an empty rum-keg, and were grated with sand as they emerged.

He was seated at his desk in the center of the small, well appointed cabin. A large, black-haired and bearded man of generous girth, his eyes were on a ledger held open between his stomach and the edge of the desk. "State your business, sir," he grumbled without looking up.

"I'm Franklin Edward Ross, Captain Evert, son of the late Captain Edward Ross. I'm seeking passage to..." He stopped mid-sentence and half smiled as Evert looked up at him, pushed the ledger onto the desk and stood, smiling, his hand extended.

"Welcome aboard, lad." He grasped Frank's hand and shook it vigorously, "And sit ye down." Then his tone was solemn. "But what's this, the *late* Captain Ross, you say?"

As he listened to Frank's story he ran thumb and forefinger over streaks of gray extending downward from the corners of his mouth through his black beard. His large, dark eyes expressed unmistakable sadness, then sudden anger as Frank finished.

"Brophy an' Dunlop are scoundrels!" he bellowed, banging his huge fist on the table. "Charlotte was long overdue for replanking. Your father knew it, and they knew it. He told me in Sydney. 'Just one more voyage,' they'd said, and she'd be dry docked. They told him he'd a bonus get... and a new ship--a clipper--they told him." He folded the ledger and slammed it on the table top. "Bastards! Scoundrels! That's what they are, and not deservin' of a fine Captain like your father." He shook his head slowly, his eyes cast downward. "Of course, you can't sue, claimin' she wasn't seaworthy without embarrassin' your father's name, for he took her out knowin' her true condition." He looked up into Frank's eyes, and his voice softened. "But don't blame him, lad. Any Captain would have done the same, else never sail as Master again."

Frank nodded his agreement. He knew how the companies postponed overhaul and pressured their Captains to save money. He had never for a moment considered his father's judgement to be poor, or Charlotte substantially unseaworthy. "I don't blame him, Captain. I think that storm would have been a threat to any ship carrying ore, even with new planking. I'd never seen such a confused sea. There seemed to be no proper way to run. And dark --it was like all the light had been sucked out of the air around us. It was a miracle we got the boats launched."

Captain Evert lit a calabash pipe and puffed 'til volcanic eruptions of smoke filled the cabin with a blue haze and the spicy aroma of turkish tobacco. "I'll wager," he said, pausing to tamp the glowing shreds with a crusty thumb, "I'll wager the lads in those boats were swamped an' drowned before they'd pulled ten strokes. It's lucky you are to be alive, lad. I'm truly sorry about Captain Ross. He was hurtin' though, you said?"

"Aye, green water set him hard against the taffrail. I'm sure some ribs were broken, and his lung punctured." The memory of his injured father coughing foamy blood bothered him and he was anxious to get to the subject of transport. "Captain Evert, I'm seeking passage to Glasgow, or to Boston where the owners have an agent and I have a relative--my mother's sister. I've sent out letters, but I want to make a personal report of the ship's loss, and turn over the logs and the money."

The Captain's eyes widened. "The money?"

"Aye, sir, the payroll and supplies money. My father put it in a sea chest we managed to get into the boat. I've got it with me, and the accounting book. I took five pounds to buy clothing, and my coach ticket and noted it in the book. I figured they wouldn't mind; it'll be against the wages I've got coming."

"I'm glad to see you are your father's son, lad. There's them that would say the money went to the bottom wi' the ship." He rubbed his beard and extended his lower lip. Closing one eye, he looked at Frank and nodded his head slightly. "It's more than those bloody bastards deserve, having men like Edward Ross and his son looking after their interests."

With obvious disgust, the Captain shook his head, slapped his huge hand onto the table before him, rose and walked to the open porthole in his cabin. "And the pity is," he said, still shaking his head while looking out the port, "you'll no doubt have to hire a blinking barrister to prove your entitlement to what was due your father, an' then they'll prob'ly try to cheat on that, the stingy sons o' bitches."

Frank was surprised at the Captain's low opinion of Brophy and Dunlop, for his father had spoken well of them. "It's not my business, Captain Evert, but you seem bitter toward the owners of "Charlotte". Have you had…" The Captain turned, interrupting him.

"Oh, it's not just Brophy and Dunlop, lad--they're all alike. In my experience, one's no better than the other. They all play your benefactor 'til you lay a claim against 'em. Then you become the scum o' the sea who's done nothin' but rape the company wi' poor seamanship an' extravagance. Twelve days late, I was, after a Cape storm bloody well blew us apart. Two men were lost. I put in to the Falklands to put ashore three men wi' broken bodies in need of a surgeon, and for the mendin' of our riggin' and morale. We took aboard live sheep for mutton and five apprentice hands willin' to work their passage back to England, plus two payin' passengers.

"It wasn't to their likin' that I'd paid a few Islanders to help wi' the mendin' o' the canvas, and took aboard 'alf dozen bloody woolies. They docked my pay, an' when I bellered over it, I was put to sea in this bloody scow, for just this trip, they said. Take it, they said, or lose my seniority an' chance for a clipper. As if that weren't enough, I'm at three-quarters the pay I had as master of a full-rigged ship." He spit through the port and turned back to Frank. "And this after fourteen years wi' Shaw, Maxton and Company!" He flicked the cover off a huge watch he drew from his vest pocket. "We dine in forty minutes. You'll be my guest, of course. Where are you staying?"

"I haven't taken a room yet, Captain. I saw the house flag when I got off the coach and put aside doing anything else until I could inquire about passage." He was glad for a chance to remind the Captain of his quest.

"Ah, you'll have to forgive an old man his ramblings, Mister Ross. As for passage, you're welcome aboard. You'll sign on as Supercargo.

I've got a full crew of Mates, but I can use a man good with figures to do the paperwork. As I recall, your father said you had your Certificate of Competency as Third Mate. Is that correct?"

"Yes, sir."

"Good. You can take watches as Assistant to the First. He's a good man, but not a well one, and I fear sometimes his attention is more on his health than on the ship. It will worry me less to have you about with him. We sail the day after tomorrow." The Captain strode to his cabin door, flung it open and yelled for the Steward.

Frank was overwhelmed. He had passage, but to where? "Thank you, Captain. I'm grateful for your consideration. By what route are we sailing?" The question was intentionally without mention of destination.

"Ah, of course. Forgive me again. We will take lumber to Shanghai, tea to Australia and New Zealand and grain from Australia to England. We will be in Bristol in May of next year. That is, of course, if we don't get pooped or shredded at Cape Horn." He laughed, "I don't think I can afford to put in at the Falklands again."

Frank winced. Eleven months! Why, suddenly, did he feel almost ill at the thought of such a voyage? So frozen was he in thought that the Captain's instructions to the Steward seemed barely audible in the background, as though they were outside the cabin, instead of a few feet away.

"Simmons here will show you to your quarters, Mister Ross. I will join you and the other officers in the Dining Room in twenty minutes."

Dinner was a pleasant affair, except for having to recount some details of the wreck of Charlotte. His account of the MacLean's and his week's stay with them seemed of particular interest to his listeners. Most agreed they would have given Adam's offer a try--one or two admittedly motivated by Frank's description of Robin. The Captain openly declared Frank daft for his decision.

Afterward, he was given a tour of the schooner by the First Mate, a tall, thin man of about forty with a peculiar gray skin color and a wretching cough. Frank guessed he had consumption.

It was dark when he returned to his cabin. All work had ceased topside. He lay back on the bunk, listening to the creaking groans of "Persevere's" planks and timbers as they adjusted to her cargo and to the cooling temperature of evening. He closed his eyes and Robin's face was in his mind's view, her blue eyes glistening behind the tears. It was the way he'd seen her last, before she turned away and ran back into the house. He'd felt an impulse then to take her in his arms again; to kiss her on the mouth and tell her he would stay. Now, more than ever, he wished he had. The same conflicting emotions tugged and flung his thoughts from Robin to "Charlotte", from Adam to his father, from Lillie to his aunt Marie in Boston, and from ranching to seagoing. "Damn me for this... this stupid changing heart and mind!" he said aloud. Angrily, he swung his legs off the bed and sat on its edge, shaking his head as despair cloaked him in physical pain. "Damn it all!"

His sleep had been fitful, and he heard three bells before opening his eyes at the steward's knock. "Five-thirty, Mr. Ross. Breakfast is on."

"Aye, Simmons, thank you."

"The Captain's compliments sir, he'll see you in his cabin at seven to sign papers."

"Aye, I'll be there."

He was uneasy as he rapped on the Captain's door. Still confused about his feelings, he wished he had more time to think, but knew that more time would only cause him more of the pain. He'd made his decision and he should be man enough to stick with it.

"Come in," boomed the voice inside. He sounded more cheerful than the afternoon before.

"Well, lad, I hope you had a restful night and a good breakfast.

"Both fine, Sir," he lied. He'd hardly slept a wink and had no appetite for what he considered a handsome and hardy meal for such a vessel, even in port. A malaise seemed to have settled on him and he wondered if he might be coming down with something.

"Good. I've the papers here. They're simple enough. You will be paid two pounds ten each month plus berth and rations until reaching Bristol plus three days. Your duties will be as administrative assistant to me and assistant to the First. You will get one twentieth of any bonus to the crew, and one eighth of the officer's bonus, if there should be one." He pushed the papers toward Frank along with a quill and ink. He gave a good natured laugh. "Take time to read, if you'd like. I labored o'er them in my best script to be sure they were legible."

"I'll take your word, Captain." Forcing a weak smile, he took up the quill, then the Captain caught his hand.

"Now hold there, Mister Ross, me lad. Are you downright sure this is what you're really wantin' to do? Listenin' to you talk last night an' all, I'm wonderin' if you aren't bein' driven to do this against your actual wishes, by some feelin' that you're obliged to the Company, or to your father, perhaps."

Frank hesitated before deciding to be truthful. "A bit of each, I guess."

"Aye, a *lot* of each, I'll wager." He released Frank's hand, plucked the quill from it and returned it to its holder. "Now, be honest lad, are you anxious to go to sea again?"

He thought for a moment and knew he would feel ashamed to say "no". "Well, sir, not exactly *anxious*."

"Are you homesick for Scotland?"

"No sir, but I..."

The Captain waved his hand to interrupt. "I've the feelin' that you really would like to have stayed longer wi' your new friends in Oregon, am I right, lad?"

"Yes sir, but..."

Captain Evert's palm came hard down on the table. "Then for God's sake, *stay*, man, *stay*. Go back to them and try a different life than you've had. This is a new land, man, with opportunity and new challenges. And if you don't like it, if you should go daft, you can always return to the bloody sea again."

"There's the money, and the log."

"I say keep the bloody money, after what you went through. But if you want, I'll give you a receipt and return the money and the log to their agents in Bristol. How much is there?"

"Nearly two-thousand pounds, sir."

"We'll take out your wages, and the Captain's, since you're 'is only heir. What's due is due, I say."

Frank went to the porthole. Looking at the blue, glass-slick water of the bay and the calm sea beyond, he felt a twinge of the loneliness that the monotony of such undefiant, placid beauty brought on when at sea. He preferred the challenge of the more tempestuous weather; he wasn't keen for the discomfort it caused, but it kept him too busy to be lonely. Without turning around, he said, as though to himself, "Sometimes I really liked being at sea. More often, I hated it. But I know my father would be disappointed if I were not to follow the sea."

"Captain Ross might be disappointed that you couldn't see to make it a career as he did, that I'll grant you, lad. But he'd feel a damn sight worse if he knew you chose to live in hell just to keep from disappointin' him. He was too great a man for that." Frank felt the big man's arm drape over his shoulder. "Your father was proud to have you sailin' with him, he told me that in Sydney. You made him proud while he was alive. You can't do more for him now."

As he walked up the hill toward the Peter Ruffner Hotel, there was new strength in his legs, a spring to his step, and a bold sense of purpose to his stride that one feels as the result of sudden success--or sudden relief. No longer depressed by guilt, trapped by obligation, nor agonized by indecision, for the first time in five years Frank caught himself whistling--a practice sailors believe to invite bad luck aboard ship. He had made his report to the Port Authority and was saddened that there had been no news of survivors. But he would not dwell on that now, for their fate was beyond his influence.

His plan was simple. A room at the Hotel, the day to shop for proper clothes. A lavish dinner, a good night's rest, a leisurely breakfast before catching the southbound stage for Gold Beach. He could not subdue his grin as he walked into the hotel, envisioning Robin's reaction to his return in rancher's clothes.

CHAPTER TEN

Seeing Frank's clothes neatly folded on the storeroom shelf, Robin took the shirt and held it to her breast. She thought of him on the porch steps, his head supported by her hands as Papa Mac fed him water. She sniffed the cloth, hoping a trace of his odor might still be there. She would even have welcomed the scent of salt water and seaweed, but there lingered only the acrid reminder of its recent lye soap laundering.

"Forget to give Frank old clothes. Hope he not need them."

Startled at the sound of her mother's voice from the doorway, Robin hurriedly returned the garment to the shelf and got the sack of cornmeal she came for. Embarrassed, she avoided Lillie's eyes as she walked past her into the kitchen.

"Maybe good sign," added Lillie, "Maybe sign he come back."

Robin shook her head. "He'll never come back, Mama. He wants to be with his own kind of people, on ships, or in Scotland, or... or Boston." She wanted to say he wasn't interested in a half-breed Indian, but knew that would cause her mother great hurt. A glance at Lillie's face told her she'd come too close to saying what was on her mind. "I mean, I think he was homesick."

She saw the tears in her mother's eyes as Lillie turned away. Flinging her arms around Lillie's waist, Robin hugged her tightly. "I'm glad you're my mother, and I'm proud to be the daughter of the famous Charlie Burns." But in the privacy of her thoughts, Robin wondered why the children of Indian women and white men were considered by white people to be Indian, not white.

"We will go to Gold Beach and buy white girl's clothes for you so you not have to dress like Indian."

Robin turned around quickly and stared unbelievingly at her mother. She felt as though Lillie had somehow read her thoughts and was offering a plan to give her white status. Her wide-eyed, expectant look, as she awaited her daughter's reaction, made Robin smile while fighting tears as love for her mother surged. "I like my clothes, Mama. They have more color and are better, too, for living on a ranch."

After dinner, Robin sat alone on the veranda and looked out to the ocean, dark gray and shimmering in the late afternoon sun. Her thoughts wandered. Mondays were always busy days, catching up on Sunday's neglected chores, but today she felt unusually tired. Papa Mac had been quieter than usual, and it seemed his thoughts were somewhere else most of the time.

He hadn't said much about his Sunday afternoon visit to the Hogan's. Aside from assuring her she'd done the right thing, he told her only that she was to stay away from them and was not to ride alone away from the ranch ever again. He needn't have said anything, for she would never be of a mind to go near the Hogan's again. As for riding alone, she seldom did so after her experience with the young Rogue river Indian, who'd caught her while she was picking wild blackberries. She recalled how frightened she was, and how they wrestled and rolled on the ground as he tried to get between her legs; and how she hesitated to use her knife on him until, in his attempt to subdue her, he struck her in the face; she stabbed him in the buttocks. That ended the attack and he limped hurriedly away, bleeding heavily. She was still shaking when she got to the beach and washed his blood from her skirt and legs in the surf. She often wondered why he had done that. He was a nice looking young man. Maybe they could have been friends. Did he think she was white and would have nothing to do with him? After that, and until yesterday morning, she hadn't left the ranch alone, except to search for moonstones on the beach nearby.

The sound of hooves shifted her attention to the path from the beach. With the sun behind the rider, she couldn't see his face, but it wasn't a familiar silhouette. A cowboy looking for work, she guessed. "Mama, Papa Mac, there's someone on horseback coming up the path!"

He was ten feet from the hitching rail when she saw his face. She sucked a sudden breath as her heart quickened. "Frank!" she shouted, jumping from her chair. She was down the veranda steps two at a time. "Oh Frank, it's you, you're back!" Tears filled her eyes as she reached to take his hand. The horse, wide-eyed at the onrush of sound and movement, spun to his left. Unprepared for the sudden change in direction, Frank followed his outstretched arm over the right side of the horse and landed on his back at Robin's feet, in a cloud of dust.

Dropping to her knees at his side, Robin smeared a tear across her cheek. Through her watery eyes he seemed to be smiling. "Frank! Frank, are you hurt?"

Reaching up, he took her by the shoulders and pulled her down to him. "Only my bloody pride," he said, hugging her tightly, "But I'd be obliged for a hand up."

Sobs and laughter burst from Robin as she pulled him to his feet. She could not withhold her joy and threw her arms about his waist. Hugging him, she nestled her head beneath his chin and kissed his chest. His arms pressed her to him and for an instant her emotion soared to a level she had only fantasized before. "Oh Frank, I love you so." She heard the voice and knew it to be hers, as was the thought itself; a thought 'til now expressed only in special, silent words of mind and heart with little hope of being spoken. Now, emotion had purged those special words from her inner soul and laid her feelings bare.

Embarrassed by her revelation, she awaited some response from him to ease the blush she felt. When, after breathless seconds waiting, no such response came forth, she slipped free of him and started toward the house to hide her shame.

"Robin, wait! I... I'm glad you... that is, I... wait, please."

She heard a tone, a sort of pleading, in his voice that made her stop and turn around. Too late; her mother and Papa Mac had reached him and he seemed to be in spirits happier now than hers. I'm being a fool, she thought. I should not turn my back on him just because he doesn't feel the way I do. And I don't have to be ashamed of my emotion, nor of what I said because of it.

With renewed pride, she raised her head, forced her shoulders back, then strode proudly to where he stood. The conversation paused as she approached, and Frank looked as though he were sorry for her. Her voice sounded throaty but the words came clear: "I'm really happy you came back, Frank, and I hope you'll stay." She smiled and made no attempt to hide her tears. His grin was all the salve she needed for her hurt.

Adam was jubilant and it pleased Robin to see him so.

While she had always liked trying to be like a son to him, she saw in Frank someone to better serve in that role and give her a chance to be a woman. She noticed that her mother, who normally remained at disciplined calm in times of high emotion, smiled, nodded, fluttered and flitted about in short but telltale bursts of excitement. "You good for Adam and this place," she heard her say. Aside from her own hope and desire, she had the comforting feeling that her mother was right.

As Adam hustled his "new hand" off to pitch his gear in the bunkhouse, Robin cared for Frank's rented horse. Then Lillie served tea and cakes as they sat on the veranda, and Adam served scotch whisky in little glasses to Frank and himself. It was an occasion, Adam announced, requiring a tipple of the sauce of Scotland. Scotch whisky, he claimed, was a blend of Bonnie Prince Charlie's blood with highland dew.

Long after tall shadows diffused into darkness, they sat and talked.

Frank told of his trip to Port Orford and his reasons for returning to the ranch. He told of his childhood in Glasgow and of his mother, and of the five years with his aunt in Boston. Relaxed by the whisky, he talked more, and with more detail than he had in the week of recuperation. His voice was stronger now, without the hoarseness it had when he was weakened by his ordeal after the shipwreck. Robin loved his trace of accent--Papa Mac called it a Scottish burr--and while she didn't understand some of the words and expressions he used, she didn't want to stop the flow of his words to ask questions. She was relaxed now, content to be near him, happy that he was again in her world.

The signal that the evening was over came from Adam, whose sudden snore broke a momentary silence.

"Adam not mean insult," Lillie commented, "he work hard today and drink too much. We all go to bed now, sleep good." Rising, she picked up the dimly glowing lantern next to her chair, turned up the wick and handed it to Robin. "Light Frank's way to bunkhouse', she said, "and make sure lantern in bunkhouse have fuel."

Frank stood up and took a deep breath. Robin thought he weaved a little, then he clasp Lillie in his arms and hugged her for what seemed a long time. As he spoke he seemed to be carefully selecting his words: "I want you to know, I'm very happy and ah, obliged, that Adam offered to let me stay and, ah, to help him with the farm -- the ranch work. I feel that you all are my, ah, my family now. I hope I can be worthy of you."

In the faint light of the lantern, Robin thought she saw his eyes fix on her. When he dropped his arms, Lillie stood on tip toes to kiss his cheek. "Have son now," she said.

A hundred feet east stood the log bunkhouse, its roofline silhouetted against pale silver light from the rising moon. Robin led the way, smiling to herself at his slight unsteadiness, liking the feel of his arms around her shoulders. Inside, she put the lighted lantern on the table, picked up the other and shook it. "This one's empty," she said. I'll take it and you keep this one."

"You'll need the light," he said.

"No, there's moonlight now, and I can see fine." Reluctantly, she forced herself to walk toward the door. "Good night, Frank," she said without looking at him. "See you tomorrow." She stepped out of the door, pausing to let her eyes adjust to the change in light.

"Robin, hold on a moment. There's something I wish to say."

She had the impulse to say "It's all right, Frank, you don't have to explain. I'm sorry I embarrassed you with what I said." She'd rehearsed it several times during the evening, but now, she stood without speaking. She felt his hand on her shoulder as he came to stand in front of her. The moonlight was on his face, and as he looked at her he smiled and the light sparkled in his eyes like glowing particles struck from flintstone.

He reached down and took both her hands in his. "From the second that I made the decision to return, I felt an excitement like I've never felt before. I must tell you, you were a major factor in that decision." He paused, cleared his throat and lifted their clasped hands to her chin. "You see, I have never before known this feeling I have for you. It... it's a feeling I'm not sure of. I just want very much to be near you."

"Whatever the feeling is, I have it too. I will always remember your words, and this moment is the happiest my heart has ever known."

He embraced her, not as before, but with a tender pressure that made her wish for more. Feeling his lips brush her forehead she raised her head. He swept his lips across her mouth then kissed her cheek. Slowly, he relaxed his arms and stepped back from her.

"I think I'd best get to bed. Your father's whisky has weakened my bloody knees."

"Good night," she said, then quickly clasp her arms around his neck and kissed his cheek. "My knees feel a little weak, too."

In her room, Robin dumped several moonstones onto he bed from a deerskin bag. Picking one, she placed it on her bedside table then put away the rest. "I'll throw it back tomorrow," she whispered, and turned out the lantern light. Closing her eyes she saw Frank in his "western" clothes, his long reddish-blond hair curling out beneath the brim of his cowboy's hat. I must have Mama teach me how to cut his hair, she mused. She was then aware that her mouth seemed fixed in a permanent smile.

CHAPTER ELEVEN

In a week Frank had been over every foot of the MacLean ranch several times on the horse he'd rented from the livery stable in Gold Beach. He thought it was a good horse, and considered buying the trail-wise gelding, but Adam judged it too old for ranch work.

"Wheezes some, too," he said, "like maybe his wind's broke. You'd best have one with good wind and a fondness for bein' in front of a string.

"There's a fella named Sellers got a horse ranch over by town. He's a feisty old fart and a caution to deal with, but he don't sell trash horses."

Seller's ranch stood a quarter-mile east of the main street through Gold Beach. Dust clouds rose from a big corral as a wrangler worked a horse through some sliding stops. Frank felt a child-like excitement about buying his own horse, and recalled a similar feeling when, on his seventh birthday, he was allowed to pick his gift from a litter of puppies.

A tall man, elbows hooked over the top rail of the corral fence, watched the wrangler and horse work and paid no heed to the buckboard till Adam drew it up behind him, then a brief sideways glance was all he gave.

"Enough for now, Ted," the tall man shouted, "Cool him off some then work his ass on the ropin' dummy. I see I got me some visitors."

Turning away from the fence he took a quick, appraising look at Frank then walked to Adam's side of the wagon. "Well, by God, my day ain't all bad when I get a visit from Adam Maclean." He smiled, showing even teeth. Pale blue eyes deep set under bushy, graying brows, looked over sun-weathered, high-boned cheeks. His nose was sharp and angular, hooked slightly over a long upper lip that could have handled a much bigger moustache than the thin, gray one he wore. Frank guessed him to be about sixty, a small bulge over his belt being the only hint that he'd given up hard riding for supervising.

Adam grasped the man's outstretched hand. "It's good to see you lookin' so well, Connie, 'though the wee swellin' around your middle tells me you're lettin' youth handle the broncs."

"Well, it's time, I figure. Ain't got any more bones that ain't been broke, least once. Now, you don't come here to admire my physique, Adam. What're yuh up to?"

"This here's Frank Ross, my new hand, and he needs a horse, Frank, shake hands with Con Sellers."

He reached toward Sellers, but the man backed away and came around the rear of the wagon to Frank's side and took his hand.

Smiling, he said: "I never liked reachin' across a man holdin' reins on a buggy horse. 'Bout time yuh do that the horse spooks at somethin', the driver's control is hindered and yuh get your feet run over by the goddam rig! Where yuh from, kid?"

Frank had the feeling he just got a polite lesson in horsemanship.

Adam filled in where Frank tried to be brief, and Sellers asked questions that further prolonged the recounting of how Frank came to the MacLean ranch.

Finally, Sellers said: "I suppose, bein' you're working the MacLean spread, you'll want an Appaloosa, right?"

"Well, I, that is, we hadn't--"

"It's the lad's choice," said Adam. "Whatever suits him."

"Come on to this other corral over here; I got a three-year-old I think you'll both like. He's Appy bred, but didn't blanket or spot out,

90

so we nipped his buds."

He was the color of red wine. White hairs sprinkled lightly through the red made him a roan--strawberry roan, Adam said, and Sellers agreed. His mane and tail were the color of flax with streaks of black here and there. He reminded Frank of a painted, wooden horse he once saw on a carrousel at a Boston carnival. He eyed the men cautiously, showing white, and flaring his nostrils as Con entered the corral carrying a halter. But he held his ground, showing the discipline of a Sellers trained horse.

"He's a beauty, isn't he, Adam?" remarked Frank.

"Aye, that he is. Fifteen-and-three, I'd say. Color's darker than most strawberries, almost a plum|. Too bad he didn't blanket; he'd made a fancy stud horse.

Sellers led the animal past them toward a small, low roofed building next to the corral. "I'll throw a saddle on him and you ride while Adam and me swap some recollections. He mightn't a told yuh, son, but him an' me rode together puttin' down the injuns in '55 an"56." He flipped the lead rope around the hitch-rail and disappeared into the tack room.

Frank looked at Adam. "How long were you in the Army?

"Oregon Volunteers, lad. Indians in these parts went on the war path in '55 against the settlers. Weren't enough of the Army boys to handle the situation so the Territorial Governor asked for volunteers to organize and help. I was in Fort Dalles at the time, tradin'. That's where I met Sellers. Just sort a got caught up in it. Gover'ment fed and that's about all. When the dust settled we got paid off in land. Arch Beeman was another of us."

Sellers quickly saddled the horse then turned to Frank. "Now I know yuh ain't no practised horseman, son, so yuh c'n be sure I ain't handin' yuh no dynamite, but he ain't no kitten, neither. We've trained him proper to cut and trail, and we've worked him on the ranch here fer two, three months. He'll know you're green afore you're on him ten seconds, but if he miscues, let him know who's boss. You know neck reinin', don'cha?"

"Aye, I know about it." He guessed it was the way he answered that gave Sellers second thoughts.

"How 'bout I give a little demonstration at what he c'n do, afore you take him? Then you'll know how he's trained."

Sellers worked the horse smoothly through backing, turning, lead changes, side passes and sliding stops. As he watched the experienced horseman perform on the well trained animal, Frank felt totally inadequate and wondered how he ever thought he could qualify as a hand for Adam. He had the feeling that he was about to make a fool of himself.

Sellers ended the exhibition by roping a post as though it were a steer to be thrown. The big roan slid to a stop and held tension on the rope. Sellers had dismounted with surprising agility before the horse had come to a halt.

Coiling the rope, he walked with the horse to where Frank and Adam stood. "Yuh know, if I weren't in the business of trainin' and sellin' horses, this is one I'd keep." He handed the reins to Frank. "Ever' now 'n then one comes along that's got somethin' special and yuh hate to let 'em go. This'n turns quicker'n a scairt rabbit. Well, you work him now. Any questions?"

"What's his name?"

"Well, he don't rightly have a real name yet Frank. But when he was gettin' broke--an" I mean ta tell yuh he threw every wrangler on the ranch, such is the spirit he has--they got to callin' him that 'pie-eyed son-of-a-bitch'. 'Course, he's all broke and quiet now, so don'cha worry none, but he was a pistol."

"Why 'pie-eyed'?" What does that mean?"

"Maybe yuh didn't notice, he's got one brown eye and one blue eye. Pied eyes, it's called, meanin' two colors. But that gets easy turned to 'pie-eyed'".

Immediately, the face of Jock MacIver, a school chum in Scotland came to mind. He wished he'd known the term back then, and he smiled at the thought of calling Jock "Pie-eyed MacIver".

Adam put down the hoof he was examining. "Well, I'll be damned," he said and came to the horse's head. Removing his hat, he waved it gently as he walked down the right side. Frank watched the blue eye follow Adam, the white showing prominent as though suspicious of the man's intentions. As Adam approached its rump, the horse turned his head and bobbed it just a little, tugging against the reins in Frank's hand. No question, the horse saw Adam's every movement.

"Don't worry, my friend, his eyes are sound like the rest of him or he wouldn't be on this ranch. Besides, they ain't a speck a truth in that crap about blue eyes bein' blind, or not seein' good. Albino eye, now that's another case, but he ain't no albino."

Adam seemed embarrassed. "Forgive me, Con. Forgot for a minute who we was dealin' with. I don't doubt your word a bit, or *I* wouldn't be on your ranch either."

"Let's have a drink on that, Adam, an' let this lad find out if the critter suits him." He turned to Frank. "Now son, there's a trail takes off behind the big barn over there," he said pointing, "an' if yuh keep bearin' left at all the forks, it makes a nice three-mile loop an' comes in back a' the ranch house. It's got some nice ups an' downs and a place er two yuh can let him out, if you've a mind to."

Frank thanked Sellers, tossed a casual wave to the two men and got in the saddle. Conscious that both men were watching, he was careful to mount and sit as Adam had schooled him during the past week.

He rode at a walk, stiff and self-conscious, until he rounded the barn. The Deringer pistol on the inside of his left boot pressed hard against his leg. He removed it and stuck it under his belt. He was reminded then, of his need to get a belt and holster for his father's Navy Colt so he could carry it western style.

Even at a walk he could feel the power and eagerness of the horse. The livery horse didn't have it, nor could he recall sensing it in the Morgans and Thoroughbreds he rode as a young lad in Boston. He felt this was an animal whose senses, nerves and muscles were set, waiting to respond to a signal--from the rider only, he hoped.

The walk had become almost a prance when, out of everyone's sight, Frank relaxed and realized he was holding too tight a rein while his knees pressed hard against the horse. As he relaxed, so did the roan. He patted the animal's neck and sighted on the path ahead through the erect and twitching ears. He leaned forward and the horse broke into an even, rythmic trot, not the stiff-legged, spine-jarring gait of all other horses he'd been on. His had a cushioned feel, as though he were trotting on spongy peet bogs. Frank could hold his seat well and had not the slightest need to post in the English manner. A touch of the heel brought forth a rocking-horse lope, a comfortable gait, easy on horse and rider. Frank felt he could ride this way for miles.

A breeze whipped strands of pale yellow forelock behind one ear and Frank was suddenly awed by the smoothness and beauty of the beast. "I hope you'll get to like me as much as I already like you," he said aloud. "Now, I must think of a fitting name."

While names paraded through his mind his attention to the path strayed, then he saw the trail fork sharply and pass down his left side. "Whoa there!" he called and reined heavily to the left. The horse reacted instantly with an abrupt change of direction. Totally unprepared for such quickness, Frank did not change direction with his mount, but landed spread-eagled on his belly on the sun-hardened dirt. The Deringer punched into his beltline like a fist.

"Bloody shit!" he grunted, rolling onto his back. He took the pistol out of his belt and rubbed the spot while getting his breath. "That pie-eyed son-of-a-bitch!" he muttered, still breathless. "He's probably a mile from here now!"

The sun shone yellow fire in his face. He closed his eyes and covered them with his arm. They'll have a good laugh at this, he thought: The new hired comes a cropper, *twice* in a blinking week! What a bloody awful show!

He sensed the shade, then a puff of hot air on his face, then prickly hairs. His arm slid off his forehead and he looked into the nostrils of a horse. He looked at a blue, then a brown eye looking back at him. "You pie-eyed son-of-a... ! That's it!" he shouted. "That's it!"

He reached up and took the reins that dangled over his chest. "MacIver, that's what it is, like my old chum Jock MacIver. One eye brown and one blue. A sturdy and loyal bloke he was, too."

Pleased, Frank got up and brushed the dirt from his clothes. As he remounted he felt great pride and confidence in the big roan. "All right, MacIver, let's get on with it, my friend."

CHAPTER TWELVE

As the trail emerged from a stand of madrone, the ranch house came into sight a short distance away. He could see Con Sellers and Adam sitting on the back porch, their feet propped on the railing. From full gallop, he brought MacIver to a sliding stop at a small corral near the house. Except for their parting of ways early on, the ride had gone well. If the horse did sense his rider's lack of experience, he never took advantage. Frank felt the same sort of infatuation with this horse that he felt about the puppy he picked out long ago.

He tried to temper his excitement as he dismounted and, with a new confidence, casually flipped the reins around the hitchrail and sauntered to where the two men sat.

Sellers smiled. "Yuh coulda just dropped them reins on the ground, son; he'd a stood there like he was anchored."

Frank felt some of the wind leave his sails. "I forgot about that," he said.

"Well, how'd it go?" asked Sellers.

Frank couldn't help smiling as his enthusiasm welled again. "The best horse I've ever been on," he said. "I won't have to look at any others, Mr. Sellers. I want him. How much is he?"

Sellers took the cigar from his mouth and studied it a moment. "Well, I know that horse'll fetch me more, but being that I'm overstocked right now, how 'bout thirty dollars?"

"Thirty dollars!" echoed Adam, rising quickly from his chair. "Come on, Con, that's twice what that horse is worth. You're forgettin' I'm here to look out for the lad. Now be fair, if yuh wanna stay friends."

Frank had no idea what a proper price was for a trained working horse, but he knew he had spoiled his bargaining position by showing enthusiasm for the animal. He didn't want a breech to develop in the friendship between these two men, yet he wanted the horse badly enough to pay what Sellers asked.

"Thank you kindly, Adam. I'm obliged. That is too bloody much, Mr. Sellers. I think fifteen is more in line." His heart jumped when he said fifteen, realizing he should have offered less, for to bargain upwards would be to ignore Adam's opinion.

Sellers looked thoughtful as he flicked the ash from his cigar. "Now Adam, if you'd let me finish afore yuh got mad, I'd a told yuh that price was with the bridle an' bit he's wearin'."

Frank saw the wisp of a smile break through Adam's beard, and realized Sellers was trying to save face and recover from an error in judgement that offended Adam.

"I figured it was, Mr. Sellers; my offer is for the same."

Both men looked at Frank with surprise. He was not just a little surprised at himself, and was beginning to enjoy the bargaining game.

"Tell yuh what, young fella, twenty dollars is as low's I'm willin'."

"Fifteen is as high as I'm willing," responded Frank. He was nervous now, but figured he'd make the same offer without the bridle, if the man refused.

Con Sellers took a long drag on his cigar, then threw it onto the ground away from the porch. "Can you shoot a gun, Frank? A pistol?"

Puzzled by the question, Frank hesitated. "Yes," he said. "I've shot a pistol, why?"

Adam spoke up: "Now what in the name of--"

"Now wait a minute, Adam. I'm bargainin' with the lad. I ain't aimin' to gunfight with him." He turned to Frank. "I got a counter

98

offer to make, son. Come with me. You too, Adam."

He led them behind the barn. Suspended on two hooks off the lowest branch of a madrone, was a small square metal plate. "From the barn to that six-inch-square iron plate is twenty one feet. Now, what I propose is each of us--you an' me-- take five shots at it. You can take aim, an' I'll shoot from the hip. Most hits wins. If you win, the horse an' bridle are yours for fifteen dollars. If I win, you've bought 'em for twenty." He stuck an unlighted cigar in his mouth. "Fair enough?"

"Wait a minute, Con, the lad's no match. He's been a sailor, not a gunslinger."

"I ain't neither, Adam. I'm sixty-four, an' not steady enough to bother with aimin' any more. I practice out here once in awhile, not often. Just thought it might add a little fun to the deal. Whadda yuh think?"

Adam laughed. "If he goes for that, I think he might as well pay the twenty an' forget the shootoff, you old rascal."

"What say, kid? You can use any pistol yuh want, includin' mine. Maybe Adam'll loan yuh his. I think that Deringer tucked in yer belt is a bit short for the distance."

He had the feeling that Adam was right. The man was going to win his twenty, but it would be more fun this way. "I'll give it a try," he said. "Adam, may I use your gun?"

Adam handed Frank his Remington Army .44. "Use both hands for steadiness, an' take your time, lad."

"Your choice, first or last?" Sellers offered.

Frank thought a few seconds. "You shoot first."

With his back against the barn, Sellers drew and cocked his pistol, a Colt .44. From waist level, his first shot rang the iron like a gong. His second shot, taken before the metal plate had ceased its swing, missed. The third shot was a hit. As the target stopped swinging the forth shot boomed out and swung it again. Sellers relaxed his arm and waited until the target was still before taking his last shot. Air moved the plate slightly as the next projectile sped past, but there was no clang of metal. He had missed.

"Well, three outa five ain't so bad," he said, then shook his head slowly. "And not so good, either."

Frank hadn't fired a pistol heavier than the 36 calibre Navy model Colt that had been his father's. Adam's .44 was larger, heavier, and didn't feel as comfortable in his hand. Stepping into Seller's footprints he raised the gun with both hands to eye level. He thumbed the hammer back and sighted at the approximate center. His hands had begun shaking as he squeezed the trigger. The gun roared but there was no sound from the metal plate.

When the smoke cleared he saw the target gently swinging. "High," he muttered, and figured he must have hit the tree limb--about two inches above the target--to cause the plate to sway like that.

The second time, he aimed at the lower edge of the plate, held his breath and squeezed the trigger before his hands began to shake. A loud clang accompanied the roar of the gun as the target jumped crazily on its suspending hooks. He smiled and looked over at Adam. He was smiling too. Still a bit high, he thought to himself and brought the aim-point a bit below the bottom edge of the target.

The next three shots were solid hits, the last of which brought a "Whoopee!" from Adam that drowned the clang of the iron.

Sellers stuck out his hand. "Good shootin', son. Yuh beat me, 'though I'm thinkin' I made it too easy for yuh. For someone who ain't shot much you seem pretty handy with a gun."

"Beginner's luck, really."

"I'll accept that. And now I've got another proposition for yuh."

"What's the proposition?" asked Frank.

"Come on now, Con, no more of your propositions."

"Well now, leave the boy hear me out, Adam. He don't have to take it, yuh know." He jammed the chewed end of the still unlit cigar into his mouth. "Here's my proposition: If I win the next shoot-off, I'll throw in that saddle and blanket and you pay the sum total of thirty-five dollars. If I lose, yuh get the whole shebang for fifteen. Even if yuh lose, yuh win. Couldn't get a better deal than that for thirty-five, nowheres, eh Adam? And we're havin' a little fun, to boot."

Frank liked the saddle. Sellers called it a California "center-fire" rig, and it appeared in good condition. "Is the saddle worth gambling twenty dollars, Adam?"

"I'd say ten is closer to right, maybe twelve."

"Now wait a minute gents, I'm riskin' the whole saddle if I lose. And if I win, I think you'll have to admit you won't be gettin' cheated payin' thirty-five dollars for the horse and all the riggin'. 'Taint as though yuh was gamblin' anything much. By your own accountin' Adam, if I win, all I'm really gonna make over the value you set on everything is eight, maybe ten dollars. A man's entitled to some profit, ain't he?"

"I reckon," Adam admitted with a nod. "Same game?"

"I'm not *that* big a fool, Adam. I'll do all my shootin' from the hip, as before, but this time Frank can take aim for two, and shoot three from the hip, like me. That's fair, ain't it?"

"No, Con, that ain't fair, 'cuz you've been shootin' from the hip, an' he ain't never, have you lad?"

"No, but I -- "

Sellers interrupted. "Tell yuh what, then, I'll only take four shots, an' the lad gets five. Best score wins. Can't be more fair than that, wouldn't yuh say?"

Adam threw up his hands. "You make deals faster than a card shark, Con, but it's up to the lad. I'm through interferin'. An' it's his money."

Frank thought a minute as the men looked at him, waiting for his decision. He had the feeling now that the old cuss had set him up for this by letting him win the first time. If he wins again he'll be getting a bargain. If he loses, which is most likely, Sellers will be satisfied, but so will he, really. He was having fun, and would have been glad to pay the thirty-five dollars just for MacIver.

"Let's do it," he said, "but I'll need to reload the pistol."

"On my belt here," said Adam, unbuckling his gunbelt, "Everything you need."

When their guns were loaded, Sellers took his position at the side of the barn. There was a breeze now, and the madrone jostled enough to cause the target to move. He took a deep breath and triggered the first round. It was a solid hit. The second round was a hit, a trifle high, as Frank's had been, and the target danced crazily. Sellers fired before its motion ceased and scored another hit, then another. Four rounds, four hits, in less than thirty seconds.

A scowl hardened Adam's face. "I think you've dry-gulched the lad, Sellers, and that don't keep you in high esteem with me."

"Just luck, my friend. Remember, he's got an extra shot to beat me with."

Frank knew he was getting a lesson in horse dealing and, along with it, gamesmanship as played in western America. "It's all right, Adam. I got myself into this."

Frank was more relaxed than he was the first time. The eratic up-and-down movement of the target made it tough to hold a constant point of aim. But his hands were steady, and when the motion was minimum, he fired. It was a hit. He lowered his gun and waited. He would take his time.

His second shot was a duplicate of the first. Now for the hip-shots. There was no sense in wondering how he would hold, for this would be shooting by pure instinct. He knew it was senseless to think he could beat Sellers. Chances were he wouldn't hit once from the hip, save the three times it would take to win. He told himself he was really just doing this for the sport of it, and the challenge was the game. Still, there was a never-say-die spirit within him that encouraged him to attempt the improbable.

Finally, he laid his elbow against his waist, cocked the pistol, fixed his eyes on the target, moved his arm until he felt as though the barrel pointed in the general direction of the target, and fired. The "clang" so surprised him that he lowered the pistol and looked at the two men.

"Well done, laddie."

Frank looked at the ground, embarrassed by Adam's praise. "Ha! Just bloody luck, that was."

He cocked the pistol, stared at the target and triggered the next round.

Adam's shout almost obscured the sound of the hit. "Holy Mother, he did it again!"

Sellers stared unsmiling at the swinging iron square, took the cigar from his mouth and ground it under his boot. "Maybe I'm the one being dry-gulched Adam. I can't believe this boy ain't shot a whole lot before."

"This was your idea, Con, not his."

It bothered Frank that Sellers might think he had lied about his experience with a pistol. But, no matter, he told himself, this was indeed, Sellers' idea. At first he didn't really care about winning, but now he had to try. They were tied at four hits; if he missed, they would just have to go through the business again. Fun as it was, he was anxious to get aboard MacIver for the ride back to the ranch, and to share his excitement with Robin.

Jamming his elbow tight against his hip, he cocked the pistol and pointed. Somehow, he didn't feel right this time and lowered the weapon. He shifted his feet, squared to the target and raised the pistol to waist level. Looking first at the gun barrel, then at the target, he tried vainly to judge how well the gun was pointed. No use trying to aim it that way, he concluded, just point it by instinct, pull the blinking trigger and get the silly business done with. He took a deep breath, expelled it quickly through his nose, and pulled the trigger. There was a muted "clink" and the target jumped crazily, then dropped down and swung slowly from only one hook.

Adam let go a "Yeaahoo" that likely was heard in town.

"Now wait just a damn minute, Adam," said Sellers, walking toward the target, "before yuh start celebratin'. I don't think he hit the target. 1 think he jus' hit one of the hooks that was holdin' it up an' broke it off."

Frank felt drained and leaned against the side of the barn while the two men went to the target. He knew it was over when he heard Adam's "Yeaahoo" again.

"Lookee here," Adam shouted, "he busted the hook off where it went through the hole in that hunk of iron. Hit it dead on, and there's lead from that .44 slug plastered all aroun' that hole."

"By God, you're right." Sellers shook his head in disbelief. "Can't believe no young sailor, fresh off the boat, can come here and beat me at my own damn game." He walked up to Frank, smiling. "Congratulations, son. And let me tell yuh, if you done that without no practice, you're either the luckiest damn beginner, or the best natural gunslinger I ever seen."

"I'm more surprised than you are, Mr. Sellers."

He put an arm around Frank's shoulders. "Well, let's go in an' have some coffee, an' settle up. I'm just glad I didn't suggest double or nothin'!" Taking two cigars from his shirt pocket, he offered one to Frank. "Mexico's best," he said.

"No Thanks, Mr. Sellers."

"Con to you, son. Now, speakin' of Mexico, I got a fancy, full-stamped Mexican double-rigged stock saddle, that would look right smart on that roan. I could let yuh have it for say, ten and that center-fire yuh won, or we could have another shootoff: best of five from the hip, double or nothin'--nothin' meanin' an even trade if yuh win."

Frank smiled. "I really like the saddle I've got, Mr. Sel... I mean, Con. But thanks for the offer."

"You never quit, do yuh, yuh old rogue?" quipped Adam.

"Nope, but mebbe I should. Reckon I'm just too easy a mark for my own good." They'd reached the house and Con held open the door. "Come on in, gentlemen," he said, with a sweep of his arm. "Today this place is mine. Tomorrow... well, some greenhorn just might beat me out of it."

CHAPTER THIRTEEN

"Well, I'm sure glad the boy's workin' out good fer yuh, Adam. He struck me first off as a real nice feller. Sure tickles me how he lucked inta beatin' Con outa the tack fer that horse." Archie Beeman gave a gleeful laugh. "Cain't wait to rib the ol' horse thief about it, neither."

"I'm tellin' yuh, Archie, it weren't dumb luck. I think the lad's a natural wonder with a gun."

"Well, docs seem thata way. Ain't two outa ten men c'n hit a danged buffalo from the hip at seven paces, 'less they's been doin' a heap a' prac-tizin'. How big did yuh say that hunk a' iron was, Adam?"

"Six inches square, so Con said. Looked about right."

Archie spat into the cuspidor at his feet. "That's the vital area in the middle of a man's chest that gunfighters go fer. But they ain't many c'n hit it when somebody's a shootin' back. A sidewinder name a' Slauson--Harvey Slauson--only man comes to mind that's a expert at killin' with one shot to the chest, and from the hip."

"Seems I've heard tell of him. Bounty hunter, ain't he?

"Sorta." Archie paused reflectively, then spat again. "A murder in' snake, in my book."

At the sound of approaching horses, Adam rose and peered out the window. "It's a possee a' two, Arch, comin' to drag me on home, I reckon." He took his glass from the table and drank the remaining whiskey. "Thanks for the drink, Arch. We'll expect yuh Wednesday 'bout one o'clock for Robin's Birthday party."

"Wouldn't miss it for anything," said Rilla. "And give my best to Lillie." She started for the kitchen, then turned as Archie followed

Adam through the door. "Supper in thirty minutes, Archie."

"All right, woman, I'm jist gonna take a look at Frank's horse, then I'll feed Toad an' come in."

As he watched the two young people ride up, Adam took note of the way Frank seemed now to be one with his horse, and was amazed at how much he had improved his seat in the four days he'd had the big roan. Well coordinated, the lad was. Of course, he'd been riding the horse nearly every minute his chores didn't keep him from it. And Robin, her heart on her sleeve, was his constant companion, radiant in her obvious infatuation with the young Scot. Adam couldn't imagine a better prospect for Robin, and the idea of their union so excited him and Lillie, they avoided talking about it for fear of disappointment should it never come to pass.

"Howdy, young folks. Reckon yuh come fer this here fugitive from Lilliesville. That's a mighty handsome critter yuh got there, young feller. Looks smart enough to be part mule, don'cha think?"

"Aye, that he does, Mister Beeman, but I been keeping the fact from him, fearing he might try to sing."

Archie expelled a loud 'tee hee'. "By gum," he said, turning to Adam and poking a thumb over his shoulder toward Frank. "*That* Scotchmen has a sense a' humor. Where's yours?"

"I'd laugh if yuh ever said anything funny, yuh old grizzly."

"Some folks wouldn't know funny if yuh stuffed their ears with it," returned Archie, with a wink toward Frank. "I heared how yuh beat Connie Sellers outa all that tack. I know fer a fact yuh gotta shoot pretty danged fancy ta git one up on him. Boy, I'd like t'uv seed that."

"I was lucky."

"Well, mebbe. Adam here reckons yuh got a natural good eye an' hand fer the gun. That's a jenna-wine God given gift, if yuh got it, kid. I know, 'cuz I usta have it. How'd yuh like ta pop a few caps at a target er two with me, some day?"

"I'd like that, Mister Beeman."

"Archie, son. 'Mister Beeman' is the callin' I reserve fer strangers and them I don't cotton to friend with." He arched a stream of tobacco juice a good seven feet, sleeved his mouth and turned to Adam. "You come along wi' the lad. Might be you c'n use some prac-tizin' too, wha'cha think?"

"Good idea, Arch. Tomorrow, 'bout four?"

"Jist right."

"Is it all right if I come too? asked Robin

"Why, yuh betcha can, Robbie." Archie put on a serious look and shook his finger at Frank. "One thing, though, young feller."

"What's that, Archie?"

"They ain't gonna be no wagerin'. Cain't afford losin' nothin' I got."

"Agreed," responded Frank, smiling. "I can't either."

Adam smiled too, for Archie probably had won more shooting contests than any man in Oregon. Rifle or pistol he was good, but with a pistol he could shoot better from the hip than most men could shoot using gunsights to take their aim. Of course, he was some younger when his skill was at its peak. "Mount up, troopers," he called. "Thanks for the squeezin's, Arch. See yuh tomorrow."

Astride Feather, Robin watched while Adam held the post upright in the hole and Frank shoveled the dirt in around it. Frank had gained weight, she noticed, and his nose didn't seem too long and thin for his face anymore. The sun reflected coppertones from his hair, trimmed to ear-lobe length by her mother. He looked strong and determined now, his jaw muscles flexing as he tamped the dirt around the post. She smiled as he extended his lower lip and, with a sudden blast of breath, blew away a pearl of sweat that had gathered at the tip of his nose.

"Soon's this one's set firm, we'll quit, Frank, and head for Archie's.

We'll start settin' the fence rails tomorrow."

Seeing the two men work together made Robin aware of her shortcomings as a substitute son for her Papa Mac. Adam had wanted to cross-fence the large pasture for nearly a year, but since the last hired-man quit, he kept putting it off. Frank was the incentive and physical help he needed for the big jobs he talked about from time to time. It wasn't just a matter of strength, but there was a dependency developing between them she saw as man-to-man, and realized why--though she knew Adam loved her like she were his own--no daughter could be like a son to her father, any more than a son could fill the needs of a woman for a daughter. Aside from her own feelings for Frank, she knew he was good for Adam and for her mother, too.

When they were through working, Frank looked at his watch. "Good timing," he announced. "We're due at Archie's in thirty minutes." He looked at Robin. "You *are* coming with us, aren't you?"

She had already made her decision not to go, yet she hesitated. "Well, I... no, not this time. There are some chores I have to do for Mama, and the stock to feed."

"I should be feeding the animals, not you."

"I like to feed the animals, and there are things my mother needs me to help her with. There will be other times when we can shoot, right here on the ranch. Besides, I know Uncle Archie is really interested in shooting with *you*. You see," she teased, "you have a reputation now."

"May be just as well you don't see me make a blinking fool of myself. Beginner's luck has a habit of leaving one on the second try."

"You'll learn a lot from Archie and papa Mac. Archie, he's *really* good with the pistol. Papa Mac is best with long guns." "Come on, laddie," shouted Adam from the buckwagon, "get aboard an' let's roll, unless yuh plan to double with Robin on ol' Feather there."

"I'm not going, Papa. I've things to do here."

"All right then, tell your Ma we'll be back in two hours.

110

Have yuh got your pistol, lad?"

"Aye, it's in a bag here, under the seat."

Robin watched for a moment as they drove off, sad that she was not going with them.

Back in the kitchen, she laid her head against her mother's shoulder as Lillie worked at the sink. "Mama, I really wanted to go with them, but I think it is better that I didn't, don't you? I have a feeling the men want to be by themselves. Besides, I think it is better if I am not around Frank too much, then maybe he will not tire of my presence and will seek my company."

Lillie turned and took her daughter by the shoulders. "You have shown wisdom which makes me proud."

"Thank you, Mama, but right now I don't feel so good about not going."

"I know, but pain will soon be washed away by happy, knowing you did right thing."

Frank scored two more hits on the pendulum target with his last three shots from the hip, then turned to Adam, seated now with Archie on a log a few yards behind him. "Adam, do you mind if I try another five shots at it before we leave? I think I'm getting the feel of it now."

"Not a'tall, laddie. Have another go at it." Then he leaned toward Archie: "Looks to me like he's got a right good feel of it already, whatta *you* think?"

"I think he's about the most natural borned gun hand 1 ever seed. I give him a few pointers, he winds up out shootin' us both."

"Damned if his eye an' his gun barrel don't seem like they're linked up somehow, Arch."

"His are, an' that's the makin's of a good hipshooter--gun hand pointin' natural-like to what the eye looks on. A little prac-tizin', an' he'll be a hunnert percent deadly. Look how quick he cottoned to timin'

111

on the swingin' target. Musta tooken me hours to git that right."

Their attention was on Frank again as the Colt barked and the swinging disc klinked and spun on its vertical axis. His next shot missed.

"Keep that elbow into yer side, Frank. If it splays out, yer point ain't gonna be true," advised Archie. "An' be keepin' the gun out in front of yuh. The farther back it gits, the harder 'tis to point where yer lookin'."

Frank nodded, and the next three shots were hits.

"All he's gotta do now is work on speed an' the draw, then folks 'ud pay money to see him shoot. An' some 'ud clear the country to keep from it." Archie gave a little chuckle. "It's a dang good thing he ain't bent to go agin' the law."

The thought that Frank could ever be anything but honest had never crossed Adam's mind. He suddenly realized how lucky he was that it was Frank who came into their lives, and not someone of doubtful character. Now *that* was something worth thankin' the Lord for, he mused, and he'd do it that very evening.

"He needs a holster. Reckon we c'n get one for that Colt of his at Hollister's? It's been a popular gun, that '51 model."

"I was a thinkin' 'bout that, Adam. I got one--belt, pouches an' all -- that was made fer my ol' Colt Navy, which I don't use no more since I got me the .44. I'll make him a present of the ol' rig. It's done a heap a' service, but it's still fit t'do more."

"That's a nice thing to do, my friend. He'll like that, comin' from you."

"Well, I've took a likin' to the boy, an' I'm gonna git some pleasure outa seein' he learns to shoot proper. The way I got it figured, can't hurt bein' good."

Frank was smiling as he came to where the men were standing. "You've helped me a lot, Archie. Thanks."

"Well, help ain't over yet, young fella. Be a waste fer someone as natural good as you not to learn the fine points. Come around when yuh can, an' we'll work some more. An' look to Adam fer teachin' the long gun. Now, c'mon in and say howdy to Rilla while I fetch yuh somethin' fer carryin' that Colt at the ready."

They took the east trail back because it was the shorter route. The sun, now in the northwest sky, warmed their backs as they turned south off the Beeman ranch and onto the wagon road that bordered the west end of the Hogan spread. As two men on horses approached, Adam felt the hair rise on the back of his neck. "Oh shit," he said aloud and instinctively his hand went to loosen the gun in its holster. He wondered if Frank had bothered to reload his gun after the last shots he'd fired.

"What's the matter, Adam?"

"Hogans. I'll explain later, but they ain't friends."

Perhaps it was because Adam's face was in shadow, the sun being to his back, but it was obvious to Adam that Cyrus was startled when he recognized him as driver of the buckwagon. Then came the sneer, already seemingly permanent on the face of Carl, his right arm still bandaged. Moving their mounts to the side of the road, Hogan spewed sarcasm as he recovered from his surprise.

"Well, looka here, Carl, it's that nice gennelman that come our place awhile back to 'polagize for his breed daughter cuttin' on yuh. Whupped any cripples lately, Mister MacLean?" Cyrus folded his hands on the saddle horn, sneering as he looked down, first at Adam, then at Frank.

Slowly, Adam shook his head and smiled wanely to control anger he knew was apt to become rage. "Surprises me your mouth hasn't already got you killed, you yella-livered pile a' pig shit. You're packin', an' so's your louse of a son. Why don't you both draw so's I can kill you legal-like?"

The sneer faded just a little on Cyrus Hogan's face and he turned to his son. "Don't let him temp' yuh, Carl. Cain't yuh see he's a baitin' us 'cuz he's hired hisself a gunfighter to back up his threats."

Adam's surprise at that remark nearly caused him to take his eyes off Hogan for a glance at Frank, whom he was sure was wondering what this was all about. "Don't need a hired gun to take care of cowards, Hogan. This young fella's my new hand."

Hogan's sneer crept to its fullest again. "*Gun* hand I reckon, judgin' by the fast-draw rig he's got a housin' that pistol. Looks well broke in, I'd say. Nope, you ain't gonna trick me or Carl inta goin' fer guns, MacLean. It's *you* that don't seem willin' to settle nuthin' in a peaceable way. Come on, Carl."

As the Hogan's horses began to move away, Adam turned to Frank whose eyes still followed the Hogans. "Ain't no man on earth ever made me madder'n that mangy ba…"

"Look out, Adam!"

Even before he heard the warning, he felt his right shoulder pushed down as Frank rose from his seat and spun to his left. Out of the corner of his eye he saw the blur of metal an instant before muzzle blast slammed against the left side of his head. Thunder rocked his senses; silver light flashed against black then scarlet, and the flesh of his cheek and ear stung with the pricks of a thousand needles. Like listening through a giant sea shell, Frank's voice was faint against the constant roar.

"Leave the gun lay where it is, you bloody, skulking freak. Mister Hogan, take your pistol from its holster very slowly and drop it on the ground."

Pressing a hand to the side of his face, Adam sat up and looked at Frank standing gun in hand, jaw set hard beneath those cold steel eyes. Carl was holding the trigger finger of his left hand, wimpering that it might be broke. The sneer was gone from Cyrus Hogan's face and it was turning red with obvious rage as he unholstered and dropped his gun. He looked at Adam, his mouth quivering as he spoke.

"Not a hired gunfighter, eh MacLean? Now whose a coward, an' a liar to boot? It's plain that innercent folks ain't safe with the likes a you an' yours aroun'."

"I'm not a gunfighter, or I would have killed your sneaking son for trying to backshoot Adam. It was pure accident--and bad shooting on my part--that the ball struck his gun instead of his gut. I'll try to do better next time, if the need arises."

The sneer was back on Hogan's face. "He lies like you do, MacLean, tryin' ta twist the truth aroun'. Well, the Sheriff ain't gonna believe that my son here is gonna try drawin' agin' a hired gun. He's gonna know the truth, that he was jist tryin' ta keep his daddy from gettin' back-shot."

"Shut your lying mouth and get straight away from here, both of you," ordered Frank, a menacing tone to his voice that surprised Adam.

"What about our guns? I s'pose yuh'll add 'em to yer collection."

"You can come back and get them later, but I want to see you put some distance, between us, *now*"

Adam briefly watched them over his shoulder then turned to Frank. "As I was sayin' before I got interrupted, ain't no man on earth's ever made me so mad as that mangy bastard."

Frank smiled. "I soon got the idea there was a bond of mutual dislike between you and Hogan. I thought your description of him rather colorful."

"I was just being polite. I get tongue-tied when I try to control my anger. " They laughed as they moved on toward home again.

"I'm sorry I had to fire so close to your face, Adam. I just couldn't take time to be more careful when I saw Carl Hogan draw his gun. I hope the blast didn't damage your hearing."

"Better the hearin'" than the damage that boy's lead might have caused me. I'm mighty grateful to you lad, an' to the good Lord for givin' you the quickness an' the eye. Tell me, did you really mean to shoot the gun from his hand?"

"The truth is that my eyes were on his gun when I drew and fired, and that's where the ball struck. It wasn't that I meant to. I had no time to think about it. It's instinct I guess, like Archie says. In my case, the gun points where my eye is focused. I guess it's a good thing I didn't take my eyes off his gun, and a better thing I didn't miss. I was really just looking at his bandaged arm, and thinking of Robin. I was so surprised when he reached for the gun, I just might have looked at his face."

"I'm thinkin' it's too bad you didn't".

There was still ringing in his ear, and white flashes in his left eye when he blinked. And there were black things floating around in his vision. He held a hand over his left eye. The other eye was normal.

"Are you all right, Adam?"

"Oh, sure," he lied. "I've a wee ringin' in my ear, but that'll go away. It ain't the first time I've had a gun muzzle close to my head when it's been touched off." He took out a cigar, and lit it. After a few puffs he gave a sigh and said, "Now I'll tell you how this all started. By the way, lad, you've now the reputation of bein' a gunfighter 'cuz of that holster an' all Archie gave you. What do you think of that?"

"I think I should get another holster, or go back to being a sailorman, or else practice a lot."

"I'm hoping you won't have to do any of those things, Frank."

"What about his threat to get the Sheriff?"

"He won't. Weren't nobody hurt, an' he knows the Sheriff won't believe that you drew first, then waited to shoot the gun from Carl's hand. Don't make sense. And it would call for further explanations of what the trouble's really all about--which is what I'm about to tell you--an' I don't think Hogan wants to open that keg."

"Then I guess the matter's done with?"

"Maybe. Let's hope it is." But instinct told Adam it wasn't.

CHAPTER FOURTEEN

Her gay spirits in command, Robin pulled the Chilkat blanket tightly around her shoulders and whirled several times around the room, until she tripped and nearly fell over Frank's outstretched legs. Slumped in a chair, chin on chest, he did not stir. His faint throaty sounds were weak competition for the vibrant, guttural rasps from Adam, slouched in a chair alongside.

She smiled. At least they had waited until her party guests were gone before giving in to the effects of their overindulgence in food and drink. Into the kitchen she glided and threw her arms around her mother. "It was the best birthday party I've ever had, Mama. I even *feel* a year older."

"You are young woman now."

"Old enough to marry and have..." Robin paused thoughtfully, then spoke in the Nez Perce language of her mother. "Do you think Frank understands that I am old enough to be married now?"

"I cannot see in his head what he does not tell or show in some way. You are in his shadow more than I; what image do you think he has of you?"

"Sometimes the sun rises in his face when he looks on me, and his rock-gray eyes smile. My spirit soars because I think he sees the woman in me. But since the day of his return I have not again known the harbor of his arms, nor affection from his words. Therefore, 'though I know he is a friend to me, I must believe he sees only a child."

Lillie's look was quizzical. "You said 'he is a friend'; you did not say 'like a brother' to you." A slight smile crossed her face.

After a coy glance at her mother, Robin looked down and her fingers toyed with the large, gold locket that hung at her bosom. "*All hope has not bled from my heart, Mama,*" she said, trying not to smile. "This is a beautiful locket he gave me, isn't it? He said it was his mother's, and her mother's. Would he give such a thing to someone he did not think of as a sister?"

"I believe he would give such a thing only to someone he thinks would bring joy to his mother and her mother."

"Then why does he not tell me how he feels?"

"Young men think it more man-like to show strength of arm and mind, than tenderness of hand and heart. They are silent in fear their mouths will betray them. It is woman's task to understand her man's values and encourage him to arrange them in order of importance to her."

The pause was filled with Frank's voice as he stood in the doorway to the kitchen area. A surge of embarrassment flushed Robin's cheeks until she remembered they had been speaking a language he could not have understood.

"Goodnight, ladies," he said. "And, once again, many happy returns of the day, Robin. I hope you'll forgive me for falling asleep. Thank you for inviting me to the party."

"Thank you, again, for the beautiful locket, Frank, but I worry about wearing it, knowing how much it must mean to you."

"It means a lot to me to have you wearing it."

His words excited her. She wanted to believe they meant she was more an object of his heart than a "little sister". She took a quick glance at her mother. Their eyes met, but Lillie's expression told her nothing.

Then Lillie said, "Tomorrow is fourth of July. In Gold Beach will be parade at noon for Independence Day of America from King George." Obviously embarrassed, she looked shyly at Frank. "Not mean

118

to make offense."

"No offense taken," he said with a broad smile, "That was a bit before my time. Besides, we Scots tried for our independence from England, but lost the ruddy war."

"I forget," she said, looking relieved. "Maybe you and Robin like to go."

Robin had to restrain herself from clapping with enthusiasm. "I'd *really* like that," she said, then worried that she may have sounded too eager.

"I'd like that too," Frank said. "Will we all be going? I mean, you and Adam will go too, won't you?"

"I think I stay here and rest. I am tired with busy day. Have seen parade many times. Besides, I think Adam Mac not feel good tomorrow. Too much party today." She smiled, nodding her head as she said it, then added, "Maybe you like to take surrey, with my horse. She not have work in many days."

"Frank probably wants to ride MacIver, Mama."

"No, no. I can ride him anytime. I think the surrey a champion idea, really."

"Champion, what is champion?" asked Lillie.

"Means the best, Lillie; a winner; a first-rate idea."

"Thank you, I learn new word. Now, what time you want to go?"

"Oh, about mid-morning I think. Then maybe we can get a good spot to view the parade." He looked at Robin. "Is that all right with you?"

"Fine. We can take a lunch."

"Ah, we have a new Champion," Frank chortled, and put his arm around Robin's shoulders.

Robin looked at him in pleasant surprise, and grinned. Aside from the gesture of affection it was the first time she ever heard him laugh.

She gave her mother a sly look; Lillie too, was grinning.

In Gold Beach they found a good vantage point on the main street in a large, open area between buildings, where several other carriages were already parked.

The parade was small, but colorful. A crowd of perhaps three-hundred formed along the street and provided flag-waving enthusiasm... and noise. A twelve piece band composed of volunteer firemen led the parade followed by the shiny, black, horse-drawn firewagon, its bright red pumper elegantly trimmed with gold-leaf and appointed with gleaming, polished brass fittings. Smoke belched from the boiler, set to provide pump pressure in the likely event people got careless with their Chinese fireworks, firecrackers or other miniature explosives, already in abundant use.

Four elderly men in Cavalry uniforms were a mounted color-guard leading a rag-tag group of several dozen men of varying ages in various dress including military uniforms, or parts thereof. They shouldered a variety of weapons and marched to what seemed a variety of cadences. They had, however, one trait in common that Frank noticed: to a man, they held their bodies erect, chins high as though defiantly proud. The banner that preceeded them proclaimed the reason: DIRECT DESCENDANTS OF VETERANS OF WAR FOR INDEPENDENCE 1776 - 1781. Behind the descendants, an assortment of Indians--men, women and children--walked, waving just about anything that might draw attention. Conspicuously absent was the presence of U.S Army regulars. When war between the states became imminent, garrisons in the Pacific Northwest had been reduced to maintenance status or closed altogether, and the troops committed eastward.

"What tribe are they?" asked Frank

"Mostly Rogues and Tututnis, I think. Some of them come off the reservation, some never went to the reservations. The Indian

Agent lets them come, saying it makes them feel good being part of an American celebration. I don't know why they want to celebrate America's Independence from England. The English never took their land."

Frank looked at Robin and his brow furrowed as the Delawares, Powhatans and Algonquians came to mind. After a moment, he said, "They would have, in time."

They were preparing to leave when he spotted Carl Hogan in the crowd across the street and watched him for a short time before Robin noticed where his attention was directed. He heard her suck in her breath and knew she'd seen him.

"That's Carl Hogan with his brother," she said. "Has he seen us?"

"I think so, but he quickly looked away, as though pretending he hadn't."

Without taking his eyes off Hogan, Frank reached over and put his hand on hers. "Don't worry, he won't bother us, I'm certain."

"I feel safe with you."

"And I with you, lassie," he said with a chuckle and gave her hand a squeeze, "After all, you hurt him more than I did."

She turned her hand over and their fingers entwined. He liked the feeling of her closeness and wanted to look at her, but was compelled to watch the Hogan boys. He pulled his arm toward his leg and she slid closer to him. Even above the odor of firecrackers, he could smell the scent of honeysuckle she was wearing.

Finally, Carl pushed Billy into a store and, after a brief glance in Frank's direction, followed his brother inside.

The crowd had thinned in front of them and their path to the street was clear. "We seem to have forgotten to eat the lunch you prepared. Shall we eat here, or would you rather find another place?"

"Another place." Her grip tightened on his hand. "I don't want to be this close to the Hogans. The Rogue River is just a short ride from here. I'm sure we can find a spot along the bank where there's plenty grass and shade."

She wore a blue, narrow-skirted dress with beadwork at the neckline and hem, and on the deerskin belt around her waist. Beaded deerskin mocassins adorned her feet. Her long, dark hair, even in the tree-filtered sunlight, flashed auburn highlights from braided coils over her ears.

They had finished the lunch, and as she sat across from him, propped on one arm, legs pulled up, her attention was on the locket she turned in her fingers. He noticed--as though for the first time-- the honey-maple color of her legs and visualized the contrast with the pinkish tan of his arms and hands.

She now seemed more than just a girl for whom he felt a fondness. There was an ache in his heart that pulsed a new and fevered emotion. She was no longer merely pretty, she was beautiful. He wanted to be closer, to put his hands on her. Her skirt, gathered tightly around her legs above the knees, displayed melded outlines of hip, buttock and thigh, and provoked in him a sensual urge to run his hand along those voluptuous curves. He yearned to pull her to him and press himself firmly against her.

Yet his was a gentle passion. He wanted to brush his lips across her cheeks and eyes, to touch his mouth to hers; to stroke her hair; to caress her breasts and feel the softness he could only imagine. He knew now what his feelings were; there was no doubt in his mind.

He moved to where she was and knelt beside her. "Robin." his voice was thick with emotion. "Robin, what I've got to say may not be welcome, but I've got to get it off my chest before I bust."

She looked up at him and the blue of her eyes seemed to darken as they widened. He sensed it was a fearful look she had and cursed himself in silence for his clumsiness. He quickly, gently, clasp her hand that held his mother's locket. "I mean to say I know now that I love you."

The look that came upon her face made his heart rejoice with a happy feeling no words could express.

"Oh I've wanted so to hear that from you, Frank. I love you, too."

He slipped his arm beneath her shoulders and pulled her to him. His lips touched hers, gently at first, sensing their soft fullness; tasting their sweetness, feeling their responsive movement against his own. Moving from her mouth he lightly kissed each eyelid and her cheek. Still kneeling, he held her half-cradled in his arms, then cheek on cheek he whispered that he loved her. "It sounds so simple when I say it. It seems not to express all that I feel for you."

He felt her arms around him tighten as she held him close. "I know; my words, too, seem empty of the real feeling in my heart."

As he eased her to the ground and lay beside her, the flare of passion that earlier produced his sensuous thoughts, cooled to a glow of prudent gentleness. He stroked her hair and face and kissed her mouth again, and smelled the sweet, erotic scent of her body, but let the softness of her breasts remain untested.

"I'm so glad you love me," she whispered. "It's a dream come true."

They sat up, startled, as the clatter of nearby galloping horses spoiled their moment. Only the backs of the two riders were visible as they rode away.

"It was the Hogans, I'm sure of it," muttered Frank, through clenched teeth.

"Do you think they saw us here?"

"I would guess they did, the horse and carriage in plain sight, like they are."

"Do you suppose they… they've been watching?"

Angered by the thought that they may have, Frank paused before answering. He wanted to relieve Robin of embarrassment. "I don't think so, any more than just in passing. And don't be concerned about them. I'm sure they're just on their way home."

She sat close and held his arm as they drove. His heart was filled with the emotion of their love, and his mind wandered down a dozen paths his love created. His proper Boston aunt would no doubt swoon at the news he'd taken a half-Indian bride. It's all the Captain's fault, she'd say, making a sailor of him whilst just a boy, and hauling him off to all the seamy and uncivilized parts of the world. He smiled at the thought. He loved his aunt; she was a fine lady, dignified but compassionate, and he knew she would love Robin too. Robin in Boston; Robin in Glasgow... the thought of that delighted him, and his smile broadened.

"What are you smiling at?"

"I'm having some happy thoughts," he said, "about us. Maybe someday I can take you to Boston, and Scotland."

She was silent as she took the locket in her hand, turning it over several times. Then she opened it. "Frank, what is the word that's written on the inside? I can't make it out very well, and it's in fancy writing."

"A Bellendaine! It's the war cry of the Clan Scott. My mother was a Scott, you see. A place called Bellendean was the gathering place for Scotts in time of war. The words are in the Gaelic tongue, meaning 'to Bellendean'."

"Who did they war with?"

"Oh, in early times with other clans, mostly."

"Like different Indian tribes fighting each other, wasn't it?"

"Much the same, I guess. We also fought the English. In those days they seemed to regard *us* as savages too." He knew that was the wrong thing to say. He looked at her and she was staring straight ahead. There was an awkward silence while Frank tried to think of something to say that would clarify what he meant.

"Most whites here consider me a savage. In Boston or in Scotland, they surely would."

Frank brought the rig to a halt, turned and took her hands in his. "I suppose I should have used the terms ruffian and rebels to describe what the English used to think of the Scottish, and the Irish, too, for that matter. But people change and so do their concepts. All peoples were primitive and uneducated in the beginning." He could see worry in her face and it pained him. He kissed her and laid her head against his shoulder. "It really doesn't matter to me what others think, and I can tell you this: You and your family are far more civilized than the crew of the Charlotte; civilized enough to live anywhere in the world. She looked at him with a wan smile.

"Besides," he added, "I have no intent of ever leaving here." "There can be problems here, too," she said. "I think we should get home now, before my parents worry. We can pick up the East road from here; it's the shortest way home."

"Problems or not, Robin, I want to marry you." She said nothing, but took his arm again and nestled herself against him.

They were above the deepest section of Caves Canyon when a bundle of firecrackers exploded in a volley a few feet in front of the horse.

"What the bloody hell!" Frank shouted, as the startled animal made a sudden turn away from the canyon, then bolted over a ditch at the side of the road. The buggy bounced violently as it was dragged across the ditch and into a brush covered field before Frank regained control. Pitched from the jolting vehicle, Robin lay on the ground some yards behind, clutching her leg below the knee. Jumping from the vehicle, Frank ran to her.

"The rear wheel ran over my leg, Frank."

His stomach knotted when he saw blood gushing through the fingers of her hand that only half covered the deep gash in the calf of her leg, cut by the wheel's iron tire.

"I'm all right, except the blood scares me a little." She looked up at him and gave a nervous laugh. "It really doesn't hurt."

"It doesn't look bad," he lied, as he moved her hand from the wound, then put it back. "Just lie still and hold pressure on it whilst I make a bandage." Folding his kerchief into a narrow band, he wrapped it tightly over the wound.

"That's fine," she said, as he helped her to her feet. "I can walk on it."

"No, don't. I'll carry you."

As he put her in the rear seat he saw blood oozing through the kerchief. "Keep your foot up on the back of the front seat to slow the bleeding, and hang on."

With pistol drawn, he lead the horse back onto the road, hoping the open presence of the gun would discourage further pranks. He wanted to look around through the brush on the canyon side of the road, to see if he could find who threw the firecrackers, but dared not delay in getting Robin home for aid as quickly as possible. Probably youngsters, he thought, and shouted as he climed into the surrey, "Whoever threw the 'crackers, if I find you, you bloody idiot, you'll wish I hadn't." Then he rein-whipped the mare to a gallop.

No doubt sensing trouble from the way Frank was driving the rig, Lillie and Adam rose quickly from their chairs on the veranda and were waiting at the foot of the steps when he pulled up. The concern in their faces added new guilt to the remorse he already felt for Robin's injury while in his care.

"Robin has a nasty cut on her leg," he shouted, looking first at Lillie, then Adam. "She'll have to be carried inside. We'll need hot water, soap, and cloth for bandage. And maybe a doctor."

Lillie started up the steps then paused and gave a worried look back.

Robin waved her hand. "I'm all right, Mama. It's really not so bad," she said cheerfully. Lillie hurried on into the house.

Adam had moved quickly to Robin's side of the surrey and reached for her. I've gotcha, Honeygirl," he said. "And don't worry lad, we've our own hospital right inside. So long as her leg's still attached, her mother an' I can likely do the doctorin'. Now come on in an' tell us what happened."

While he sat talking to Adam, Lillie tended Robin. After a few minutes she came to them with a smile that lifted a ton from Frank's heart. "Cut is long, not deep, not in muscle. Will heal good in week, I think." The smile faded and she looked at Frank with a solemn, pained expression. "Most pain Robin suffer now is from loss of locket. She did not know of this until now, and thinks chain maybe broke in fall from surrey." Lillie put her hand on Frank's shoulder. "She wants to go back now to look, but I think maybe you and Adam go. She cannot see through tears she is making."

Let's go, laddie," said Adam, rising from his chair. "From what you've told me, the place ain't far from here and there's not likely to be traffic over where she fell. We'll find it, I'm sure, lad."

They searched in vain in a wide radius from where she fell, in case it might have been flung away from her somehow.

"It sure ain't around here," said Adam. "It's tough to read the signs in this hard ground, but I say someone else's track's have walked all over yours."

Frank stood where she'd lain, pushed back his hat and looked around. "Now why would anyone come in here off the road unless... unless this is where they were hiding when they threw the 'crackers?"

"That's possible," agreed Adam as he walked to a large, wild bush. "It's right across the ditch, and near this bush that's large enough to hide a moose." He laughed. "Yuh know, it might be that yuh damn near ran over the bastard when the horse came chargin' in here." Adam paused and looked around, then went on, pointing. "An' if he hid right *here*, he might just have seen the locket layin' *there* when you'd gone."

"Are there youngsters living around here that might do such a prank?"

"I've been givin' that some thought for quite awhile an' keep comin' up with the same answer: Hogan boys. You saw 'em earlier, you said, an' they coulda guessed you'd be comin' home this way from where yuh had the picnic. Wouldn'ta been much outa their way to be waitin' here. The west line of their property runs along Caves Canyon there, the other side of the road. If that mare had spooked the other way, you'da gone down in the deep, rocky part of that gulley an' things woulda been a whole lot worse."

"Maybe that's what they were hoping would happen."

"I reckon," said Adam. "I reckon that's *just* what they were hopin', an' prob'ly why they hid on this side of the road."

As he started to move away from the bush, he stopped and picked something off the ground. "This sorta proves my theory," he said, holding a small copper object between thumb and forefinger. "An unfired primer cap. Skirt's spread a bit, so its been on a nipple, but musta fell off, as they will if they ain't on tight. Ain't been here long enough to tarnish. I'd say the slimy bastard gave some thought to bushwhackin' yuh, Frank."

The term was new to Frank and seemed to fit what he thought Adam meant, but "What's a bushwhacking?" he asked.

"That's an ambush, hidin' in the bushes an' attackin' someone without warnin'."

A hot collar seemed to tighten itself around Frank's neck as he envisioned Carl Hogan hiding behind the bush. "I wonder why he didn't."

"Hard to say, lad. Scared, maybe. Excited... couldn't steady his hand enough. Maybe if that young brother of his was with him, he didn't want the kid to see what a sneakin' coward his big brother really is. An' the kid would be a witness."

"What do you think we should do, Adam."

"Nothin' right now but go on home. We'd get no place with the father backin' up the lies they'd tell, an' we've got no hard evidence that proves it was them that did it. After the threats I made to 'em, if we was to approach their house, we'd prob'ly get rifle-shot before we got too close. I don't think we're ever gonna draw them Hogan's to a fair fight."

"I wish he'd tried to bushwhack me."

"No, it's glad I am he didn't. He might've gotten lucky, then he'd surely have killed Robin too."

Frank was embarrassed by the brash overconfidence his statement implied. "You're right. And I forgot, for the moment, about Robin."

Adam walked over to Frank, smiling, and gave him a pat on the back. "You're true grain from a Scottish glen," he said. "Now let's get on home before--as my mother would say -- 'the spirits of your ancesters stir you to foolish deeds to prove what men you are by how well you can die.' She hated violence."

As they drove back Frank was deep in thought. It was revenge he wanted, and he knew that his desire to punish Carl was giving him rash ideas as to how he could achieve it and recover the locket. "The idea that Carl Hogan might have the locket makes matters worse," he said finally.

"I know, an' I'm truly sorry about the loss of it. But I've a feelin' that--assumin' he has it--that heirloom piece is somehow gonna be a curse to that boy."

"I hope you're right, Adam."

"Well, patience ain't one of my virtues, laddie, but I think it may prove rewardin' in this case." He nodded his head several times, as if in self approval. Then he said, "Yuh know, I think Lillie's influence is beginning to show in me."

"And your mother's."

"Aye, my mother's too, I suppose. It's been a long time comin', but this is the first time I can remember turnin' away from any excuse for a fight, an' feelin' right about it. It don't feel *good*, but it feels *right*."

CHAPTER FIFTEEN

At better than a hundred yards, the coyote's yellowish coat made him a tough target against the background of tall, summer grass. If he was aware of the riders, he failed to show it as he tugged at his morning leg of mutton.

Without dismounting, Adam leveled his 54 caliber Gemmer-Hawkens and fired. The half-ounce lead ball from the plains rifle threw the coyote six feet from his final breakfast.

Frank, ready for a backup shot, took his rifle from his shoulder. "That was a bloody eye-blinker! A really first-rate bit of shooting, Adam. Glad I didn't have to back you up on that; I could barely see him."

The dead ewe lay in the corner of the northeast pasture, close to the fence. Frank's nose wrinkled at the stench of sour blood and flesh.

Kneeling beside the carcass Adam examined the partially mutilated remains. "She's been chewed some, but this critter didn't do the killin'. The critter that done her in was two legged an' used a knife." He pulled the head back exposing the bloody throat area. "See here, throat's cut right through the juggler. Sliced. Teeth don't do it that way."

"You'd marked her as having a lamb, Adam."

"Yep. Well, we'll look for the bummer, but my guess is that it's stew meat by this time." Adam plucked a handful of grass then angrily threw it down. "Sons-a-bitches!" he exclaimed.

"Who you think did this?"

Still kneeling, Adam cocked his head toward Frank and squinted against the early sun. "Same as you're thinkin', I'll bet."

"Hogans."

"Sure as hell weren't renegades. They'd a left nothin' here but guts. This is an act of revenge, to get me stirred, an' that points to the Hogans." He stood and began reloading his rifle. "Well, they've got me stirred, an' I've half a mind to go over there an' get *my* revenge once an' for all."

Frank shook his head. "I know the feeling, but unless we can prove somehow that--"

"I know, lad, I know. I'm just losin' my patience over this ... this harassment. If it keeps up, 'fraid I'm gonna blow up an' do somethin' that'll put *me* in jail instead of the Hogans."

Frank rubbed his palm slowly over the butt of his holstered pistol. "Seems that Carl's the source of all the trouble, Adam. Maybe I can get him to face off with me; I'm sure I can do away with him rather easily." Even before he finished saying it, he felt a quiver of excitement, but he knew it was a suggestion too cocky and imprudent to have made.

Adam gave him a stern look. "Don't even consider it, lad. Don't let your bein' handy with the gun lead yuh to lookin' for a fight. Not ever." He paused, as he put a cloth patch over the end of the rifle barrel then carefully placed a lead ball on the patch. "No, we'd best wait. Common sense tells me they'll make a mistake," he said, and grunted as he ram-rodded the lead ball down the barrel, "I just hope *they* do before *I* do." He replaced the spent primer cap with a fresh one and put the rifle in its saddle scabbard. "Speakin' of mistakes reminds me, there's somethin' I should show yuh when headin' back to the house. Right now we gotta bury these carcasses, then look for an orphan lamb tryin' to bum milk from another mama."

They stopped at the stump of a lightning-struck tree, its splintered remnant standing eight feet tall at the head of a row of summer corn. Dismounting, Adam slapped his hand on it and gave a little chuckle.

"There's a story connected with this stump," he said, and chuckled

132

again. "An' even though it's a bit of a joke on me, I get to laughin' when I think about it."

Frank sensed humor by the way Adam was was acting, and he couldn't help smiling. "I'd like to hear about it," he said.

"You couldn't keep me from tellin yuh."

Adam took a swig from his canteen, rinsed his mouth, then took another. "When we was puttin' this place together we'd cleared land out to here and was puttin' in vegetables an' things. Ol' Magic here, was only green broke at the time an' whilst I was busy hoein' I had him tied to this here snag with about fifteen feet of rope to his hackamore. Well, I'd been workin' awhile when I got a call from nature, so I put down the hoe, picked up my rifle and walked a ways into the woods.

"Now the woods weren't very thick an' I'd no sooner finished my business there when I found myself being watched by a black bear no more'n a hundred feet away. I just knew we'd have bear steak that evenin'.

"The shot was easy an' that fifty-four ball, well placed as I thought it was--in his big ol' head--shoulda dropped him right there. So I just couldn't believe it when it come runnin' at me after I pulled the trigger. Well, there's no time to reload, so I took off runnin', an' when I got to ol' Magic I jumped aboard an' jammed my heels in him to put some distance between us an' that bear, an' Magic takes out like he was scalded. Yuh mighta guessed, I forgot to unhitch him from the stump. By the time I remembered, I musta been ten feet in the air on my way to re-plowin' some of that garden plot with my chin. The sight an' commotion of both me an' the horse gettin' throwed musta scared that bear, 'cuz when I picked myself up, he was haulin' himself back into woods, an' ol' Magic was standin' there spraddle-legged, shakin' the dirt off.

"Do you know, for months after that, I had to walk that horse a hundred yards before I could spur him into as much as a trot! But since then I can tie him to a twig an' he won't budge."

Frank convulsed with laughter. When finally he could talk, he looked at Adam, who was grinning broadly. "That's a grand story, Adam, a grand story. A king's ransom would've been a fair price to see it. But why haven't you taken the stump out?"

Adam looked down and flicked a bit of dirt with the toe of his boot before he looked back at Frank and answered. "Well," and he paused thoughtfully, "you might say it's my piece of humble pie. It reminds me that a man never gets so good he can't make a mistake."

Their eyes met in a steady gaze while Frank marveled at the cunning way the old trapper got his point across. After a moment he nodded slightly, grinning. Adam smiled and winked. "Now get on down here lad," he said, "There's somethin' I need to show yuh about this stump."

He showed Frank dynamite sticks with blasting caps, wrapped in waxed canvas, placed in a metal tea cannister and stuffed in a hole at the base of the stump. Two wires, concealed under ground, ran from the explosive to the plunger-operated magneto in the ranchhouse storeroom.

"Me, Archie, an' three of the other ranchers within earshot have dynamite buried somewhere on the premises to be blown in case of a need for help. Thought about it after the Wigginses got murdered, not that it would've helped them poor kids any, since they got slaughtered in their bed. But we figured we needed some kind of a signal we all can hear an' can use from inside the house if we're attacked. Buried mine where I ain't apt to forget where it is."

"Has anyone used the signal?"

"Nope. Things been kinda quiet since the Wiggins. There was such a ruckus about it that a vigilante group formed and scared hell outa every stray injun in these parts. Mosta them mavricks are just thieves at worst, not murderers. An' they seem to be keepin' outa sight for fear of being lynched."

"Did they find who committed the murders?"

"No. More'n likely done by drifters lookin' for gold, or valuables, or such as that maybe. Renegade Indians usually try burnin' everything down out of revenge for takin' the land away from 'em. Their place was left standin', just a few livestock run off. Didn't make sense."

Frank looked at his watch. "It's nearly eleven Adam; you wanted to get some hardware in town today."

"Aye, that I do. We'll go in now, get some grub under our belts, then head over to town. Yuh know, Frank, reckon I didn't 'preciate how well-off I was when I only had Indians to worry me."

"Watches, Rings, Fine Jewelry" read the sign on the window. A wooden replica of a pocket watch was hung over the door to mark the store's presence to shoppers up or down street. Adam stopped and peered at the array of gold and jeweled articles displayed in the window. "I never owned a time piece," he said. "Always feared I'd let my life be governed by the damn thing. Bad enough havin' to put up with sunrise and sunset."

Frank smiled as he reflected on Adam's words. It seemed that time-pieces had always been important to his daily life. Until now.

"You've got a point, Adam. Sailors are slaves to time." He compared the set of his pocket-watch to the chronometer in the window. "My father's," he said. "I carry it more out of sentiment than need, 'though it's bloody accurate. Little more than a minute off since..." His eyes swept across a familiar form, then focused on it. He leaned forward for a closer look till the brim of his hat struck the window.

"Adam, there's my mother's locket--the one I gave Robin!"

The proprietor listened politely to Frank's story, but seemed sceptical. "Well, the young man that brought it in--about two weeks ago I think, said it was his mother's and she was selling some of her jewelry to buy livestock. The chain was broken. Just yesterday I repaired it and put it in the window. Are you quite certain it's the piece that was lost?" He moved toward the window. "I'll get it. Perhaps on closer inspection…"

Frank swallowed and tried to curb his impatience. "Sir, I can identify the piece: The side that's down will have the crest of the Clan Scott engraved on it. Inside the locket, engraved in old style English letters, are the gaelic words *A Bellendaine!*, the clan's war-cry. Hand painted on the porcelain side that is shown, is the clan's badge--the blaeberry, or bilberry shrub."

The jeweler seemed depressed when he returned to the counter with the locket, his manicured hands caressing it admiringly. "I suppose you're right. The other fellow knew nothing of it's meaning, and seemed to hold it in no special esteem. However, I had no reason to doubt him, you understand, I…"

"I'm not blaming you for buying it, I quite understand. Was the man who brought it in named Hogan?"

"Well now, that sounds familiar. I'll just have a look in my record journal here. Let's see now. Yes, here's the entry. July 9th. Carl Hogan. I paid him six dollars for the piece. Rather a fair price, don't you think?"

Angered at the thought of a price on it, Frank snapped, "I'm no judge of it's worth in coin, sir. Just tell me what I must pay to get it back."

Tapping his fingers on the counter-top, the jeweler's eyes darted quickly to Frank's gun belt, to Adam, then to the locket on the counter. "Well, sir, I do wish to recover my costs. The eight dollars I paid out, plus my material and labor to repair the chain. Twelve dollars should be fair I think."

"You told me you paid *six* dollars for the piece."

The jeweler's face flushed. "Oh, yes, quite right," he said, running his finger to the journal entry. "Quite right." He gave a little laugh.

"Ten dollars, then."

He placed it carefully in a chamois bag which he closed with drawstrings and handed to Frank. "No charge for the pouch," he said, smiling. "But tell me, how did you know the man's name?"

Frank handed him the money. "He was there when it was lost."

The man's eyebrows raised. "Then he knew who it belonged to?"

"He damn sure did," blurted Adam.

"Then that makes him a thief!"

"Among other things," said Frank.

Chapter Sixteen

"Lemme buy us a drink before we go back, lad. It's the least we can do for ourselves after the day we've had."

Preoccupied with thoughts of how he'd like to punish Carl Hogan, Frank was a few steps past Adam before he heard his voice and turned around. They were in front of the Quiet Woman Saloon.

Walking in from bright sunlight, Frank could see no more than those he stood near at the bar. As he sipped his whiskey he tried not to choke, and looked around as his eyes adjusted to the dim light. He'd given no thought to the name of the place until he saw the broken wood sculpture of a nude woman posted at the end of the bar. It appeared to have once been the figurehead of a ship. Probably wrecked on Oregon's rocky coast, it now posed headless to be toasted by those who preferred their women silent.

The tall, narrow man to his left suddenly backed against him, then turned and put his back to the bar-rail as Frank moved aside. The man held a glass from which he sipped while looking straight ahead. Frank judged him to be about his own age, and noticed the pistol stuffed in a holster on his left hip. He was about to switch his attention back to Adam when the man turned his face toward him. He knew he'd seen the face before, but it was a few seconds before he realized it was Carl Hogan's. Their eyes met and Hogan's narrowed some, but he seemed uncertain until he looked past Frank toward Adam; then his mouth twitched at the corners before his lip curled into the Hogan sneer.

"Well, if it ain't Mr. MacLean and his hired gun. Beat up on any cripples lately, MacLean?" He looked away, still sneering, as he put the glass to his lips.

Frank's fury exploded as he knocked the glass from Carl's hand, then grabbed his still upraised arm by the wrist. "You bloody sneak-thieving bastard, I've a score to settle with you about the firecrackers, and the locket. Let's go outside, *now!*" He nearly jerked Carl off his feet.

Carl paled and his mouth twitched again as the sneer left his face. "I ain't gonna fight no gunslinger, an' I don't know nothin' about no locket, an' no firecrackers, neither."

"Yes you do, you swine. You found the locket Robin lost in the accident you caused, then sold it to the jeweler down the street. I just bought it back from him!" He gave Carl's arm another jerk. "Let's settle this outside."

Glancing around, Carl pleaded to the patrons who were nearest to him. "He's lying, the locket was my mother's. He's a gunman. I cain't fight him." He struggled to free his arm.

The bartender, a large man with the muscular build of a wrestler took hold of both men. "Please, gentlemen," he said in thick, Irish brogue, "Settle the matter outside, if yuh will."

"He's a gunfighter; he'll kill me!" pleaded Carl.

"I'm no gunfighter," said Frank. "I'll use my bare hands. Take my gun, Adam."

Adam removed Frank's gun and turned to the bartender. "Take the other's gun, McGuffy."

"Come on lad, gimme your gun now, unless you'll be puttin' your tail 'tween your legs an' runnin'. Now, that's all right by me, but I'm thinkin' you'll just have the other lad runnin' after you."

"I don't have no reason to fight him, anyways. An' you got no right to hold me. Lemme go."

McGuffy released his hold and with a jerk, Carl wrenched his arm from Frank. Half screened by McGuffy's huge frame, Carl managed to draw his gun and when he side-stepped clear of the bartender, it was pointed squarely at Frank. Frank's hand flashed to his empty holster, then his body tightened as he waited for a bullet.

"Now, you shithead, squaw-fuckin', English bastard, I'm gonna settle *my* score with *you,* an' *Paw's* score with--"

McGuffy's move was fast and the gun fell to the floor as the big man's arm came down on Carl's hand. There was a look of panic on Hogan's face and Frank lunged for him as he started for the door.

"Get him!" someone shouted, but he was already in Frank's grasp.

Pushing him against the bar, Frank shoved a hand under Carl's chin, forcing his head back. As Hogan's arms came up, Frank hit him twice in the stomach, stepped back and punched him solid in the face with his left and drove his right again to the gut.

Gasping, arms covering his midriff, Hogan doubled up and Frank's knee smashed into his face. Blood spurted from his nose and lips as he hit the floor and rolled onto his side, groaning, sucking breath through a bloodied mouth.

"If I were you I'd kick the shit outta him now," someone said.

"He's had enough," shouted McGuffy, "It's over, in here anyway." Frank watched as the big man carried the moaning Hogan by his collar and belt out the door to the boardwalk, then threw him onto the street. "Don't be comin' in here again," he said, and tossed Hogan's gun beside him.

Frank was breathing heavily although he hardly exerted himself. He took a deep breath as Adam looked into his face sayin, "You all right, lad?"

"I'm fine. Just need to calm down." He took another deep breath and shook his head. "Can't remember ever having such a hate. I wanted to kill him."

He smelled foul breath, sweat and cigar smoke, and was suddenly aware of the men gathered around him--his shoulders heavy with the weight of hands whose owners he didn't know. There were pats on his back from those he could not see, and a jumble of words from too many mouths. He drew another deep breath and turned to the bar. McGuffy was uncorking a bottle.

"I'm obliged to you for savin' my skin, Mr. McGuffy."

"Glad I managed, son. I don't favor gunplay." He poured into a shot-glass and pushed it at Frank. "You're a mean brawler for an Englishman."

"Scotchman."

McGuffy nodded, grinning. "Aye, that explains it." He raised the bottle and looked out across the bar. "Belly up, boys," he announced, "You'll be havin' one on the house."

"What's the occasion, McGuffy?" someone asked.

"The lad's a Scotchman, that's what. An Irishman's pennance for savin' one o' them is only half what it is for savin' a bloody Englishman!"

Frank squinted against the bright splash of sunlight as he and Adam stepped out of the saloon. They headed for the livery, where they'd left the buckboard with its load of supplies. An off-shore breeze wafted salt-air freshness across his nose and cooled the sweat spots under his arms and down his spine. It was pure perfume after the odors of bodies, spitoons, cigars, whiskey and farts in the close quarters of the small saloon. After a few steps he noticed a stiffness in his right knee where he'd hit Carl Hogan's face. He smiled. It was worth a bruise.

"This has been a day and a half, and it's still more'n three hours 'til sunset," observed Adam. "'Bout the only thing could make it seem longer'd be to lose a wheel on the way home, then get there and find we're havin' mutton stew for supper."

Frank laughed. The idea of mutton didn't please him, either. He wondered if the Hogan's would be sitting down to a lamb supper.

"I should've asked Carl if they planned to invite us over for a lamb supper. Forgot about the ewe, I was so mad about the other things when I saw him. Had I remembered, I'd of kicked his groin before putting my knee in his face."

"You surprise me, lad. You can be a lot meaner than yuh look. You don't seem like much of a brawler."

"Bein' in the crew of my father's ship, edging my way up, I had to work hard for respect. Sometimes I had to fight for it. On a merchantman, bein' a good brawler is as much important as bein' a good sailor, 'specially if you're the Captain's son, else you're soon put to the blush."

They stopped at the street corner to let a carriage pass. Frank stooped to rub his knee and heard the call behind him.

"This'll even the score, you... !" The last word was blanked by a gunshot.

Still bent over, Frank turned and saw smoke belch from a stairway on the side of the corner building. His gun was out at the second shot. From a crouch, he fired at the smoke-fogged outline of a head and shoulders. The sound of his shot blended nearly as one with the other, and the target seemed to dissolve in the haze. Then, what was clearly Carl Hogan--in a half-sitting position against the building--slid sideways a foot or two before toppling over and skidding head first to the boardwalk. He lay sprawled grotesquely, legs across the bottom three steps, the side of his face against the boardwalk, eyes open, a puddle of blood forming around his head from a purple hole in his throat.

Frank's stomach pumped sour mash to his throat as he looked at Carl, and he re-swallowed it several times as he stared. Hypnotized by the sight, he realized he even hated the corpse of Carl Hogan.

"Good shoot in', lad."

Adam's voice jarred him from his trance. "Jesus, Adam, I'm glad

143

you're all right!" Then he noticed Adam holding his right arm above the elbow, blood visible between his fingers. He felt guilty, responsible.

"Damn! You were hit. You need a doctor." He shouted to the gathering crowd. "Where's there a doctor?"

"Never mind lad. It's a wee flesh wound, a scratch, nothin' more." He turned to a man next to him. "Did you see what happened?"

"You betcha. From right across the street there," he said, pointing. "Dead man there shot first from them stairs. My son here seen it too, didn't yuh boy?"

The boy, looking at the body, nodded his head and threw up. His father grabbed him by the shoulders and turned him away, explaining, "He's only twelve; never saw a man shot before."

"We'll need yuh as witness," Adam said. "What's your name?"

"Smith, Roger Smith."

"Adam MacLean, Mister Smith. Will yuh try to find the Sheriff, please?"

"Yes, oh yes," Smith answered, taking his son by the hand.

"Never mind, Smitty, I'm here," boomed a bass voice behind Frank. "An' any you folks that seen what happened here, step up and gimme your names."

Frank turned around expecting the man with that voice to be a giant. Instead, he looked at the tall hat of a compact little man whose face was hidden under its wide brim.

"You a witness?" he asked without looking up.

"No, sir, I'm the one that shot him."

The sheriff's head snapped up like he'd been hit under the chin. "Oh. Figured 'twas the Maclean feller done it since he's the other one got shot." He twirled the point of a pencil in his mouth and fished a piece of cardboard from his shirt pocket. "What's yer name, son?"

"Frank Ross. The dead one is Carl Hogan."

The words were hardly out of his mouth when a moaning "Oooh

144

no!" came from a man kneeling at Carl's body. "Who done this?" he screamed, turning toward the bystanders, "I wanna know who killed my boy!"

Frank pushed his way between two spectators. He saw the redness of fury and anguish in Cyrus Hogan's face. "I did."

Cyrus glared at him; eyes narrowed, jaw muscles worked and his chin quivered. He appeared unarmed and Frank half expected a bull-like charge.

"Murdering bastard!" Cyrus raged, "You'll hang!" He looked at the Sheriff who now stood at Frank's side. "He'll hang for this, won't he?"

"'Tain't likely," came the bass voice. "Folks're sayin' your boy bushwacked these fellers." He pointed to Adam. "Got this 'un in the arm."

Carl's gun lay near where his father knelt. "He weren't no gun fighter, just a boy," he said, his voice tapering off. Then he picked up Carl's gun.

"I'll take that," said the Sheriff, and as he spoke, Frank heard the clicks of the hammer as Hogan thumbed it back and swung it in his direction. Frank drew and the Colt bucked in his hand as smoke billowed in front of him.

Hogan's arm jerked violently. The gun fired, kicked out of his hand and into his chest. He grabbed his gun hand as he fell sideways against Carl's body, screaming, "My thumb! Oh my God, my thumb! My thumb's tore off!"

A man carrying a black valise hurried toward the injured man, paused a few feet away and looked toward Frank, perhaps to be sure the shooting was over. "I'm a doctor," he said.

Aware now that his gun was still leveled toward Hogan, Frank lowered his arm. The doctor gave a quick nod and went to the loudly moaning Cyrus Hogan. Some of the crowd followed.

145

Someone said, "Jesus! D'yuh see that draw? 'Aint never seen nobody that quick. *Gotta* be a hired gun."

"He's fast," said another. "Ain't no gunman though, or he'd fed him another ball. Lucky hit on the feller's hand, I'd say."

Frank mulled over the words "lucky hit" and wondered, then holstered his gun and turned to Adam. "Your arm, I think you should get--"

Adam cut in sharply, "Lillie will take care of the arm, Frank. Yuh shoulda killed that son-of-a-bitch. If yuh'd missed, he prob'ly wouldn't have."

The Sheriff stepped up. "Agree on both counts, MacLean." He looked Frank in the eye. "Yuh had a right, kid. Self defense, like the other." He removed his hat, revealing wavy brown hair too youthful for a man whose face bore the map of a thousand trails. Frank studied him as the little man looked him over as if to fit him with clothes. The hint of a lower lip was all that showed of his mouth beneath a thick, long-horn moustache, its waxed tips extending past the borders of his square-set jaw.

His voice thundered again, "Yuh got the hand an' rig of a gunman, kid, but I'm guessin' yuh ain't... on accounta yuh didn't settle the kid's paw--settle him permanent, that is." Elbows tight against his sides, he made a little hitching motion. "I sure as hell would've." he said, "Dead men don't worry me none." He motioned with a jerk of his head. "Let's get to my office. I gotta know what this was all about."

CHAPTER SEVENTEEN

The Sheriff claimed the shoot-outs were the most excitement Gold Beach had witnessed since the massacre by Indians in '56. Beware the publicity, he warned Frank, "It'll bring all sorts of vermin to your self: killers, and them wantin' someone killed."

Beemans saw the story in the Crescent City "Herald" a couple days later, Archie said, and he "come straightaway" to be sure Frank realized what he was up against. "Drifters from all over these parts'll mosey in lookin' fer Hogan to hire 'em ta gun yuh down," he told him. "An' I'm thinkin' Cyrus ain't 'zakly 'posed ta seein' yuh dead."

It was plain that his friends were worried about the consequences of what had happened. He wasn't feeling good about it either. He felt no remorse for having killed Carl, but the fact that he hadn't killed Cyrus worried him. He was certain that Cyrus would do something for revenge, and he was concerned about Robin and the MacLeans being drawn in.

He was also bothered by the fact that of the three times he had drawn his gun against another man, he twice left his opponent alive. The way Archie put it: "Blastin' guns outta fellers hands is tidy shootin'. But even if yuh c'n do it ever time, which the odds don't favor none, it ain't likely a lastin' fix fer the problem." Archie insisted Frank practice every day to hone his reflexes and learn to shift his eye from his opponent's gun hand to the torso at the moment of draw. Practice and more practice, Archie claimed, was Frank's best insurance.

And practice he did. He built a man-size target with a six-inch circle drawn in the chest area. It had wooden arms another person

147

could move suddenly by rope to simulate an opponent's draw. During the next three weeks every-one practiced their marksmanship. Because the healing wound in Adam's right arm hampered his use of the pistol, he practiced only with the rifle, and carried it everywhere.

Frank watched carefully as the old Indian's hand moved the trimming knife slowly around the underside of MacIver's hoof. "Not good to hurry," he said. "Bad work here make horse lame." Adam said it was unusual for a Rogue Indian to have a horse, let alone know anything about its upkeep, but added that old Solomon Tip-su and his wife Polly were exceptions to the rule. Befriended by the MacLeans, they'd been coming out of the hills to the ranch twice a year for five years, camping on the ranch for a few days, doing odd jobs in exchange for a live goat or sheep, a few staples and perhaps a slab of bacon or dried beef to take back with them. Solomon was chief of a small band of Rogue River Indians that had avoided being hustled onto the Siletz reservation in '56. Adam considered friendship with the old chief good insurance.

Solomon lowered MacIver's hoof to the ground and motioned to his rear with a quick movement of his head. "Someone come," he said.

Frank looked up. A quarter-mile away on the north road, two men on horses rode slowly toward them. He flipped the tie-down loop off the Colt's hammer and looked at Solomon. "Two men on horses. How'd you know someone was comin'?" "Horse tell me," he answered. "Body get tight." Frank looked at MacIver; ears forward, body still rigid as the men approached. He shouted toward the barn, "Men riding up, Adam."

The riders were just a short distance away when Adam came and stood alongside Frank. "Damn! he said, adding, in a lowered voice, "Left my rifle in the barn. Forgot I ain't wearin' my--"

"Mornin' gents," shouted one. Raising his arm, he waved his hand from side to side.

Both men were smiling as they approached. They were a scruffy pair; one in his twenties, Frank guessed. The other looked older, maybe forty. Sweat streaks ran through the trail-dirt and stubble on their faces. "Drifters," he heard Adam mutter. "Saddle bums."

There was nothing special about their equipment; standard cowboy outfitting as far as Frank could tell. Nothing special about their holsters either. But as they reined up, his gut tightened when he noticed the tie-down loops had already been slipped off the hammers of their guns.

He watched them as they talked to Adam, and though he heard them ask for work he knew that wasn't really why they'd come. His thoughts were racing through the scene of two on one, or would one go for Adam? No, they both would go for him and gun down unarmed Adam--perhaps old Solomon too--at their leisure. Which one first? The closest. Then the other with a second shot that had to come off fast and true as any he'd done in practice; faster, if he could. The voices were heated now and he listened. The older man was nearest to him and seemed to be the spokesman; the other kept quiet and looked at him.

"Oughta be a law again' givin' white man's work to redskins," said the older one. "Seems to me a man does that must sure favor them heathen bastards. Agree, don'tcha, Mickey?"

Without taking his eyes off Frank, Mickey answered, "Yeah, but that figures. Didn't we hear he's shacked up with some squaw an' her half-breed daughter."

No doubt now who sent these two. The heat began to rise in Frank's face, and he wondered when they'd get around to insulting him, or if they'd even bother. They could afford to insult Adam, he was unarmed. To insult an armed man is to force him to draw. He hoped they'd give him that advantage, but didn't think they would. He figured they'd both go for their guns on signal.

Adam was not taking Mickey's insult. "Get off the horse an' stand down here, you mangy saddle tramp son-of-a-bitch, an' we'll see if your fists can defend your mouth."

Mickey's eyes widened. As though surprised at Adam's challenge, or uncertain as to what he should do, he glanced at his older partner.

"Mick," said the spokesman, "We're wastin' time." His gun arm twitched as he emphasized "time."

Like the strike of a coiled snake, Frank's hand went to his gun. Webbing between thumb and forefinger cocked the revolver as it was pulled from its holster, and the shot was triggered before the gunman's piece cleared leather.

Swinging to Mickey, his left palm flicked the hammer spur. The youngster seemed to lurch sideways as Frank fired. His hat flew off and he fell from the saddle, smoke exploding skyward from his pistol.

Frank looked back to the other man, slumped over, hanging to the pommel with one hand, gun in the other. He fell as his frightened horse spun, but held onto his gun. Groaning, he struggled to his knees and raised the weapon unsteadily, weaving like a drunk. Frank hesitated, then shot him in the head.

Turning away, he felt sick, and guilty. He wished that shot hadn't been necessary, then wondered if it was.

He walked a short distance away then stood looking at the ground. He was trembling. Thoughts of his mother, his upbringing, his father's hopes for his future, all floated through his mind's eye like writhing ghosts. If they could see it they would not like what they saw now. In two and a half months his life had changed and he was not sure he wanted to go on being what he'd become.

He stood there alone for what seemed a long time, breathing deeply, trying to shake the sick-body feeling he had. He felt an arm on his shoulder, then Adam's voice, calm, fatherly, reassuring:

"It was a bad situation that yuh handled very well, lad. Yuh had to do what yuh did, there."

"I hated to shoot him again."

"It was the only way."

"Like shooting an injured animal."

"Aye, a mad dog."

Mickey was belly up; his hat covered his face but not the puddle of blood around it. "I thought he'd get me," said Frank as they approached the body.

"So did Robin, and he might've, hadn't been for her."

Puzzled, Frank was about to ask what he meant when Adam removed the hat. He was startled to see bloody bone fragments and brain matter emerging from a large hole in Mickey's temple, and the adjacent eye protruding horribly from its socket. There was a smaller hole in the other side of his head above the ear.

"Jesus, my shot couldn't have done that."

"Robin's did."

"Robin? How could... that is, where... ?"

"From the barn. I'd left the Hawkens there. She took it up and figured *she'd* have to shoot one of 'em." Adam looked at him and smiled. "Else she wouldn't have no one to moon over anymore." He put the hat back over the dead man's face.

Frank recalled that as he shot Mickey, the man seemed to be lurching to one side. It was now apparent he was falling, killed by Robin's shot.

"And I thought I'd gotten him."

"Oh, yuh got him, all right." Adam pointed to the red splotch on the shirt, just under the breast bone. "But he'd already taken a good bump on the head, as you can plainly see."

"Now what happens, Adam, do I get the Sheriff?"

"Not unless yuh want the news of this spread over three or four states, drawin' more of their kind this way."

"What'll we do?"

"Bury 'em here, on the ranch. Don't think anyone's gonna be askin' about them two. Keep Hogan guessin' awhile." Solomon had gathered the gunmen's horses and stood quietly nearby. "Let me take dead ones away in darkness. Drop them in old mine shaft. Very deep. No one find them ever, I think. Few months just bones. My people can use horses."

They put the bodies in the barn. That night Chief Solomon Tip-su and his squaw hauled away the evidence.

Frank and Robin sat together in darkness on the veranda. For a long while they were silent; entwined fingers expressed their mutual understanding of the melancholy that gripped them.

Lightening slashed the ocean sky revealing mouse-gray clouds, low and rain-filled, moving eastward with a cooling off-shore breeze that raised goose bumps on his arms. He thought about the old Indian and his wife and wondered how they ever find their way in the blackness of night.

Robin broke the silence: "Do you think this will end it?"

"No. There'll be others. Can't hide the fact I'm alive."

Alive. To Frank the word seemed now to take on special importance. He used to take being alive for granted. Not even his survival from the shipwreck had changed that as much as the gunfights. He suddenly realized how quickly one's condition can change from being alive to being dead. Alive is a temporary condition. Dead is forever.

"I think it's best if I move on," he said, staring into the dark."

"Don't go, Frank, please don't go away."

He turned to her and in the mirror of her moist eyes a flash of distant lightning flickered for an instant like a candle's flame. He kissed her mouth and felt the wetness of her tears against his cheek. "I love you Robin, I truly do. I know I shouldn't say it now that it's plain to me I must leave here, and I'm sorry for the time it's taken me to know my heart and mind. But--"

She was sobbing now and gripped his hand with both of hers and drew it to her face. "You don't have to leave. You don't have to... please don't. I love you, don't leave."

He put his arm around her, pressed her close to him and brushed his lips across her eye. The salt of Robin's tears reminded him of those he tasted kneeling, crying, at his dead mother's side. "Mum, oh Mum, don't leave me, please," he'd sobbed. The central figure in his ten year life had left him, her role unfulfilled. He felt cheated by her death and he still felt sick with sorrow whenever thoughts of her crept in.

And now he was experiencing the same ill feeling. With mutual love discovered, he would leave it, its joys unrealized; its passions unfulfilled. Feeling cheated again, he forced the words he didn't want to say: "I must go. You're all in danger as long as I stay here."

She pushed away. "Then, if you really love me, take me with you, and I will be your woman."

Her words surprised him. "I… I can't ask you to do that."

"You're not. I'm asking you."

"What I mean is, it just wouldn't be right."

"Why? Because I'm part Indian?"

"Don't be foolish. I'd want you to be with me, but we'd have to be married."

"Well?"

In the faint glimmer of lantern-light from within the house, he watched her wipe her cheeks, her face tipped up to his. His heart pounded as he realized that what he would say in the next minute or so would have a lasting effect on his life, and on Robin's too. "I want you to be my wife, and it was in my mind to ask you someday soon. And if you were willing, then to ask the consent of your parents. That's the truth."

She moved to him and laid her head against his shoulder. "Oh Frank, I want so much to be your wife."

"I'm glad for that," he said, and kissed her. The warm softness of her lips, the scent of honeysuckle she wore, filled his mind with thoughts of loving and living with her, of lying close to her, caressing her, caring for her. The things they wanted of each other, in marriage they could share. And for a fleeting moment, the burden of his dilemma was lifted. Then a flash, a rumble of thunder, and the pain of his predicament returned. "But how would it seem now, to ask for your hand at the same time I announce that I'm leaving, without knowing where I'm going, or what I intend to do? The situation wouldn't please them at all, I'm certain."

"It won't please them to learn you plan to leave here, Frank. Papa Mac looks at you as his son, and my mother loves you in that same way, too."

"And I love them. But I'm sure my being here endangers them, and you too, of course. Leaving seems to be the best thing for me to do." Just saying it, made him feel sick.

"I think you should talk to them before you decide what is best."

"All right." He said it, but he didn't mean it. He knew what they would say, and he would not then be able to leave. He had made his decision. He wanted Robin, but could not allow her to go with him under the circumstances. His stomach was sour and he thought he might get sick. "I don't seem to be able to think clearly any longer. I'll talk to them in the morning," he lied. "I'll go to bed now."

He kissed her--a casual kiss--and rose abruptly to leave. "I'll see you in the morning," he said, and we'll make plans." Guilt agitated his stomach, and as he left the veranda he was surprised that Robin said nothing. As he walked to the bunk house rain began to fall. It would be miserable, but if it were still raining at dawn, the noise would cover his departure. He swallowed hard against the taste of bile.

CHAPTER EIGHTEEN

He lay watching the window gradually lighten and become a square moon in the dark bunkhouse wall. He hadn't slept, and though he was awake his body resisted the commitment of his mind to get him up and on his way.

The sick feeling in his gut hadn't gone. Over and again he'd told himself that leaving was the right thing to do. If he stayed, and harm were to come to Robin or the MacLeans, he would bear guilt and remorse the rest of his life. He'd written her a note, and one to Adam and Lillie.

He got out of bed and went to the window. It was nearly an hour before sunrise, but light enough to see his way. Without lighting the lantern, he dressed and rolled his blanket around the few clothes and articles he would take with him. Perhaps leaving the bulk of his belongings would convince Robin he fully intended to return.

The storm had passed. The dawn air was crisp and a slight breeze from the ocean stirred the fragrance of rain-freshened earth and grass. As he passed the corral near the barn, a horse neighed. Then a sheep baaed, its bleat echoed by others throughout the meadow. The rooster crowed his alarm, and it was officially morning. The sounds, the smells: he loved them all.

As he opened the tack-room door he was startled by Adam's voice behind him:

"Now yuh weren't gonna leave without a goodbye, were yuh, lad?"

He shook his head slowly, chin on his chest; ashamed, like a kid caught stealing a cookie. "I'm sorry, Adam. I was making it a bit easier on myself."

"I think yuh need to come into the house and talk things over with us--Lillie and me, that is. Come on, Lil's got coffee a brewin'."

Walking to the house, Adam's brawny arm hung from Frank's shoulder, his hand now and then administering a comforting pat. "I understand your feelin's, lad, but I want yuh to come in an' see if yuh can understand ours."

"How did you know I was leaving? I was trying to be quiet and be gone before you were up."

"Robin. The poor lass was in a lot of pain about your wantin' to leave, and told us she thought you'd be gone before daylight."

"But I told her I'd see her in the morning."

"She's got her mother's sense of knowin' whether you're truthin' with her or not. She was set to go along."

He turned his head and looked at Adam. "I wouldn't have let her."

"We were sure of that."

Lillie, in a white robe made from a Hudson's Bay blanket, poured coffee into three cups. As she sat down she gave a practised toss of her head that laid every strand of her long, black, unbraided hair behind the back of the chair, then smiled at Frank. There was visible moisture in her dark, compassionate eyes. "I am glad you not leave yet."

The hot coffee warmed his stomach. His body tingled from the effects of no sleep, but he wasn't feeling sick any more. "I thought it would be easier for me if I left without saying goodbye. I thought you might try to talk me out of it." He looked at Lillie, still with a kindly smile on her face, then at Adam who sat staring into his coffee.

"Simply put," said Adam, "we don't want you to leave. There ain't no reason for yuh to go... none that *we* know of, anyway."

"Surely, Robin told you why I feel I should leave."

"Aye, that she did. And I admire yuh for your noble, unselfish reasonin'. Our reasons for wantin' yuh to stay are just plain selfish. Yuh see, you're a wee bit of help to me and, well… ," Adam paused, looked into his coffee cup, then back into Frank's eyes with a pleading look. "Truth is, your bein' here just kinda suits all of us."

Frank shifted his eyes to his own cup, cleared his throat and hoped his voice wouldn't crack under the strain of emotion. "Truth is, I don't want to leave, but stayin' will surely mean more trouble and--"

Lillie interrupted: "You must not think you bring trouble. You bring joy. Trouble with Hogan family start without you. If you go you will give us much pain, for we will have lost son, same as Hogan."

Deeply touched, Frank rose from his chair, went to Lillie and embraced her. He felt awkward and self-conscious, but it was a gesture he wanted to make. Kneeling at her feet, he gently wiped the tear that had spilled onto her cheek, kissed her and turned to Adam. "If staying is a better way of showing how much I love you both, then I shall stay."

A small sound, like the joyful whimper of a dog at the sight of its master, came from Lillie's throat as she threw her arms around Frank and hugged him with a rocking motion.

"Good lad!" he heard Adam say. And as Lillie released him, he felt Adam's broad hand clap him on the back.

Frank got to his feet and tried to swallow the emotional lump in his throat. Looking first at Adam, then at Lillie, "There is one thing I must tell you," he said, surprised at the hoarseness of his voice: "I'm in love with Robin, and she says she loves me. I want to marry her, and I'm asking you now for her hand."

Lillie stood and took Frank's hand and placed it against her cheek. "You make my daughter good husband, I think. But many times not good for white man with Indian wife, even part Indian. Many see only Indian blood. Do you think of this, Frank Ross?" Releasing his hand, she gave him a solemn look.

"Aye, I'm aware, and I've thought on it plenty. I know I'll never regret my choice of a wife, nor will my love be affected by foolish words or acts of bigots."

Adam clapped his hands. "Oh, well said, laddie, well said!"

Frank felt the color rise in his cheeks. He exchanged smiles with Adam, and looked back to Lillie.

Her eyes moistened as a smile broadened across her face. She took his hand again and said, "I hope Robin make good wife for you."

"Eeeyahoooo!" Adam shouted, raising his coffee cup. "There's your answer, and it's happy I am for yuh both."

Frank had barely enough time to brace himself as Robin rushed in from the doorway and threw her arms around him.

"Oh, Frank, I'm so happy. We can make plans now." Keeping one arm around Frank, she turned to her mother whose eyes were wide with obvious surprise. "And thank you Mama, for your permission."

"You hear everything we say?"

"Most everything, I guess. I was awake before Frank woke up the rooster. I heard Papa Mac go out. When they came in I got up, but I didn't come in here. I waited to see if you talked him into staying. Then I... well, I just sort of stayed in the other room and listened." She looked up at Frank, grinning, and gave him a quick squeeze. "You've got to get up pretty early around here to sneak off without waking somebody."

His arm was around her shoulders; it felt good to have her close to him. Now he felt right about staying, and the sick feeling was gone from his stomach. "Now that I've wakened everybody, including the animals, I'll get out there and feed 'em. You folks all go back and get some more sleep."

"Now that's a dandy idea. Come on, Lil'. Yuh know, I think I'm gonna like havin' him around as a son-in-law. He respects the need us older folk have for sleep." As Lillie rose from her chair, Adam gave her a pat on her behind.

"Yes, Adam Mac. And young men have need for food. You go sleep. I will have breakfast ready for Frank when he finish chores."

"I'll help you, Mama. We've got to make plans."

"It is you and Frank who must make first plan for when you want to marry."

"Oh, as soon as possible, I..." She looked embarrassed as she turned quickly to Frank, "I guess," she continued, her eyes fixed on him.

"Well, we'll have to have a place to live, first," he said. "We can't just--"

"The bunkhouse," interrupted Adam, "We c'n make the bunkhouse into a mighty nice little place for yuh. We'll put in a cook-stove an' a sink, take out them bunk beds--I'm sure yuh won't wanta sleep in sep..."

"Adam Mac! You have good idea, and say enough. How long to fix bunkhouse for their place?"

"Oh, couple weeks oughta be plenty."

"Two weeks from now will be a Thursday. I want to be married on a Sunday--the following Sunday." Robin turned to Frank, who was feeling a bit overwhelmed by the speed at which the mood and tempo of events had changed since he got up. She went to him and took his hand. "Is that all right with you?"

He looked down at her. The nightgown she wore was thin and loose fitting, yet it revealed the plumpness of her breasts. Pert nipples poked through strands of unbraided hair that cascaded across her shoulders and down her back.

"Yes, if we have... that is..." With a flush feeling in his neck and cheeks, he cleared his throat and shifted his eyes to her face. He thought for a moment. "That will be Sunday, September Fifteenth, just seventeen days away."

"Is that too soon?" Her eyes were wide with concern as though she feared she was rushing him.

"Not a 'tall," he answered, smiling, and put his arm around her shoulders. "That's just right with me. The sooner the better."

Robin thought the following two weeks were filled with the happiest days she'd ever had. The days were long and warm, the evenings cool and fragrant. Frank was far more attentive to her that he'd ever been. At first there was an air of uneasiness about Frank. Although he didn't talk about it, she knew he expected trouble again. The Beemans came over almost every day to help, and Frank and Archie always spent an hour or so shooting. As Adam's arm got better, he joined in a little more each day.

While she and her mother made curtains and decorated the inside of the bunkhouse, Adam and Frank built cupboards, shelves and a bedstead, painted and patched until the transformation from bunkhouse to cottage was complete, except for a cookstove. It was to buy a cookstove that had Frank and Archie Beeman on an overnight trip to Port Orford with the buckboard. They left on Thursday, September 12th, to return on the 13th, late afternoon.

She'd been excited before, but not like this. She couldn't sleep for thinking about what their first time in bed together would be like. Sometimes when they stood and kissed, holding each other close, she felt him grow large and firm as he pressed against her. His hands had explored her breasts, lightly, tenderly. And when he kissed them through her clothes, she wanted to expose them to his eager mouth. She wondered if her desire to have him kiss her breasts was something she should be ashamed of, or if wanting the man she loved to do it was a sign of wanting to nurse his child. She decided she would ask her mother, but not until after she and Frank were married. There were other things she secretly thrilled at the thought of him doing, but was so embarrassed by her thoughts that she tried not to dwell on them.

On the morning of Friday, September 13th, Robin was awake before dawn. Spurred by the added energy of youthful excitement, she decided to get up and hang the curtains in the bunkhouse. She had finished adding beaded flower appliques to them the night before. It would be nice, she thought, to have them hanging when Frank returned with the stove that afternoon.

Choosing a buckskin skirt and blouse against the cool air, she dressed quickly, gathered up the curtains and ran, lantern in hand, to the bunkhouse. Inside, she lit another lantern and went to the bedroom. Looking at the bed, it seemed very large compared to her single. Frank and Adam built the bedstead; she wondered what they talked about while they were building it. The mattress was a gift from Rilla and Archie Beeman. Stuffed to a high loft with lamb's wool and goose feathers, it looked very comfortable and inviting.

It bothered her a little that Frank would sleep on the new bed for two nights before she could share it with him. She wished she didn't have to wait. She sat on it and laid back. It *was* comfortable! Moving her hips up an down, slowly at first, then faster and higher until the wood creaked and the rope network beneath the mattress squeeked as it stretched away some of its newness under her bouncing body.

Against the noise of her own making she heard another sound, a click, like that of a latch. Or was it more of a snap? Abruptly she sat upright and listened. Had she broken one of the pegs that held the ropes on the bedstead? Her face flushed as she wondered how she'd explain that. Then, from the corner of her eye she thought she saw movement outside the window. Motionless, she strained to hear the slightest sound. Her throat constricted in sudden fear as she forced her words: "Mama, Papa Mac, is that you?"

As she looked toward the kitchen, the light given by the lantern she had left there, faded to darkness.

"Whose out there?" she cried.

No answer, but a noise, like the shuffle of feet. She stood, terrified now by the unseen. Sensing movement, she made a futile grab for the knife strapped to her thigh, as a grayish blur sprang at her from the darkened room.

She managed a brief shout before her neck was in a powerful grasp. Her hands dug at his eyes; her knee jerked wildly toward his groin. But as strong hands applied their deadly pressure, the savage face dimmed and faded before her eyes, and the sound of her pounding heart grew faint in her ears.

CHAPTER NINETEEN

Suddenly awake, Lillie sat up and listened, straining to sense whatever brought her out of her sleep. In the silence she could not hear her husband's breathing and guessed he, too, was awake and listening.

"Adam, you 'wake?" she whispered.

"Aye."

"You hear something?"

"Don't know. Somethin' woke me. Don't hear nothin' now."

She put her hand on his arm and felt goose-bumps--a sure sign of his uncertainty--and a shiver of fear ran through her as her own flesh suddenly felt cold. "Papa, go see if Robin all right."

Without a word, he patted her hand and got out of bed. In the dusky gray light of dawn, she watched as he put on his trousers and took the revolver from its holster by their bed.

Their sleep had been disturbed before, but this time seemed strangely different to Lillie and not knowing why unsettled her. Rising, she donned her robe from the bedside chair and took the Deringer from under her pillow.

Noise of a scuffle came from the living room. Her heart throbbed frantically as she cocked the Deringer and came out of the bedroom. "Adam! What--?"

She flinched at the sudden flash and roar of gunfire in the semi-darkness. A figure fell backwards, crashed heavily into the wall, then slid to the floor with a groan.

'Indians!" Adam shouted, breathing heavily, "Robin's gone. Send th' sig…"

She saw the movement behind him, but couldn't get a warning out before he was dropped by a blow to the head.

Apparently unaware of Lillie's presence, the assailant must have been startled by the gutteral sound of anguish she made as she rushed toward her fallen husband, for his mouth was open as he looked into the Deringer's stubby barrel an instant before she shot him in the face.

Even in the dawn light, the blood gushing from Adam's head wound was bright against his hair and the tan wood floor on which he lay, face down. Pressing her palm against the gash, her mind raced. Were there others? Where was Robin? She had to get cloth to cover the wound. Signal: Adam wanted her to blast the dynamite. The storeroom: the plunger for the signal was in the storeroom, and there was cloth in there for dressings. She had to get to the storeroom.

Hunkered down next to Adam she listened and heard nothing but the rapid throbbing of her own heart. She saw Adam's .44 Remington an arm's length away. Slowly, she reached for the gun, every fibre tense, expectant. She felt as though she was being watched and was even more frightened as she carefully picked it up. Gun in hand, she thumbed the hammer back, reassured by its noisy clicking as it ratcheted into the fully cocked position.

Removing her hand from Adam's head she felt a twinge of panic as she looked at the blood streaming from his wound. Confident there were no others in the house, she rose and walked quickly to the storeroom. As she opened the door light flashes burst and sparkled in the back of her eyes, then her head hit the side of a dimly lit tunnel that narrowed sharply as she sped to its dark end.

Adam could not focus his eyes. Closing them against the light that gave them pain, he struggled briefly, futilely, against the bonds that held his hands behind his back and hobbled his feet. His head throbbed and he felt that any second he might throw up. Why ain't I dead? he wondered. What's happened to Lillie and Robin? Nausea brought stomach juices to his mouth. He spit onto the floor that pressed against his cheek, then moved his head back from the sour smell.

A splash of water hit his head and caused the scalp on top to sting. He felt the hard sole of a boot against his neck, and heard the distinct sound of of a revolver being cocked. His first thought was that Cyrus Hogan was about to take his revenge, and he never wanted him to have that satifaction.

"MacLean, you're gonna tell me where the gold is hid, or your women'll be the first to pay for you bein' stubborn."

Adam was relieved the voice wasn't Hogan's. He opened his eyes and tried to focus on what he figured was a pantleg over a black boot, the other of which was on his neck.

"What about my wife an' daughter?" His voice didn't sound like his own. He tried to turn his head up so he could see the man's face, but the boot on his neck got heavier.

"They're just fine. But they ain't gonna be if we have to use 'em to get you to talk up. You folla me, MacLean?"

Adam felt sick again. He closed his eyes, swallowed, and tried to think. 'We', he said. Then there were others. Oh God, Lillie and Robin in their hands. Gold? Where'd they get that notion? He had no gold stashed.

The boot got heavier on his neck.

"I ain't very patient, MacLean. Got four Injun's here'd be glad to make your squaw an' that pretty li'l breed pay for the two you an' her killed. You ever seen how them savages can mess up a woman?"

He tried to block the thought of it from his mind.

"Where are they?"

"Well, the girl's in the li'l house yonder with an injun watchin', an' your squaw's locked in the storeroom where she ain't likely to cause no trouble."

The man took a deep breath and exhaled, moving his foot back and forth with heavy pressure on Adam's neck. As he did so, Adam was able to turn his face up enough to see a thin, hawk-nosed face with close set eyes looking down on him. "Now open up an' tell me where it's hid, *now*!

"How do I know they're alive?"

"You don't. But we coulda killed alla you people right off if we'd wanted. We didn't 'cuz all we want's the gold we know you got stashed somewhere." He took his foot off Adam's neck and knelt beside him, then poked the barrel of his revolver into Adam's nose. "Look, I'll be honest with you MacLean: you ain't gonna live through this day whether you tell me or not, so the gold ain't gonna do you no good, evermore. But you can save the ladies' asses if you cooperate. Now I *know* you can tell me what I want to know. I *don't* know if they can. If you make me ask 'em, and they really don't know nothin', then they'll have you to thank for whatever those redskins put 'em through before I'm convinced. An' I won't guarantee their future, neither. Understand?"

"If I cooperate, what happens to them? I can't believe you'll leave witnesses." He knew it was a foolish question; he couldn't rely on the word of this man. Still, he was compelled to ask, and he needed time to think. Obviously, Lillie hadn't sent the dynamite signal. But why?

"Ain't neither of 'em seen me. Witness again' a bunch a renegade 'skins ain't worth the breath. Now, tell me where the stuff's hid an' they'll be alive when we leave here."

Adam's mind was clearing. He knew the leader could never be convinced there was no gold. Now that he knew they were going to kill him, a plan formed--a desperate plan--that would only work if Lillie was, indeed, alive. If she was, and locked in the storeroom, then it was probably the only chance she and Robin would have for survival.

"All right. Show me Lillie--my wife -- is alive, an' I'll show yuh where it's at."

"An if she ain't?"

He felt like something pierced his guts as he heard those words and looked at the cruel grin on the man's face. "If she..." he paused and swallowed hard, "then show me that my daughter's alive, else it won't matter what yuh do to me, yuh'll never find any gold."

"Horseshit. Them injuns c'n make a deaf-mute talk." He chuckled at his little joke.

Adam thought of how he'd like to put a bullet through the deep dimple in the man's pointed chin.

"But I'll show yuh she's alive." He waved his arm. "Bring the squaw out here."

Adam's hopes raised. Now he'd need somehow to get the message across to her that she was to blow the dynamite at his signal--a shout from the field he hoped she could hear. Chinook trade jargon might be understood by the Indians he supposed were standing nearby. He would try Nez Perce. He heard the storeroom door open and a man's voice he judged to be young and American, said "Get on your feet, we gotta show yuh off to your man. Come on, get up."

After a long interval, the leader shouted his impatience. "Come on, get her out here. What in hell's keepin' ya?"

Footsteps and the young man's voice grew louder as he entered the room, talking.

"ol' Feathers here musta split 'er skull bone with his li'l hatchet, 'stead a jist tappin' 'er one to put 'er down. She's deader'n hell, Jim."

Adam's guts contracted like they'd been kicked. The moan that escaped him sounded to his ears like the bawl of a fresh-branded steer. He had never before felt such agony of mind and body. "Aw, you filthy bastards," he yelled, straining against his bonds with all the strength he could muster. "You shitty, no-good bastards!" He tried to curse them more, but grief overpowered his anger, and sobs overwhelmed his words.

He heard the word "sorry" then felt the weight of the boot on his neck again, as the voice of the man called Jim came through.

"It weren't meant for her to get killed, MacLean, but then she had a gun and had shot one of them, so he had to hit her. I guess he did it too hard."

He felt sick, but his anger flared. "You stinking, goddam, murderin' thieves. You sonsabitches." He wanted to bang his head against the floor in anger, grief and frustration. "Who put you up to this, Cyrus Hogan?"

"Never heard of him. Now, we're wasting time. Where's the gold? Remember, we've still got your daughter."

"Show me she's alive an' unharmed." He realized the scheme he'd devised had no chance of being implemented without Lillie, unless he could maneuver Robin into Lillie's role.,

"All right, MacLean, I'll get the girl in here." He pushed hard with his foot against Adam's neck as he turned and ordered someone to get her.

Miserable at the thought of her being in the storeroom with her dead mother, pained by the shock and grief she would feel, he discarded his plan.

"No!" Adam shouted, "Take me to her. I don't want her to know about her mother--not yet."

The booted foot pushed roughly on his neck again.

"Well, all right. I'm bein' easy, I think, but maybe it's better this way. I don't wanna have no wailin' squaw around me. Ain't never seen one that didn't wail an' squall somethin' awful over dead kin." His foot came off Adam's neck. "Cut his hobbles."

There was a grunt from a fat Indian that knelt and slashed carelessly at the ankle bonds. Before the rawhide ties were severed, he had sliced

168

deep gashes in Adam's legs. Then looking him in the eye he said, "You kill brother. You bleed little now; bleed plenty later. Die bad way."

Adam's foot caught the Indian under the jaw and bowled him onto his side. "Fat pig," he said, "Go to hell." Then added, "Along with your brother!"

The Indian got quickly to his knees and lunged at Adam, knife poised. Adam tried to roll away, but it was Jim's kick at the Indian's arm that saved him and sent the knife clattering across the floor.

"Back off!" Jim shouted, pointing his gun at the Indian. "I aim to keep him breathin' awhile." He looked down at his prisoner. "MacLean, that was a dumb goddam move. You dying before yuh tell me where your stash is, will make it rough on that breed kid of yours."

"She don't know nothin' about any gold."

"Then don't do nothin' foolish again so's we don't have to make sure. Now get on your feet."

Dizzy, head throbbing, fighting nausea, Adam staggered to the bunkhouse in company with the two white men and three Indians.

The door was open. He winced as he saw Robin, sitting at the table with a rope tether around her neck, held in check like an animal by an Indian across the table from her. Jumping up from her chair when she saw him, she burst into tears.

"Oh, Papa Mac! I heard the shots," she said, her voice hoarse with sobs. "I thought maybe they'd--"

"I'm all right, Honeygirl. He saw that her hands were bound together in front of her. "Are you?"

"Yes, I'm all right. Where's Mama?"

"Locked in the storeroom, she's fine." He hoped Robin didn't notice the catch in his throat as he lied about her condition. "Tied up, of course," he added, so Robin wouldn't wonder why Lillie hadn't touched off the dynamite charge under the old stump.

"What do they want, Papa?"

He tried to walk to her, but someone grabbed him. "They want my gold, that's all."

"Gold?" Surprised registered in her voice as well as on her face. Adam hoped Jim saw it and would be convinced she knew nothing.

"That's enough jabber, MacLean. You've seen her, now where's it stashed?"

He gave Robin a reassuring wink. "I'll show yuh," he said. "It ain't far. But you'll need shovels. There's a couple in the barn."

"Let's go," Jim said, "An' bring the girl along."

Adam's heart sank. It was getting close to his time to die, and he didn't want Robin to be a witness to it. Maybe he could talk the leader into sending Robin back to the bunkhouse when the time came. He said a silent prayer that maybe something would happen pretty quick to get them out of this nightmare.

The lightning-splintered stump of the dead tree cast a long shadow from the rising sun. As they approached it, Adam could hear Frank's laughter as he told him the story of Magic and the bear. "This is the place," he said.

"You mean the gold's in the stump?" asked the younger of the white men.

"Nope," answered Adam, "Under it."

"How far under?" asked Jim.

"Oh, 'bout four feet down, I reckon. Right next to the tap root, in a little' wood chest wrapped in waxed canvas, if someone ain't sneaked in here an stole it already. I ain't had the need to dig it up in quite a spell." Am I crazy? Adam wondered. Where is this gonna get me? Just stallin' for time, waitin' for a miracle to happen, 'cuz they'll never believe there ain't no gold.

"Where should we dig from?" Jim asked.

"Between them two exposed roots." It was a mighty slim chance, Adam thought, but maybe the dynamite was old enough to be unstable, and just maybe it might get struck hard enough by a shovel to set it off.

"All right," said Jim, "tie MacLean to the stump. We'll burn him there if the gold ain't where he says. An' gimme the girl." He turned to the oldest of the Indians. "Seven, get your braves to diggin'."

Lillie looked at the ceiling, and at the shelves. I'm in the storeroom, but why am I down here on the floor? She sat up and sharp pains stabbed at her eyes and deep in her head. Her right ear burned. She put her hand to it and felt something caked over the ear and in her hair; and there was something warm and sticky there too. When she took her hand away and looked at it she saw traces of blood.

I must have fallen, but what did I come here for? Oh, bandages... bandages for Adam's head. Oh, poor Adam is hurt. I must hurry to him. And what else?

With deliberate, painful effort she rose unsteadily to her feet and reached for some cloth on a shelf. There's something else, something else I must do. She shook her head to clear her confusion, and the pain--like an explosion in her brain--forced a moan and sent her staggering against the shelf-lined wall. Then it came to her: signal... I must send the signal!

Steadying herself against dizziness that began to make her feel sick, she half-stumbled to the corner of the room and fell to her knees by the magneto. It seemed to take all her strength to raise the plunger. When she pushed it downward, she slumped, exhausted, over the box. I'll just rest here awhile, she murmured. The explosion sounded far, far away.

CHAPTER TWENTY

Robin remembered turning her head away, crying, not wanting to watch as one of the Indians threw a shoveful of dirt at Adam, lashed to the stump. Then a sharp, violent jolt. She looked up into Jim's narrow face, and realized she was on the ground. There was a ringing sound in her ears.

"Well, you've finally come around," he said. "Don't look like you're hurt none." Grabbing her arm, he pulled her to her feet. She was dizzy after the sudden movement, and fell against him. He put his arm around her.

"You hurtin' any place, girl?" he asked.

"No." She tried to push away, but he held her tight.

"Good. Wanna keep that body of yours in shape."

The way he said it made her afraid, and she tried not to think about what he meant.

"What happened?" As she spoke she smelled the odor of dynamite and knew. Then she saw the bodies of three Indians sprawled near each other. She turned away fearing she might get sick. Jim relaxed his arm and she moved a step away; he still held the tether around her neck.

"The sonofabitch had a charge under that tree stump," he said. "One of them injuns musta set it off somehow while he was diggin'. Killed them poor bastards outright and knocked the rest of us on our asses. You were standin' in front of me an' musta caught more of the blast."

Looking at the ground, fearing the answer, her voice was hardly above a whisper. "My father, what... ?"

Jim grunted a forced laugh. "Ha! He musta thought he was ridin' one a them Chinee sky-rockets. Threw him an' that stump fifty feet. Layin' out there face down with that tree trunk an' all--what's left-- strapped to his back."

She was crying before he finished. "Let me go to him, please," she begged.

"Ain't no use, an' here come Seven an' Rollo with the horses. We're moving out." They were coming from the direction of the beach where they'd left their horses and sneaked up to the house on foot.

"What about my mother? Where is she?"

He turned and looked away, avoiding her eyes. "She ain't comin' with us."

"She's dead, isn't she? You've killed her!" She started toward the house but was jerked to a halt by the rope around her neck. Tears flooded her eyes as she dropped to her knees crying with grief and anger. "Why don't you kill me too?"

"Got plans for you--big plans, unless you can tell me where there's any gold stashed around here. Tell me an' I'll let yuh go."

Sobbing, she shouted angrily, "I don't know about any gold. I didn't know Papa Mac had any."

"Well, if it was under that stump like he said, then it's scattered to hell-an'-gone now."

The two men rode up, each with three horses in tow.

"Well, I see little bright eyes waked up," said the one called Rollo. "Get anythin' outta her?"

"She don't know nothin'. You took long enough gettin' them horses."

"What the hell's your hurry? I figure we oughta go through the house pretty good. Maybe he had some gold stashed in there."

Jim shook his head. "Naw, the gold wasn't as important to him as protectin' his family. He woulda showed us the stuff right off, if it was in the house. I figure he put the charge there plannin' to blow that stump, then changed his mind figurin' it was a good place to stash his poke." He turned to the Indian. "Put the girl on one a them ponies, an' ride lead with her. Anyone seein' us'll think she's your squaw, or your daughter. It'll look natural. Rollo, turn the rest of them injun ponies loose."

"Why turn 'em loose, for Chris' sake? We can sell them critters to other injuns. Barter for stuff with 'em."

"Turn 'em loose, goddammit. Anybody seein' us trailin' them ponies and hearin' about what happened here will sure as hell remember seein' us. Might as well carry a damn sign. Now mount up and let's move."

"Well, shit, Jim. I still think we oughta see what's worth takin' from the house, then burn the fuckin' place down."

Jim shouted back at him: "You're a stupid ass, Rollo! That blast was heard by everybody within' two, three miles. Prob'ly won't take too much notice, 'cuz lotsa ranchers blow out stumps. But add smoke from a house-a-fire, an' you'll have the whole goddamn population hurryin' down here." He lowered his voice, "Now, the farther away we can get before anyone comes here, the better off we'll be. So unless you wanna be amongst the casualties, get your ass on your horse and keep your mouth shut. And one more thing, *kid*, keep your hands--and the rest of yuh--off that girl, *savvy?*"

Rollo spun angrily from Jim, his fair-skinned face so flushed his blond eyebrows stood out like huge scars. He muttered something and glared briefly at Robin. The cold, pale blue of his pink-rimmed eyes gave his pudgy face the look of a bad tempered boar hog. In spite of her grief, he frightened and repulsed her, and she looked away with tear-flooded eyes.

The Indian they called "Seven" looked about forty years old, she thought. She hadn't heard him speak, and his facial expression seemed frozen, except for his eyes. He checked the bonds on her hands, then lifted her onto a skewbald pinto.

As they rode off, she glanced back. She had never known such grief, and the tears she was shedding neither relieved nor satisfied her anguish. As they passed the bunkhouse that was to be her wedding cottage, the arrow of pain that pierced her heart brought forth an outcry that shock and dignity had, until that moment, surpressed. "Frank, oh Frank," she sobbed, "Oh God, why has this happened?"

The wagon ride back from Port Orford was a painful one for Archie. He'd hurt his back when helping to load the stove. At the last stop, Frank had to help him back in the wagon.

It was late afternoon when Frank brought the rig to a halt at the outer gate to Beeman's ranch. Nailed to the top rail, next to the large, closed padlock, was a folded piece of paper.

"Now why in tarnation did Rilla lock the dang gate?" spewed Archie as he handed Frank the key. "She knowed dang well we'd be a'comin' through this way today." Retrieving the note, Frank handed it to Archie. It was with a rare display of impatience that he tore the paper as he unfolded and held it at arm's length. The scowl left his face as he read, and Frank thought some of the color did, too.

"Nothing wrong, I hope." It was wishful thinking, for he could tell that Archie wasn't cheered by what he'd read.

"Dunno," he answered, handing Frank the note, "but let's get movin', son, and pay no heed to my gol durned back."

The note from Rilla was brief: *I'm at MacLean's. Hurry along, there's been trouble.*

CHAPTER TWENTY-ONE

The ride from Archie's ranch was fast and rough, but not fast enough to keep a score of worrisome thoughts from running through Frank's mind; nor rough enough to break up the rock-hard knot that had formed in the pit of his stomach. The two men spoke not a word during the two-mile trip. Even Magic acted as though he sensed the urgency as he seemed eagerly applying new-found energy to haul the heavily laden wagon at more than a mere head-for-the-barn gallop.

Rilla's buggy and another were at the hitchrail along with two other horses. Two men stood on the veranda. Recognizing the short man with the tall hat as Sheriff Rufe Pickens from Gold Beach, Frank was off the wagon before Archie brought it to a stop; "What's happened?" he shouted, taking the porch steps three at a time.

The Sheriff's bass voice boomed out as though he were addressing a crowd: "The MacLeans, they's both hurt some, but alive. Doc's in keepin' tabs on Mac, bein' he was busted up pretty bad." He smiled and and put out his hand as Archie came slowly up the steps. "Damn good to see yuh, Arch. Your wife's inside nursin' Missus MacLean. How've yuh been, yuh ol' horse fart?"

"What about Robin?" interrupted Frank, his voice pitched high with panic. "Their daughter, where is she?"

"Don't rightly know, young fella, but from what Mac was able to tell us, what was left of the gang that raided the place this mornin', has prob'ly made off with her. Last he saw, 'afore the 'splosion, he an' the girl was held by two whites an' four Indians. Well, three of them redskins is dead in the field there--blast made a mess of 'em--which

177

leaves one Indian, two whites, an' the girl unaccounted for. Oh, an' they was two shot-dead Indians in the house."

The knot in Frank's stomach got bigger and tighter. "Has anyone gone after them?" he asked, his voice hoarse with emotion.

"Nope."

"Why not, you intend to get a posse together, don't you, Sheriff?"

Rufe Perkins tilted his hat back off his brow and looked at Frank a few seconds before he spoke, his voice seemed even lower, but softer, quieter. "I'll level with yuh, son. They ain't a whole lotta menfolks in the area that I could talk into formin' a posse to rescue a whore-house madam if'n they were to get free passes for the rest of their lives. Meanin' no disrespect to the girl, there ain't a prayer of gettin' anybody to ride after a kidnaped half-breed."

"Wrong, dad burn it Rufus," said Archie, "I'll ride!"

Frank looked at his friend. Archie had been in pain most of the trip home, from his back. He knew he was still hurting, bad.

"Well now, that's fine, Arch. But lemme remind yuh, them renegades already has a… ," he looked at his pocket watch, "… a ten, 'leven hour jump on yuh. An' yuh don't know which way they went."

It was the first that Frank knew when the incident had taken place. "Then it happened this morning?"

"Yup, long about first light, I'm told. Neighbors heard the 'splosion little after sun-up an' figgered somethin' was wrong. Group of three joined up at the pre-arranged meetin' spot, then rode in. Sons-a-bitches were gone by that time."

Suddenly Con Sellers came to mind. "Con Sellers!" he blurted out, "I'm sure he'd ride, and maybe some of his men will--"

"Sellers an' a couple a his boys left yesterday to fetch some horses outta California somewheres," said Perkins.

The sheriff clapped his hand on Frank's shoulder. "I can understand how yuh feel about takin' out after them bastards, but I doubt yuh got a frog's chance in a snake pit of catchin' up with 'em. They could be anywheres in these woods. The best bet is I get some flyers printed up with the descriptions I got, an' get 'em mailed out north, south an' east."

Frank knew he couldn't sit back and wait. He would have to ride in search of them or he would go crazy. "Which way do you think they'd go, Sheriff?"

"My guess is they'd head inland, then make their way north or south--most likely south--to minin' towns, or on into California."

"I agree," said Archie, "an' if that injun's a-ridin' with 'em, they won't foller no stage routes, neither."

"But why south, why California?" Frank knew it was but wishful thinking to hope they'd remain somewhere within easy reach, but California? The knot in his gut tightened.

"This time a year--mid-September -- they'd be ridin' into warmer, better weather," said Archie.

Mid-September, thought Frank, Sunday, the Fifteenth--just two days away--he and Robin were to be married. He felt sick.

Sheriff Pickens tucked his thumbs under his belt and flapped his hands against his pants. "Yuh know, it's my guess them scoundrel's mighta took that girl to sell her."

"Sell her?" shouted Frank. "What do you mean?"

The Sheriff reached out and put both hands on Frank's arms. "I'm sorry, son, I keep forgettin' your interest in the girl. But the truth is, women--'specially Indian—is bein' sold to miners, mostly by their own kinfolk. But a young gal--'specially one that's half white--will bring a hefty price. I'd say they aim to sell her, 'less one of them bastards that stole her aims to keep her hisself."

Not that he'd ever been in doubt as to what he had to do, but now he felt urgency and frustration worse than he thought possible.

"I'm starting after them… now," he said. "Where's the first place they might try to sell her?"

Archie put his hand up as though he wanted to stop the proceedings. "Now jist a dang minute there, Franklin," he said, louder than necessary, "there hardly more'n an hour's daylight left, and yuh ain't a gonna leave without me goin' an' I gotta get on home an' get Toad an' a change a travelin' gear an' leavin' today we ain't gonna make no real progress 'afore it's dark." Archie paused, breathed in and out. Frank could see him wince when he inhaled, and knew he couldn't let Archie come with him, as much as he knew he'd need him. "'Sides," he went on, "*they* ain't gonna travel after dark, neither. We can ready-up proper tonight an' move out at daybreak."

"I'm going as soon as I can get ready, Arch. I know you want to go, but I also know your back's bloody well got the squeeze on you, much as you're tryin' to hide it. Hard ridin' is the first thing you *don't* need. Now, my friend, help me by telling me where they're most likely to try to sell Robin first, and how to get there."

"But you ain't--" started Archie.

"Kerby. I'd say Kerby." suggested Will Handy, interrupting. It was the first the old pioneer had spoken since Frank's arrival. "Some calls it Kerby*ville*," he added. "Ain't much minin' activity close in, no more, but it's a place miner's come to stay, get drunk, get supplies, an' get laid. Good hotel there, the Union. Got ever'thin'."

"What about Galice?" asked Archie. "It's some closer."

"Tough up there," said Handy. "Men there either got a squaw, or if they ain't it's on accounta they ain't got enough in their poke to buy one. "

"I'd say Will's right," said Rufe Pickens. More money around Kerby. It's the county seat. Besides, them renegade bastards might figure anyone chasin' 'em would go to Galice first, so they'd prob'ly stay clear, don'cha see?"

"Kerby-how far?" asked Frank. "How do I get there?"

"Ninety, hunnert miles. Follow the Rogue to the Illinois, then up the Illinois thutty, thutty-five miles."

"Thanks. I know Adam's got some maps. I'm going in now to see him and Lillie."

Carilla Beeman was at the door as he was going in.

"She's in Robin's room; heard your voice and wants to see you. Talk softly, her head still hurts pretty bad."

Shocked when he saw her head swathed in a bandage extending down heavily over her right ear, he knelt beside the bed and took the hand she held up to him.

"I'm going after them, Lillie," he said. "And the Sheriff is putting out bulletins. We'll find her. Please try not to worry."

Tears oozed from the outside corners of her eyes. "I worry also for you now. Be careful. I will be all right."

He kissed her hand. "I must go now. There isn't much daylight left."

"Take Adam's saddle bags. There is dried food in store room; tea, things for travel."

"Archie is going with you, of course," stated Rilla, in a matter-of-fact tone. "I'll have to--"

"No' Mam. He wants to, but I can't let him. His back and hip are bothering him so he can hardly walk. 'Course now he won't admit it."

"Sciatica," said Rilla, nodding, "and his old back injury teaming up on him again. Poor Archie. You know Robin is like a grandchild to us. But you're right. Once astride his mule for a few miles, you'd have to lift him off, and you'd need block and tackle to get him back on. But he's more stubborn than that mule of his; he'll not want to stay home."

Frank thought a moment. Archie hadn't made much of a protest over not going. That could have been a sign he was planning to go

181

anyway, so wouldn't argue. Wanting to start in the morning--actually sound logic considering the mere traveling time lost, and their need for preparation and rest -- might have been with the hope that his back 'would be better by then. But the hope of a miraculous, overnight recovery was not realistic. If he came anyway, Frank would worry about him.

"I think I'd best tell Archie I've decided to go in the morning as he suggested, and that I'll meet him at your ranch." He detested the idea of lying to Archie, but it seemed the easiest way.

Rilla's look became thoughtful--worried perhaps, and Frank sensed an aversion to his scheme, compounding the guilt he already felt. "I really hate to deceive him," he explained, "but he's in no condition right now to make a hard ride. I don't know how else to get on without him."

"Don't worry," she said finally, and smiled. "*I'll* tell him, and get him on home so you can leave."

She gave him a strong hug then held him at arm's length and looked at him, her dark eyes darting over his face as though looking for something. "We've both come to love you, like you were our own. Because you came into our lives so late, we cling desperately to the pleasure we get from you, and from your romance with Robin." She hugged him again, saying, "Do be most careful. I'll pray for God to help you... to help you both."

For Carilla Beeman it was a rare display of affection.

About forty minutes remained before the sun would set, and as he rode northward toward the Rogue River, his thoughts were a jumble of concerns--and worry.

The visit with Adam had been brief, for he was painfully hurt, and so heavily drugged he was almost incoherent. "Too much," he kept repeating, over an over.

"Too much of what, Adam?" Frank asked.

"Dyn'mite," was the groggy answer.

The doctor had done most of the talking, partly to express his awe of Adam's miraculous survival after being blown into the air on the roots and stub of a tree trunk. In spite of a broken shoulder, several broken ribs, a badly broken leg and ankle, the doctor said Adam would recover, 'though minus, he reckoned, some of his prior mobility. "His recovery was assured the instant he learned Lillie was alive. And she's gonna be all right too," he added. "The split ear, the hand-sized bruise on the side of her head, and a pretty severe concussion--while it bears watchin'--won't keep her down long, unless her skull is fractured which I firmly doubt. It's my guess whoever hit her wasn't meanin' to kill her, because it looks like she was hit with the flat side of somethin', like a rifle stock, or a hand ax, maybe, like Indians carry... a tomahawk."

MacIver was fresh and willing as he covered ground in a smooth, easy canter. They turned upriver at the time the sun settled below the western horizon. For another forty minutes they kept moving until darkness made further progress too difficult and dangerous. As Frank made his lonely camp, he felt the first pangs of uncertainty. And while he tried to keep his thoughts from dwelling on what could be happening to Robin, he could not shake the uneasy feeling that all was not well with her.

CHAPTER TWENTY-TWO

Having been a mariner did not serve well for camping skills, and his first night alone in the woods was a test of the stability of Frank's already strained emotions. It wasn't just the difficulty he found in the simple chores of building a small fire, heating water for his tea, and finding a comfortable spot for his bedroll, but also the night noises: the creaking and soughing of trees; and from the forest floor--the weird, clicking, scratching, snapping and rustling that had him reaching for his revolver more than once. Birds, animals, insects, and the river--their calls and sounds intermingled and magnified in the black and boundless amphitheater that was his bedroom without walls.

He was up several times before daybreak, hoping there would be enough light to find his way safely along the river; but each time, the night seemed darker than before. It was MacIver's whinnying that woke him from the only real sleep he'd had. It was simply that he wanted water, and his tether snubbed his grazing area a few yards short of the river's edge.

Surprised by the daylight he'd longed for, Frank cursed himself for having finally slept, for it was long past the time of pre-dawn light and well into the first hour of the rising sun. Hurriedly he broke camp and was on his way, angry at himself for time lost.

He rode slowly at first, looking carefully for hoof prints, horse droppings, or other signs of recent transit, hoping to confirm he was on the right track. But as the first hour passed and he found nothing he could be sure of, he abandoned the procedure and quickened the pace.

By late afternoon he reached the confluence of the Rogue and

Illinois rivers. Again, he looked for signs but saw nothing from which he could determine whether they had continued along the Rogue, or had followed the Illinois toward Kerby. "Damn it to hell!" he shouted to MacIver, obviously startled at the outburst. "I'm not even sure they're in this part of the bloody country."

Deciding to follow the suggested route, Frank veered southward along the Illinois, more uncertain now than when he'd started. Tortured by visions of Robin being mauled and ravished by her captors in some isolated place nowhere near where he was searching, he rode long after nightfall hoping to see a campfire. Finally, struck and nearly unseated by a low branch he did not see, he gave up for the , day.

On his bed he strove to keep the recurring torturous thoughts of Robin from his mind by counting the variety of sounds. Nearby, MacIver munched grass, stopping every now and then as if to pay closer attention to something he heard. During those pauses, the rest of the forest life seemed also to cease its clatter. Once he tried to fill the noiseless void with the memory of Robin's voice. He could not remember the sound. He lay, for most of a fitful night, trying vainly to recall.

First light of morning found him moving hastily, angry and impatient. At a clearing he spurred MacIver to a pace he knew was reckless for the early, still sunless time of day. A grayish sea of tall grass swished across his stirrups and brushed the belly of his horse.

MacIver seemed uneasy; his gait was stiff as though each foreleg moved with muscles taut, and his head jerked each time the lead hoof struck the ground. Suddenly, what appeared at first glance to be a tree stump rising from the ground, reared into view not twenty yards ahead--growling.

In one continuous motion MacIver planted his forelegs and changed direction ninety degrees. A split second later Frank was on the ground and MacIver was putting additional yardage between himself and the bear.

Scrambling to his feet, Frank drew his gun, expecting a charge. But none came. He watched only briefly as the animal lumbered through the grass towards the woods; then he turned to look for his horse. He was nowhere in sight.

"Oh Christ!" he said aloud, then called, "MacIver, you pie-eyed son-of-a-bitch, whoa, boy, whoa, wherever the bloody hell you are!"

Despair gave Frank's gut a twist and brought him to the edge of panic as he considered his plight. Precious time would be lost looking for his horse; and worse, what if he couldn't find him?

He looked around, trying to stay calm. "He won't go far," he told himself aloud. But he was far less than certain.

"Bears do somethin' to horses," he remembered Adam saying, "No matter what their trainin', a bear will scare 'em witless."

The grass was dry and trampled blades laid down a path Frank followed nearly to the river bank, then lost where rocks and brush confused the signs.

He didn't think MacIver crossed the river, for there was too much white water at that point for even a panicked horse to try. Or would he? He wondered. And if he didn't cross, then which way did he go, up or down river? Down river most likely, he figured, in the opposite direction from where he'd seen the bear.

It was lighter now. Although the sun had not yet cleared the tall trees to the east, it's filtered morning rays threw a much less somber light than dawn. He saw fresh droppings as he walked a ways downstream, and his spirits rose. For near half-an-hour more he walked without another assuring sign, stopping now and then to carefully scan the area, calling, whistling; spirits sagging more each step. The smell of dampened ashes cut through his worry and spun him around. A freshly doused campfire, ten feet from where he stood!

Cautiously he approached, searching the ground nearby for other signs. There were footprints, a bootprint… two bootprints! His heart pounded. He'd found their camp, he was sure! There was a canteen! Were they still nearby? Crouching as he pulled the Colt from its holster, he inched to where the canteen lay propped against a log. It had the same type wool cover others had in the MacLean household. Robin's? He picked it up. It was full. Then he noticed the knot in the leather carrying strap. "Bloody shit," he grunted through his teeth, "This is mine!"

The discovery that he was back in the camp he'd left only an hour or so earlier, seemed to sap his strength and he slumped onto the log and stared at the ground, feeling stupid and without hope. He shook his head, wondering if he owed thanks to God for having stumbled onto his canteen. "Thanks," he said, looking up. "But I need more help than this." And he stared at the ground again as his thoughts moved to Robin. "Happy wedding day," he murmured.

Self pity won't do it, he thought after a few minutes, and was about to rise when he felt a presence behind him; he was certain he heard breathing. The skin prickled along his spine. His back arched as muscles tensed for anticipated impact of he knew not what. Drawing his gun, he slid from his seat and laid against the log, using it as a shield. He imagined he was being stalked, and his pulse sounded fast and loud in his ears. He held his breath, listening, wondering... man or beast? Bear or cougar? Indian or white man? There was a mild thump on the other side of the log, close by--like that of a foot against the ground--then another. Then a snort--right above his head. He looked up, and, for the second time since their meeting, into the muzzle and pied eyes of MacIver.

Frank knew he was better for the experience, although he'd lost precious time. He rode better. Slower, painstaking and cautious at first, but alert to his surroundings and to the path of his horse. Gradually he increased the pace until MacIver was moving at a mile-gathering rocking horse lope, except through the thickest of the rocky and heavily forested areas.

It was at a clearing along the river's edge where he'd stopped to let MacIver drink that he saw the first evidence that other horses had been in the area.

The soft, damp ground near the water bore the hoof prints of several horses, some shod, some not. He tried to determine the number of animals, and was certain of only three distinctly different prints, but could not rule out a fourth. He walked from there, leading his horse, following the line of prints, and soon came upon a trail of horse droppings. Dry to the touch, but still containing moisture, he guessed they were no more than eight or ten hours old. Perhaps they had camped nearby the night before, He spent a few moments investigating places they might have camped, but found nothing. He followed the trail of hoof prints until they faded into the leaf and needle covered floor of the woods. Still uncertain, but encouraged by what he'd found, he mounted up and urged MacIver on with new vigor.

As sunset approached he'd seen no other signs to convince him he was on the right trail. He expected them to be clever and leave no obvious trail. The fact that he found no further evidence was, he reasoned, an indication that the tracks left at the river's edge were made by a party that did not thereafter want to be followed, and not by some unconcerned group.

After the sun set beneath a thin overcast, daylight faded quickly and the rising quarter-moon was no challenge to the gathering darkness. He found himself at a fork in the river that did not appear on his map. The choice of direction must wait until morning, he decided, and dismounted to make camp.

Water for his tea heated over burning twigs as the gray sky gloomed to starless black and a light wind moved a damp chill through the air. Frank shuddered and chewed on jerky as a hobbled MacIver munched grass nearby.

"Be much obliged if I c'n share yer fire." The voice, sounding old and thin, came from the riverside. "If you've a mind to talk, it'll suit us both."

As Frank eased the Colt from its holster, the owner of the voice came into view, hands held head-high, palms forward.

"I'm Curly Ford," he announced, "an' this here's Honeydew," he added as the donkey appeared in the firelight. "If you be hungry, I'll gladly share my grub." He stopped, still holding his hands up. "If'n I meant harm, I'da put yuh in my sights from a ways back," he said. "So you c'n holster that piece, young feller, 'less you'd rather I move on."

Frank suddenly felt foolish with his gun trained on the old prospector. "Just being careful," he said, slipping the Colt back in its holster. "You're welcome to join me." In almost the same breath, Frank asked if he'd seen a young Indian girl riding in the company of another Indian and, or white men. He had, he said, seen two white men--one wearing the badge of a U. S. Marshal--with an Indian man, and a young squaw.

"'Twas right about noon," he said, "ten, mebbe twelve mile back. They was headed toward Kerby. Figured them injuns to be the Marshal's prisoners, and th' other feller his depity, 'though I didn't see no badge on 'im." He scratched his head. "Yep, it shore 'nuff was a skewbald paint she was ridin'."

New energy surged into Frank's system. He started toward his horse, then, checking the impulse, stopped and moved to the fire, frustrated by the absence of daylight.

Curly Ford was anxious for conversation, and as Frank told his story they drank tea and ate the smoked fish, raw carrots and dried figs the old man offered.

"Kerby's a good twenty-fi' mile," said Curly, "an' the goin' be downright tough most th' way. Trees an' brush thicker'n fur on a beaver."

The old man drew a few more lines on Frank's crude map and told him where best to cross the river to get on the Kerby side. "Reckon the fust man I'd see when I got there'd be the Sheriff," he advised. "Howell, I believe's his name. Good lawman, I heared say, willin' ta help folks."

Frank had trouble getting to sleep, but woke to the smells of coffee, eggs, and venison sausage Curly Ford was cooking. It was still dark. "You're up early, or didn't you sleep?" he asked.

"Sleep? Sleep's fer young'uns." He chuckled. "Stayed up all night plannin' this here meal. Ain't ever' day I has me a guest fer breakfast. Now sit down here an' fill up afore yuh take out agin after them fellers."

As Frank began his ride to Kerby, the edge of morning that was dawn was just beginning to show above the trees.

Chapter Twenty-three

Robin sat, head to knees, hands bound to her feet. She shook violently, not knowing if from the cool dampness or from fear, exhaustion, or despair. In three nights she'd had little sleep. Raped, abused, terrorized, anguished by the uncertainty of her parent's fate and by her longing for Frank, she had wept until her eyes were swollen.

She was bitter now, a feeling she had never known before. She wondered about the Christian faith she was taught to hold within her heart and mind. Christ the Saviour... where was He when she needed Him. Why didn't He help her? She was a good Christian, she thought. She believed in God and she prayed. She didn't do bad things. Why was this happening to her? The images of young Mary and Judd Wiggins came to her tortured mind and ripped at her faith once more. "There can be no God, no Christ the Saviour," she whispered, "at least not for... for half-breeds, not even for young white people. Who *does* He save? And why, why didn't He save me for Frank? Sobs drowned her whispers, but not her troubled thoughts.

A gunshot tore the silence of the dewy morning, releasing Robin from the grip of despair. She looked over at Rollo Davis, squatting at the small fire, pouring coffee. As he looked around, the coffee--still pouring--missed the cup and splattered at his feet.

"Jesus! That shot maybe came from town. Whatta you think, Blue-eyes?"

"I don't know where the town is," Robin answered.

Coffee pot in hand, Rollo swung his arm around and pointed. "Off there, 'bout a mile."

Robin stared blankly at Rollo; without answering, she lowered her head to her knees as her thoughts drifted back to her misery.

A second shot pounded the air with a different sound than the first. It was more of a crack than a boom. Robin raised her head. The sound came from the direction that Rollo had pointed. The hope sprung into her mind that maybe Seven Feathers and Jim had been shot.

Rollo, standing now, put cup and coffee pot down, went to where his saddle lay and took his rifle from its scabbard. "That was a pistol shot, for sure," he said, "and from town, too. They musta run into trouble. Dammit, I bet them bastards will have the law after us. I'm gettin' ready ta move out."

"What will you do with me?"

"You're comin' with me, Blue Eyes. An' if them guys ain't back by the time I'm ready, we're pullin' out." He grinned at her. "Yuh know, I jus' might get my turn with you, yet."

Robin panicked at the thought of Rollo having his pleasure with her. Her stomach, already sour, spasmed, and bile flooded her mouth. Quickly, she turned her head and spit. The taste in her mouth was as bad as the odor and she fought against another surge from her stomach.

"You tryna spit at me, you damn half-breed?" He raised his foot near her head. "I'll kick your face in if you ever try ta spit at me again, you hear me?"

Unable to speak against the swallowing, Robin nodded her head, then rested it on her knees. Viciously, it was jerked backward by her hair. The tension on her neck muscles pulled her mouth open.

"You hear me, you *bitch?*"

She strained to close her jaw and make the words: "Didn't... spit... at... you. I'm sick... in stomach."

"Yeah, I can smell it, now," he said, and pitched her head forward as he let go of her hair.

Rollo was saddling his horse when Robin caught the sudden movement of a bird, then watched as Seven Feathers moved silently into camp and stood, unseen by Rollo, at his back.

The Indian's voice had a sarcastic tone: "You fix to leave, Rollo?"

Rollo's startled reaction jerked his body rigid. His ground-tied horse threw his head and took several steps backward.

Cursing, Rollo lunged and grabbed at the dragging reins. When he had the spooked animal under control he spun and faced Seven. His hand went to his gun, but stopped there as the barrel of the Indian's cocked rifle centered on his chest.

"Move hand from gun or you die here, Rollo."

Rollo's arm went limp at his side and the fair skin of his boyish face took on a sunburned look. "You crazy damn fool Injun! What the hell's the idea, sneakin' up on me like that?"

"Not try to sneak. Make plenty noise, like running elk. Maybe shit from brain plug ears. Now, why you saddle up?"

Rollo's face got redder. Robin wanted to laugh at Seven's insult, but was afraid Rollo would take out his anger on her.

"Simple. I heard shootin'--two shots--an' figured maybe you and Jim had trouble in town and I... we might hafta move fast when you came back. Jus' gettin' ready, that's all. Now, where's Jim? And Where's yer horse?"

Seven cradled the cocked rifle. "Horse in bushes. Jim shot by Sheriff. Hurt bad, maybe dead now." His voice was matter-of-fact.

Robin's heart pounded; her spirit lifted as she hoped he was dead, and maybe her situation would improve.

"God A'mighty, what happened?" Rollo shouted.

"Don't know. Maybe law man know Jim not real Marshal. Don't know. I watch store from far across street. Jim come out of store hands up, law man's gun point on his back. I shoot at law man an' he go down. Jim grab for law man's gun but he not dead yet an' shoot Jim

195

bad. Jim go down; scream like squealing dog. I go, come back here. No one follow, I make sure."

Rollo kicked the ground. "Damn it all to hell! I tol' Jim that Marshal's badge would buy us nothin' but trouble. Did anyone see you?"

"Don't think so. I behind tree, back from street. Not see anyone."

"What about the sheriff? You prob'ly only winged 'im."

"Man hit in chest, where I aim. Still on back when he shoot Jim. Not get up. I think he not live long."

Rollo turned to his horse and tightened the cinch. "Well," he said, "We'd best get our asses outta here. Get that squaw on her horse an' let's get movin'. An' cover that fire while 1 pack the cookin' stuff." He slapped the saddle. "*Shit!* no supplies, an' no money neither, dammit."

The Indian didn't move. He looked first at Robin, without expression, then at Rollo who was gathering up the utensils. She could see that Seven Feathers was breathing heavily and sensed his anger.

She'd noticed that Jim had always shown respect for Seven and never had she heard him order the Indian to do anything. She figured that Jim was afraid of Seven, for he seemed always to be careful not to anger him. He had even offered her to Seven, "next after me," he'd said. The offering brought an angry response from Rollo: "I ain't takin' seconds to no damn injun!" Then Jim said: "Shut up, Rollo! You ain't even gonna get *thirds* with no gal I'm layin', on accounta I *know* you got the drip from that Chetco injun whore."

Seven had refused Jim's offer. He didn't say why, but he was obviously offended by Rollo's remark and said he didn't think Rollo could take any woman who wasn't tied down. That made Rollo mad.

"Untie her, damn it," he'd screamed, I'll take her now, you'll see, you God damned injun, you'll see."

196

But it was Jim who took her. "You ain't gonna do shit, Rollo," he'd said, "not with your runny pecker. Now Seven, how's for keepin' an eye on this here 'boy' while I try on the filly?" Seven grunted his agreement.

Away from the other two, Jim had warned her, "Don't try to stop me or I'll cut your throat!" Her arms, tied behind her, ached from the restraint. Her hands were numb and swollen from the bonds at her wrists. Shocked by the day's events she became a rag-doll, limp, without resistance, without emotion, and with little feeling.

Jim had shoved her harshly to the ground then jammed his knees between her legs. She had wept silently as he forced her buckskin shirt up over her breasts, squeezing them, fingering her nipples then putting his mouth first on one, then the other, sucking and biting until she cried out in pain and her weeping was no longer silent.

Angered by her outcry, he'd backhanded her across the jaw, but without the force she wished had blotted out her knowledge of his acts. His hands then shifted to her skirt and legs, and groping thereabout had found a knife, tied high on the outside of her thigh; a small, Bowie type that Adam made for her.

Jim had grinned as he stroked her belly with the blade. "You was hopin' you'd get a chance to stick one of us with this, weren't you? But now you're the one that's gonna get stuck, 'lil squaw, but not with no knife, no siree, not with no knife!"

Thus, in the fading light of her first day as a captive, Robin experienced lust and sex without tenderness, without gentleness, without respect and, for her, without feeling except for the hurt to her body and pride.

She shook her head to dislodge the memory and was sickened by the thought that her ordeal was not over.

Her thoughts were trampled by a sudden rush of angry words from Rollo: "Dammit, Seven, you ain't moved a muscle.

Now get that bitch on her horse and let's get outta here, you hear me? I'm ready ta go. You comin' or not?"

"Seven Feathers not take orders from yelping pup."

Rollo's face cherried. He stared at the Indian while his mouth tried for words that didn't come. Seven stared back and lowered the cradled rifle.

Robin watched, anxiously hoping the two angry men would shoot each other and that the shots would bring townspeople to help her.

Cuss words spewed from Rollo. "Well, God *damn!* he shouted, shaking his head one way then the other, with each word. "You can just go ta hell. I ain't takin' no more shit from you." Dropping the reins of his horse, he walked quickly toward Robin, his scowling face beet red. "I'm takin' the squaw with me."

"No!" The shout from Seven stopped Rollo a few paces from her. A dozen feet away, the Indian took a quick step toward them. As Rollo turned to face him, Seven's arm blurred in an arc. Robin couldn't see Rollo's face but she guessed he must have seen it coming, for his hands went up as though to catch the tomahawk before it slammed into his chest with a hollow "thunk". His knees buckled and he fell heavily on his back. Breath hissed through his partly open mouth. Blood gushed onto his shirt as his shaking hands grasped the handle and struggled feebly to lift the imbedded blade.

Robin's teeth clenched against dry heaves. She watched in fright and facination as Seven stepped behind the fallen man's head, grasped the chin and, with a sweeping stroke of his knife, cut Rollo's throat. Lifeless hands fell from the handle.

Seven pulled away his tomahawk and wiped the blade on Rollo's clothes while Rollo's heels thumped the ground in brief response to the final twitches of nerves and muscles. The heavy, sweet scent of fresh blood scared her like it was her own. Soon it gave way to a more pungent, sickening odor as bowels and bladder relaxed and gave up their contents. Robin swallowed hard and dropped her head to her knees. She hated Rollo and was glad he was dead, but she had not enjoyed being a close-range witness to his killing.

A tug at her wrists and she raised her head as Seven Feathers cut the strand of rawhide that joined the bonds of hands and feet. Placing his knife between her ankles, he paused, the blade edge resting on the leg hobbles he himself had put there. "You are *my* woman now. I will treat you well, you will see. Run, and you will die as you run. If you do not please me, I will sell you, and maybe that will be worse for you."

The blade moved and the bonds on her ankles fell away. Grasping her forearm, he cut the ties at her wrists then pulled her to her feet. Gently, he rubbed her arms and hands and as he did she looked past his pocked and leathered face to the forest that filled her view. Her thoughts drifted to the trees that sheltered birds and made her long for the home and freedom she had known.

Seven's rough hand cupped her chin and turned her face to his. Smokey brown eyes looked about her face then centered on her eyes. She thought she saw the morsel of a smile before he spoke again, this time in a whisper that proclaimed a different Seven Feathers than she'd known.

"You are young and pretty. It is not in my heart to give you pain."

"I am glad I am no longer with them," she said, "but my heart is sick and I can never be your woman."

"You must try. Moon can never be Sun, but it can give light to darkness."

CHAPTER TWENTY-FOUR

Unlike the stone-block prisons of the British Isles, the jail at Kerby didn't look to Frank like it would hold anyone intent on getting out. The building was set back from the street more than the others and resembled a warehouse. A structure of poorly fitted logs, with black and yellow stripes painted diagonally across the solid door, it looked like it belonged on an Army post. A tree-filtered ray of late afternoon sun struck the door and stood it in garrish contrast to the dark, mud-brown of the building's exterior. Above the door a crude sign, chiseled out of a board with the letters painted white, announced simply: JAIL. To the right of the entrance, another sign, hand painted black on white, told the public that therein also was the Office of Jeff Howell, Sheriff, Josephine County, Oregon.

Frank pushed open the door and was confronted by a stocky man, swarthy complexioned, with a full, black moustache that swept downward below the corners of his unsmiling mouth. A double barreled shotgun, held waist level, pointed at Frank's belt buckle, just inches away.

"Move slowly, *Senor*, an' drop the gun belt, *por favor*."

Startled, Frank asked "Are you the Sheriff?"

"No, I am the Deputy. Now drop the hardware, eh?"

With his eyes fixed on the threatening barrels of the shotgun, Frank worked at the buckle and wondered why he was being disarmed. The gun and belt dropped to the floor.

"*Bueno*. Now, reach as high as you can, an' tell me what is your name an' reason to be here, eh?"

Frank raised his arms. "My name is Ross... Frank Ross. I'm--" The shotgun moved quickly, jabbing him in the belly, and he jerked back with sudden, reflex action.

"Easy, *Senor* Ross. Another quick move maybe get you blown in two. Now jus' stand still while I take that piece from onder your shirt, eh?"

With one hand holding the short barreled coach gun against Frank's groin, the beefy man pulled up Frank's shirt and took the Deringer that was tucked at his waist. "Nice little hideout you got here, hombre. A real Deringer, eh? You mus' be expecting troubles, or looking for it maybe. Now jus' turn around slow amigo, an' keep the hands high, eh? An' tell me why you have come to this place."

"I'm after three men with a young girl they kidnapped from a ranch near Gold Beach... on the coast. I want to know if anyone has seen them around here."

"You are a lawman, yes?"

"No, a friend of the girl and her family."

"*Muy bien, Senor* Ross, put your ass in that chair in the corner an' pull off your boots; then we will talk, if you don' make no funny moves."

As Frank moved to the chair he felt discouraged and wondered why he was getting this kind of treatment. Still pointing the shotgun at Frank, the Deputy sucked in his belly, stuffed the Deringer in his belt then picked Frank's gun belt off the floor. Backing to a desk, he sat on the edge and whistled a tune while Frank removed his boots. The melody sounded to Frank like one that a Spanish sailor on "Charlotte" used to hum.

Frank turned his boots upside down then pointed the tops toward the Deputy to show they were empty. "Satisfied?" he asked.

"No more little guns, eh? *Bueno.* You can dress your feet again, *Senor.*

His voice seemed less menacing now, and as Frank put on his boots the Deputy moved to the chair behind the desk. Still holding the shotgun, with both hammers cocked, he sat down and put Frank's gun belt on the floor at his side. "Now, tell me again why it is you come here, eh?"

"I'm looking for a young Indian girl... well, half Indian. She's the daughter of friends. Their place near Gold Beach was raided by a gang of renegades--whites and Indians--and she was kidnaped."

"When did this happen?"

"About five... no, four days ago." Frank shook his head. "Yes, four days... it seems longer." As Frank told of the raid, the Deputy's eyes narrowed.

"The three *hombres* with the girl, do you know what they look like... any special thing to... how to recognize them?"

"The two whites, one young, early twenties, round face, fair skin, medium height, pudgy; the other is tall, thin, dark hair, in his thirties. Lillie said his eyes are very close together and his face is long, and he had a deep hole --I think she meant a dimple--in his chin. One of the white men was called Jim.

The Indian was wearing a beaded chest plate and a small bundle of feathers trailing from a braided section of hair over one ear--the right one, I think. He was not a young buck, she said. They were seen yesterday morning along the Illinois River, about fifteen miles northwest of here, by a prospector I met. He said the tall one's wearing a U.S. Marshal's badge." Frank paused as he noticed the Deputy was staring past him and didn't seem to be listening. He studied the man's face. It was a ruddy, intelligent face; wide, with deep set dark brown eyes beneath bushy eyebrows. The black moustache turned down at the corners of his mouth, giving him a stern, but not unfriendly, appearance. Eyes narrowing, his brow furrowed and suddenly he looked at Frank as though he just realized the talking had stopped.

"A U.S. Marshal's badge, eh?"

"Aye, sir. But I'm sure he's not a genuine Marshal. Have you any information that might help me find them?"

Without answering, the Deputy pointed the shotgun at the ceiling, carefully lowered the cocked hammers then put his feet on the desk. "I got a friend that lives out that way now: Archie Beeman; you ever hear of him?"

A surge of excitement brought Frank to his feet. "Sir, I *know* Archie. He's a neighbor of the MacLean's, and a good friend."

The Deputy motioned for Frank to sit down. "You should have brought him with you, *muchacho*. You are going to need plenty help, I think."

"Then you know something of these men, and of Robin?"

"Maybe, maybe not. We get to that in a minute. Why you don' bring Archie or someone with you, like a posse, maybe?"

"Archie has a bad back; could hardly walk when I left. And there was no time to get a posse together. They already had nearly a full day's start, and I wanted to get--"

"Suppose you catch up with them, then what, eh? You are going to shoot it out with them an' save the girl, eh, all by yourself?"

Frank felt his ears get warm. "I can handle myself."

"Horseshit, amigo. You could have got yourself killed dead right here."

Frank flushed with anger, his pride jolted. "How? I mean... I didn't expect a lawman to pull down on me when I walked in here."

"Well, you got a point there, kid. But I have some little troubles here this morning an' I am not sure who is this young *hombre* who comes riding up. I think maybe you come to help the ones who gave me the troubles. But what I mean is, before you are sure who is this unfriendly *hombre* with a doublegun at your belly, you tell him all about why you are making this visit. Now, if I am not who you think, or maybe I am one of these hombres you are looking for, or maybe one of their *companeros*, I will kill you quickly when I hear your story, eh *amigo? Comprende?*"

Stunned by this exposure of his inexperience, Frank felt stupid and humiliated. "You have made your point, Sir; it's a lesson I'll bloody well remember."

"*Bueno*. Now here is your gun." Reaching down, the Deputy grasped Frank's gun belt and slid it to him across the floor.

Frank looked down at the holstered Colt that lay at his feet, but made no attempt to pick it up. Without looking up he said: "No matter how good I am with this, it won't help me if I'm stupid, will it?" It was an open expression of an inward thought; a self criticism, the first outcropping of his own doubts as to his being able to find and rescue Robin.

"Jus' remember, Francisco, it is best you don' trust nobody. Be careful who it is you talk with. It is big advantage to you if these men don' know who it is that hunt them. It is bigger advantage if they don' know they are hunted, eh?"

"I'll remember. You said you may know something of Robin and the men who have her, Sheriff… I mean Deputy." Then Frank noticed that the man who said he was the Deputy was not wearing a badge. "If indeed you are a Deputy." he added, looking straight into dark eyes that didn't seem to blink.

The thick eyebrows arched slightly. "You think I am not the Sheriff's Deputy, *amigo*? Why is that, eh?"

"You're not wearing a badge."

A smile broke on the man's face. It was a friendly smile, Frank thought. "Now you are starting to learn, *Senor* Ross. Don' trus' nobody." Without taking his eyes from Frank, he unbuttoned his shirt-pocket, withdrew an object and held it out. "Come close, *amigo*, an' bring the chair, eh?"

205

Pulling his chair to the desk, Frank sat and peered at a small metal shield. Across the top, imprinted in small, black letters, it read JOSEPHINE COUNTY; at the bottom: OREGON. In the center, the word DEPUTY formed an arc in large, bold letters over what was obviously the word SHERIFF, except the letters ERIF were flattened and distorted along a heat seared groove in the metal.

He looked up at the man holding the badge. "How did that happen?"

"Target Practice."

"Target Practice? You used the badge for target practice? Or was it on someone else at the time?" Frank smiled when he said it. He really didn't believe this man wasn't what he claimed to be. He didn't know why, but he felt he could trust the burley Spaniard, or whatever he was.

"Ha! Now it is you who is hard to convince, eh? No, I was wearing the badge an' someone is holding target practice on me, amigo. Look, maybe this convince you, eh?" Opening his shirt he pulled it aside and exposed the left side of his chest. "Look here, Francisco, look at this."

An ugly bruise was centered on the nipple of the left breast--now swollen egg-size. It spread, in greenish-tinted black, purple and yellow, from the middle of his barrel-like chest to the armpit.

Frank sucked breath through his teeth. "Holy Jesus, that's a bloody pipper, that is! Right on the tit, too. It must hurt like flaming hell!"

"Only when I breath, *amigo*. Lucky I ain't no wet nurse, eh?" Chuckling at his own humor, he buttoned his shirt and smiled broadly. "Satisfied?" he asked.

Frank nodded, smiling. "Please Sheriff, tell me what you know of Robin, and the men who have her."

"My name is Ephram Angeles," he said, offering his hand. "Call me Ephram, *por favor*."

His grip was firm and there was a competent, informal way about him that reminded Frank of Adam. Now that the matter of the Deputy's identity was resolved, he wondered why he hadn't as yet seen the Sheriff. "Where is Sheriff, ah... Howell, isn't it?"

"Si, Jefferson Howell. He is gone for couple of days to go fishing with some *politicos* from up north. He will be back tomorrow, I think. "You are a 'King George Man', eh? English, Canadian? You gotta accent like a 'King George Man' as our Indian friends say. Only it is jus' a little different, eh?"

"Well, 'King George Man', 'Boston Man', a little of each, you might say. Born in Scotland, lived five years in Boston--'til I was fifteen. Now please, what do you know about Robin?" Frank was having trouble keeping his growing impatience in check.

Ephram's eyes narrowed as he moved forward in his chair and looked sternly at Frank. "Now you listen to me good, George Boston, what I'm gonna tell you will make you want to charge out of the door an' go galloping off like Christ jus' told you where is the Holy Grail. An' that would be very foolish, amigo. So, it is bes' you sit back, have a snort with me of this good homemade whiskey an' don' pull your trigger while on half cock, okay?"

Frank's breathing quickened with anxiety and fear; fear that what he was going to hear would test his reason and restraint. The worry for Robin that had eaten into his soul and tortured his mind for nearly four days, now ravaged him even more and he found it difficult to control his voice. "For God's sake, Ephram, if you know anything that can help me, don't waste time. I've got to find her!"

"This girl, she mean something to you... special, eh?" Frank came to his feet as his emotional control cracked under the strain of anxiety. "Yes, dammit!" he shouted, "We were to be married--yesterday! Now please, tell me what you know, for God's sake, man. Don't stall me any bloody longer!" He felt the blood rush to his face as he glared down at the man who sat there appearing so calm.

Ephram turned away and unhurriedly took a bottle from the desk drawer. "Sit down, may friend. Have a drink an' try to relax or I will tell you bloody *nothing.* Now sit!" His voice was calm, but the command was firm, as though to his favorite dog.

Frank slumped in the chair and his jaw sagged as he spoke: "I'm sorry. I'm just damned tired; not much sleep in three nights, and I'm out of my mind with worry."

"You got no reason to be sorry, Francisco." Ephram poured from an unlabled bottle into two glasses and pushed one toward Frank. "Here, sip this while I talk, an' keep quiet, eh?"

Taking a sip of the whiskey, Ephram ran his hand down over his moustache and rubbed his chin.

"Early this morning a tall, skinny *hombre* wearing the badge of a U.S. Marshal, come in Tom Reddick's store -- it is next to this place an' order some groceries, .44 Ball, caps an' powder. Now it jus' so happen that I am standing in the back of the store with a glass of milk and one of *Senora* Reddick's hot honey buns. Then, this hombre say's to charge it to the U.S. Gover'ment. *Senor* Reddick asks him for his Marshal's Identification so he can put the number on the charge slip, an' for him to sign his name." Ephram paused and took a sip from his glass. "Hey, Francisco, you have not yet tried the whiskey, eh?"

Holding the glass in both hands, Frank shook his head. "No sir, I haven't yet. I've been too anxious to hear your story. Please,go on."

"Try it, *amigo.* It will do you much good."

Frank tipped the glass. Might as well, he thought, it's no use trying to hurry this man. It had a heavy, sweet-sour odor. He took more than a sip, a good mouthful. Hot to his tongue, it tasted like medicine for croup. He swallowed hard and his eyes watered as it seared a path to his stomach. He coughed, swallowed, and coughed again.

"You okay, *amigo?*"

Frank nodded. "Go on," he whispered, sleeving the tears from his eyes. "I can handle it."

Ephram sipped again from his glass, cleared his throat and went on. "Now, this *hombre* gives to *Senor* Reddick the card of Identification an' is signing the sales slip when Tom says to him: 'Marshal George Colson, eh? This here says you weigh two- hunnert an' five pounds, Marshal. You look more like one sixty, to me.' "Been losin' weight," he says. Now I have been watching this *hombre* and while I have never seen this man George Colson I have heard he's got *una cicatriz grande--*a big scar--that run across his face from his chin to under his ear. A bullet crease, they say. Now, this *hombre* has a few days growth, but I can see no scar from where it is I am standing. So I walk up to him an' I say '*Buenos dias*, Marshal. I am the Sheriff's Deputy. What brings you to this place?'" Ephram paused, picked up his glass and raised it, his eyes fixed on Frank. The heavy moustache lifted slightly at the ends, exposing a slight smile. "*Salud, amigo.* To your health, eh?"

Resolved to the price he must pay for information, Frank raised his glass. "Thank you, Ephram, and to your health also." The whiskey seemed smoother, this time warming without burning. "Go on, please," he urged.

"Well, when I ask why he is here, he tells me he's got a Rogue Indian squaw that he mus' take to Jacksonville for trial. She an' some Buck killed a settler an' his wife, he says. 'Where is she?' I ask, an' he says she is with his deputy where they are camped outside of town. Now I know that is not the way a Marshal would do. He would bring her to this jail an' he would stay at the hotel until ready to move again. So I ask him to come to my office an' have some coffee I have brewed, an' some of the *Senora* Reddick's honey buns I am taking there. Well, he says he ain't got time, so I say that is too bad and hand him one of the buns I am holding. 'You mus' try one of these most excellent buns,' I said, an' when he takes it I poke him in the belly with my hog leg forty-four. Then I take his gun an' tell him he is arrested for impersonating a U.S. Marshal."

Ephram finished the whiskey in his glass and reached for the bottle. "Drink up," he said.

The thought of Robin heated Frank's brain like the whiskey heated his belly. Quickly he rose and leaned over the desk that separated him from Ephram. "You've got him locked up here now? My God, man, what about the girl… it must be Robin… where… were you able to find them?"

"Easy, *muchacho*. Sit down. You have much to hear. I know you want to run off an' save this girl, but you mus' be patient, an' know all the story, *comprende*?"

Frank sat down and banged his fist on the desk in frustration. As Ephram continued, he filled his glass.

"Well, marchin' that hombre out the front door of Reddick's store was the mos' *loco* thing 1 have done in many years." He took a swig of whiskey, tipped his head back and gargled before swallowing. "This is the bes' medicine I know for a sore throat, also a sore tit." He pushed the bottle toward Frank. "Help yourself."

Frank shook his head. "Thanks, but I've had enough for awhile. Please, go on."

"Well, I poke this *hombre* out of the front door, like I said, an' then he walks down the steps of the porch an' I tell him to hold it. Like a fool I stand on the porch, holding my gun on him while I look around for just a secon'. Then 'boom' an' I am knock on my ass by something that hit me in the ches' like the kick of a mule. From the noise I am sure the shot comes from across the street to my right. By the Union Hotel maybe, but no matter. I think I am killed, by God, an' so does my prisoner. He comes back on the porch an' start to reach for my gun which, by some miracle of God, I am still holding at full cock. Well, as this *hombre* bend over I raise up the gun. Now it is *him* who goes loco an' try to grab for it an' I pull the trigger. But my aim is not so good an' the bullet catch him on the hip an' he goes down with a scream that would sour the milk in a cow.

"I lay still a minute, until I am sure I am not dying, then I roll off the porch an' get behind the steps in case maybe there will be more shooting. My prisoner is rolling around in the dirt an' hollering like he is being gored by a bull. I think for a minute that I will holler along with him, because I think my tit's been tore off an' my chest is broke.

"Well, after awhile I guess that the shooting is over an' I crawl to where my prisoner is puking an' moaning. Then I can see why: that forty-four ball jus' plain tore in him a hole that you could stuff your gun in, butt first. *Madre de Dios*, his blood was coming like out of a well pump." He took another sip from his glass.

"Where is he now? Is he alive?"

"Locked up in there." Ephram answered with a jerk of his head to a door behind him, which Frank assumed led to the cell block. "He was for awhile passed out after Doc stopped the blood an' we got him to the jail. Doc says the *hombre's* hip is smashed to hell, an' maybe some other things, too. It is hard to stop the blood. About one hour ago the Doc comes to change the bandages an' to give him a sed... seda... some medicine. This fellow, he is in bad shape but is able to talk a little."

Ephram took two cigars from the desk drawer that looked like dog turds, then searched through the drawers and his pockets, muttering about matches.

"You said he was able to talk. Well, what did he say?"

"Take a cigar, Francisco, an' relax. Have another drink maybe, eh?"

Frank shook his head. He felt a liking for this man, but the casual attitude had turned his patience to frustration. "Dammit, Sheriff, don't you understand the urgency of this bloody situation? I've got to find those bastards and... and..."

"An' get yourself killed, an' maybe the girl too. Now just listen awhile, *muchacho*, an' you will have the facts, eh?"

Frank angrily grabbed the bottle and sloshed his glass half-full. Setting the bottle down hard on the desk, he took a long swig, slumped in the chair and glared at Ephram. Whiskey coursed down his neck from a corner of his mouth.

Ephram mumbled something in Spanish, leaned to his left as though he intended to break wind, then struck a match across the back of his right leg and lit the cigar. A dense cloud of bluish smoke rose between them and he waved it away, all the while staring back at Frank. He didn't seem to blink his eyes, even as the smoke shrouded his face.

"My prisoner says he is Jim Whittson; that he an' his Indian friend called 'Seven' an' another white named Rollo Davis, found Marshal Colson on the bank of the Chetco, drowned dead, with his head bashed in like maybe he fell in the river an' got carried into the rocks. They took his identification figurin' they would charge supplies to the Gover'ment. Then, he says, they found this young squaw up around Pistol River an' talked her into goin' with them to Jacksonville or maybe Yreka. He said they figure they would sell her to some miner.

"Well, I don' believe his lies so I look through the 'Wanteds' an' I find this one with a picture and description that fit him pretty good, only the name is Corporal James E. Watson, not Whittson, an' he is wanted by the U.S. Army for murder of a sergeant an' deserting to escape trial by Courts Martial.

"Now this fellow that he calls Rollo Davis, I think is Private Roland David Brown, wanted also by the Gover'ment for deserting the Army after killing a Paymaster while trying to steal the payroll. The Indian he calls 'Seven' I am sure is Seven Feathers, a murdering renegade Tututni who one time ran with Crazy Enos an' was in on the massacre of Ben Wright--the Indian Agent--and many settlers at Gold Beach back in '56. These are bad *hombres*, Frank Ross; *malo, muchisimo malo*, my friend, especially this Indian. I have heard before of him. He kills people jus' because he don't like *people*, especially if they are white. *Comprende, amigo?* These two that are left with the girl are bad an' you should not go after them alone. You maybe can get help from the Army at Fort Lane, eh?"

"Well, what of the one that shot you, didn't anyone see him, or go after him?"

"Nobody claim to have seen who was it that shoot me, and nobody is fool enough to run into the woods after him. I think it was the Indian who shoot me. The woods are thick an' the way that hombre can shoot, he would kill many before they would get him. But he would have killed me sure as hell, if that punkin ball had not hit my badge at such a fortunate angle that it bounce off." He ran his hand lightly over the breast and sucked in his breath. "*Caramba!* That is one sore son-of-a-bitch! The Sheriff, it is too bad he was not here; he would have rode out to find the hombre who shoot at me and maybe find also the girl. But he maybe also get shot for his trouble, eh?"

Frank agreed, then added his thought aloud, "Although he might've organized a posse and caught them."

"No, it is very hard to get the men together in this place, amigo, unless the crime is against the citizens, an' there is maybe only one man to chase. Crimes against the law don' get much notice from nobody, I think. And by the time I get my prisoner took care of an' I can breath good again, I am sure his *companeros* are far away. An' I cannot leave when the sheriff is gone, you un'erstand, in case you wonder, eh?"

Embarrassed now, by the obvious implication of his statement about a posse, Frank began shaking his head before Ephram finished his explanation. "Please, Ephram, I didn't mean that *you* should have

213

gone after them. I realize that--"

Smiling, Ephram cut him off with a wave of his hand. "*Olvidalo*, Francisco. Forget it."

Frank was trying to keep calm and patient, but his anxiety had peaked. "Please, may I see the Watson fellow now?"

Ephram stood up, brushing cigar ashes from his pants.

"Sure, but you gotta promise you don' try to finish the job on him, eh? I would like for him to live a little longer. He don't know yet I'm gonna send him to the Army at Fort Lane tomorrow. He thinks he is going to hospital in Jacksonville. When he finds out, that soldier is gonna shit. They will shoot his ass off at Fort Lane!" Ephram laughed. "Come on, Francisco, I will take you to see him now."

CHAPTER TWENTY-FIVE

In the cell block, gray shafts of late-afternoon light streamed through barred windows, piercing the darkness. A single, flameless lantern hung from the low ceiling of the corridor between cells. Strong antiseptic vapors, like smelling salts, perked Frank's senses to the thump-clank rhythm of heels and spurs as he followed Ephram.

"He's in this firs' one, *amigo*. He's got this whole place to hisself." Ephram unlocked the cell door and motioned Frank inside as a moan came from the man laying on a cot--the man Ephram said was Jim Watson. Frank stepped in and there came another moan as Watson's arm slid limply from his chest and his hand struck the floor with a thud.

"This is him, Francisco. He don' soun' like he feel so good, eh? What is the matter, Jim boy, don' you feel good? Take a look, my friend. I will get a lantern so you can see better, eh?"

Frank moved to the cot and looked down at a tall man lying on his back. His pants and boots had been removed and he wore gray long-johns, cut off at the knees; the left leg was dark with dried blood and his feet extended beyond the cot. What seemed to be a large piece of old bed sheet swathed his midsection and looked wet-red at the side. With dark hair, thin nose, eyes set close on a long, narrow face, Frank was sure he was one of the men Adam had described. Then Watson's eyes opened.

"Who the hell're you?" he asked, his voice a grainy whisper.

The odor of urine reached Frank's nose.

"I'm pissin' myself," said Watson. "Can't hold it. Can't move, can't do nothin'. I ain't never hurt so damn bad." He turned his face toward the wall. "Jesus, I think I'm dyin'. I think my guts are smashed."

Ephram came in with a lantern and held it over his prisoner. "What do you think, *amigo*, this is one of them, eh?"

"From what I can see and from what you've told me, I'd guess that he is."

Watson turned his face toward Frank. The added light from the lantern made clear a deep dimple in his chin. Frank's jaw clenched and his pulse thumped in his temples. "Now I see. Yes, he's bloody well one of them. He's the one that Adam described as having a hole in his chin, I'm sure of it!"

Watson's eyes widened. "Who the hell're *you*?" he asked again, "an' who's Adam?"

"It was Adam Maclean who's ranch you and your bloody friends attacked near Gold Beach." Frank paused and tried to control his rising anger. "And I'm a friend, looking for their daughter that you rotten bastards kidnaped!"

Watson turned his face to the wall again. "I don't... don't know what... you're talkin' about. I need a doctor, bad."

Frank looked at Watson and felt a hatred he'd never known before. He wanted, somehow, to cause the man more pain, to make him tell what he knew, then kill him. He saw that blood was oozing through the makeshift bandage onto the cot.

"You're as good as dead, Watson. You must know that. If you don't die right here, the Army will have you before a firing squad." Frank heard Ephram's scolding whisper at his side:

"*Caramba*! Now you have ruin my surprise for him, *amigo*!"

Frank didn't whisper his reply. He wanted Watson to hear, to suffer with the thought. "I don't think he'll live to be turned over to the Army, Sheriff."

Watson slowly turned his head until he faced the two men. He tried to raise his head, but couldn't and began to breath heavily. "Sheriff, you said... Jackson... a hospital in... in Jacksonville."

"That was before I find out who you are, James Watson, Corporal, United States Army, deserter, wanted also for murder. Tomorrow I will send word to the Army detachment in Jacksonville. I think the Army will fix you up so they can have a little target practice on you, eh?" Ephram chuckled. "But you tell my friend here what he wants to know, then maybe I will feed you before they get here for you, eh?"

"Horse shit!" murmured Watson, and closed his eyes.

"What've you got to lose?" asked Frank. "Your friends don't care about you now. They aren't going to bother with an injured man; not one that can't move or help himself. I don't give a damn about your friends, I just want the girl back. Where is she?"

Without opening his eyes, Watson spoke, his voice weak and raspy, "My arm hurts. Pick it up 'n put it on the bunk, will ya, bud? I can't seem ta move it." He opened his eyes and looked at Frank. "Please, bud."

It appeared to Frank that the man was near to passing out and the gaunt, expressionless look on his face reminded him of the way his father looked, just before he died. He cradled the arm on the foot of his boot and hoisted it onto the cot. "Now, you son-of-a-bitch, tell me where I can find Robin."

Watson moved his mouth several times without speaking, then ran his tongue over his lips. When the words came, they sounded forced. "John Seymore, Yreka."

"Why John Seymore. Who is he?"

"Agent... Injun agent."

"Indian agent?" Frank was puzzled. "Why were you taking her to him?"

"Bounty."

"Bounty?" Frank shouted, "What in bloody hell do you mean,

217

bounty? She's no criminal!" Frank felt Ephram's hand on his shoulder.

"Easy. I will tell you later what this is, eh? You got more questions of this *hombre*, you better hurry. He is very weak."

Frank nodded, but he was so upset and anxious that he was finding it hard to concentrate. "Is she all right?"

"Yeah."

"How many were with you?"

"Two."

"They are Roland David Brown an' Seven Feathers, is that not true?" asked Ephram.

"Yeah. Will you... get me... blanket? I'm cold."

"One more question," said Frank, "Did Cyrus Hogan hire you to raid the MacLean's?"

There was a long pause before Watson answered. "Yeah. Said there was gold stashed there."

Frank turned to the Deputy. "Thank you, Ephram. You were right. Now I'll move on." He turned to go but Ephram held him by the arm.

"*Uno momento.* I will get his blanket then we will talk a little more before you go. You owe me that, eh?"

Frank paused, then nodded. "All right, I want to hear about John Seymore and this bounty business."

Ephram Angeles pulled open a desk drawer. Propping his feet on it, he leaned back in the chair and re-lit his half burned cigar.

"Before I forget, may I please have my Deringer back?"

Ephram's lips pursed and the corners of his mouth came down as he took the small pistol from his waist. He studied it briefly then handed it to Frank. "Ah, that is a very fine piece. A real Henry Deringer, eh? How did you come by it, my friend?"

"It was ray father's. He got it on one of his runs to New York or

Boston, I think."

"Runs, what kind of runs, eh?"

"Shipping runs. He was Master of a mercantile trade ship."

The large eyebrows lifted and seemed to pull the corners of Ephram's mouth into a smile. "Ah, that is mos' interesting! I have wanted always to go on a ship. How come you do not follow in his steps, eh?"

"I did, for a time. Too long a story for now, if you don't mind. I'd really like to get on with the business at hand."

The smile faded and, for an instant, a scowl betrayed Ephram's obvious disappointment. "*Si*, another time. Now, what of the other gun you carry in the holster? It is a Colt, is it not?"

"Aye, a Fifty-one Colt, Navy model." Frank's impatience showed in the rising tone and volume of his voice as he tried to quicken the pace of their talk. "Sheriff, I'm grateful for the help you've been to me, but you must understand that I've got to get on after those..."

Ephram leaned forward and lifted his hand as he interrupted. "Si, I understand, *amigo*. But I think you better listen to me a little more, *por favor*. As a favor to the girl, eh?" He waved away a cloud of cigar smoke that hung between them. "I want you to get her an' not to get killed. Now you want to know about this John Seymore an' the business of the bounty, so I will tell you if you sit still an' listen, eh?"

Frank nodded. "But please hurry on with it, Ephram."

"This John Seymore was a gambler 'til someone in big authority, who must have owed him much money, have him appointed Indian Agent. He is also a slave dealer, Francisco. He buys an' sells women Indians, Chinese, any kind--to the miners, ranchers, whorehouses, anyplace they want them. The Indian women who are brought to him he says he sends to the Reservation. He lies."

Waves of anger and despair swept over Frank and he felt sick. "How can he do this against their will? What about the law?" He knew his questions were naive.

219

"Well, most of the women he gets I think ain' got no will. Those that have, prob'ly have none left when those hombres finish with them. The ones that bring them in are not much at being gentlemen. And for most of the Indians it is better than the Reservation, especially when the Gover'ment's agent is selling most the supplies they are supposed to get. As for the law, I think they don' see much, don' hear much, don' care much an' don' say nothing so long as there ain' no troubles an' they maybe get a cut of it, eh?"

Rising from his chair, Frank stuffed the Deringer inside his shirt. "Ephram, I've got to go after them now. I can't rest while Robin is in their hands. Thanks for your help and hospitality. Maybe you can tell me the way to Y... Yreka?"

"*Si*, I can tell you the way. But sit down, Francisco. There is more I have to tell you that you must know before you run off." He pushed the bottle of whiskey to him. "A little more of this medicine won't hurt you none, eh?"

Frustration was all that Frank felt as he sat down again. He grabbed the bottle and poured only about one finger level into the glass. He was feeling the effects of what he'd already had. Ephram's eyebrows came together as he gave Frank an intense look. "These men, they are bad, an' have much experience with running, hiding an' killing, especially the Indian. Can you shoot, amigo, real good? I am worry because I know you are not brought up to this sort of thing you try to do. An English gentleman, eh?"

"Scotch, and not much of a gentleman, I'm afraid; not by the Queen's standards. But I can handle myself, I'm sure."

"Damn it, *muchacho*, can you *shoot*?"

"As good as Archie. He taught me and I'm as fast and sure as he is." Frank blushed at his immodesty. "*Muy bueno*, I am much impress. Archie was one of the best. A rifle... you got a rifle, Frank?"

"Yes, and a shotgun, with plenty of powder and lead."

Ephram clapped both hands against his head, jarring cigar ashes onto his shirt. "*Dios mio!*" he exclaimed, with a broad grin, "That is some load for your horse. It is a good thing you are such a skinny fellow, not like me, eh?" He chuckled and brushed ashes from his belly.

"Now listen, those *hombres* got eight, nine hours lead on you. Maybe you catch up on them before they get to Yreka, maybe not. I think it best you do not. But maybe they travel slower than you if they think nobody chase them. If you catch up--if even you can find them--unless you can ambush them an' kill them both quick, they will prob'ly kill *you*. They will use the girl as a shield if they can, an' I don' think you will sneak up on that Indian, not ever. So don' try it, eh?" He took of the whiskey while he fanned away another cloud of smoke with his hand.

Frank drained his glass. The whiskey seemed smooth and tasty now and he felt warm and confident. "I'm ready to get on now, Ephram. Where is Yreka, and how far?"

"I will tell you, but what you should do is stay here tonight, *amigo*, an' get the firs' good food an' rest you have in four days, eh? Then you will get up fresh before daylight an' ride to Fort Lane to stay the night; you have only then to follow the stage road to Yreka. That is two an' a half, maybe three days more ride if you don' wan' to kill your horse. An' you mus' travel in the daylight, my friend; you will never find your way through the Siskiyou Mountains in darkness."

"Dammit, Ephram," said Frank, getting up from the chair, "I can't rest while Robin is in the hands of those bastards. Thank you for your advice, but I think if it were your wife, or daughter, or... or sweetheart, you'd feel as I do: sick at heart, very angry, and very anxious to find her."

Ephram rose, walked over and put his hand on Frank's shoulder. "*Si*, I know, very sick, very angry, an' yes, very anxious; but not anxious to get killed, or to get the senorita killed.

"Now listen, amigo: my papa was a lawman for many years. He told me many stories an' many times about how angry men die, still angry. I, myself, have seen it. So you are anxious to save the girl from these men. An' what they maybe do to her has heat up your mind, eh? Well, I tell you like my papa tell me, the more anxious you are for water, the more slowly you mus' drink, or you will puke up the water. You un'erstand, my friend?"

Frank stood silent for a moment as a hazy recollection of Adam giving him small sips of water, surged through his mind. "Just a wee sip now, lad…"

Ephram's question, "You okay, Francisco?" brought him back. "Yes, just thinking," he replied.

"Well, I hope you are thinking good about rest before you go, an' of something to eat. You must also think about your horse. You should maybe feed an' grain him good, eh?"

Frank thought about his horse, his own weariness, the mere half-hour or less of daylight that remained. Suddenly, Ephram's advice seemed acceptable. "All right, I'll rest awhile." he said, and felt relieved. The thought of food and sleep raised his spirits. "And where, Mister Innkeeper, can I get water and feed for my horse?"

Ephram reacted with a broad grin and a clap of his hands. "*Bravo, amigo.* Now you are showing good sense. There is a small corral at the rear of this building, between where is my horse an' the Watson *hombre's.* Put yours in there. Hay an' oats are in the shed, where you can put your saddle. You will feed my horse also, and the prisoner's, *por favor?* I will go an' tell *Senora* Reddick to fix also a plate for you, Francisco. For your sleep, I have five empty cells; take your pick, eh?"

As they walked outside, Ephram turned and gave Frank a solemn look. "I know you have plenty worry, Francisco, an' your guts ache about this girl. But you have made a good decision, my friend. *Manana*

I will get you up early so you can start at firs' light. You will feel better an' think better also. I go now to *Senora* Reddick's." Hoisting his sagging gunbelt to the overhang of his belly, Ephram trotted off toward Reddick's General Store. Frank watched the stocky man hustle away, and for the first time in three days, he smiled.

Savoring the smokey flavor of the sausage, Frank pulled the watch from his vest pocket. Four-thirty. Light would be showing in about forty minutes, he figured. "That sausage is so good I hate to wash the taste away with the coffee, but the coffee's so good I can't leave that last swallow in my cup."

Ephram smiled. "Bad plannning, amigo. Next time you mus' leave a piece of the sausage for last, eh?"

"It's all so good, the eggs, biscuits, blackberry jam, everything, I shan't ever forget Mrs. Reddick for preparing this so early in the morning."

"I think she like you when she meet you at supper, las' night. A han'some young English fellow, eh?" Ephram laughed.

"Scotch," corrected Frank. He felt self-conscious as he stared down at his plate. He caught himself fingering the scar on his left cheek and quickly put his hand down.

"Ah, the scar! You worry over it, eh? It is a good one, Francisco. It gives a character to the face. How did you get it, eh? A fight?"

"I ran into a painter's scaffold when I was a lad." In a different world and a different time, he wanted to add, but didn't. "I should be getting along now, Ephram. It will be getting light before long."

"*Si,* but before you go I want to give you this note to the *Commandante* at Fort Lane. It tells him that I have the Watson hombre, an' that the Army mus' come pronto an' get what is left of him. Also, I ask that he give you some help to catch this Rollo fellow an' the' Indian."

As he handed the items to Frank, Ephram looked up at him with squinted eyes. "You know amigo, I am sorry the Watson fellow die in the night. When I hear more from you las' night about the *Senorita* Robin and what happen at the MacLean place, I wish he would have live to suffer the wagon ride to Fort Lane. It would have give him more pain an' more time to think about what is going to happen to him, eh?"

Frank nodded. "I just wish I'd been the one that shot him. At least I would have *that* satisfaction."

"There is one more thing, Francisco: each of these men you seek has a reward on his head. There may be bounty hunters aroun', an' if they find out who you look for, they will maybe offer to help, to split the reward. Be careful of them, amigo. Most cannot be trusted. Even if you say they can have the reward, they may kill you jus' to make sure you don' change your mind. It is bes' you don' trust nobody, eh?"

"Aye, I'll remember."

"*Bueno.* Now it is time for you to saddle up, my friend."

The chill of the dawn air blushed Frank's cheeks and ears. Nostril hairs stiffened as he breathed the stuff, pine scented, tinged with dampness, mixed with odors of wood smoke and cooking, and a trace of horse liniment. It coursed down his throat like a mind-clearing vapor. He sucked in deep breaths, exhaling fog into the dark gray morning. He'd had a fitful sleep, still he felt rested and alert.

Ephram said nothing as he walked beside Frank to the corrals. The horses, silhouettes in the sparse light of dawn, nickered their welcomes as the two men approached. It was Frank who broke the silence. "I'm very much in your debt, Ephram. Thank you."

"*Por nada, amigo,* for what? You owe me only to be careful, my friend. I hope to see you again, an' with the girl, God willing."

"I'll be careful."

"I wish I were to ride with you, Francisco."

"I wish you could too."

"I will try to get word to the sheriffs in Jacksonville an' Yreka to watch for these men an' the girl. The stage from Crescent City is due this afternoon. I will put a message with the driver for him to pass along."

"I should be in Yreka before your message gets there."

"Si, I know. But just in case you… well, if maybe you get lost, eh? It is good to have something to tell them what has happened. An' when the Stage comes the other way, I will put a message for the Sheriff at Gold Beach about this Hogan fellow, eh?"

Frank smiled. "Thank you, Ephram; I appreciate all your help."

As he saddled his horse Frank said, "By the way, how's that bruise this morning, Sheriff?"

"Ah, it is nothing. I forget about it already."

Frank grinned at his new friend. "You know, you've given me a lot of good advice, now I've got some for you."

"Ha, you are going to tell me to put horse linament on the bruise, eh? Well, I have already done so, can you not smell it?"

"Yes, but that's not what I had in mind. My advise is, if you ever get hurt enough to need a doctor, may God forbid, get the veterinarian to take care of you. I don't think that the man who tended to Watson knew, or cared, what he was doing or he might have kept him alive."

"Doc Briggs? He *is* the vet. But you are right, an' also he is not sober very much."

"Then go to the mortician. Surely he can do a better job of patching you up than a drunken veterinarian."

"Hmmm," was Ephram's comment as he struck a match. When he lit the cigar he held in his teeth, the match fire danced in his dark eyes and his lips parted in a grin. "There is jus' one problem with your advice, my friend."

"What's that, Ephram?"

"Doc Briggs, he is also the mortician!"

Both men were laughing as Frank mounted up. "Goodbye, my friend, and thank you," he said, offering his hand.

Ephram held Frank's hand firmly in both of his. "Not goodbye, Francisco... *adios, y vaya con Dios*... go with God. An' stay close to the stage route, jus' in case your horse, he break a leg or something, eh?"

"Aye aye, sir," he said, smiling. As he reined his horse toward the unlighted street he looked back. *"Adios amigo*, and may God be with you, also." Frank rode away wishing Ephram Angeles was riding at his side.

Chapter Twenty-six

Free of her bonds, Robin thought of escape, but knew she must plan carefully, for Seven Feathers would be expecting her to try and he would be ready.

He hardly took his eyes off her as he stripped Rollo's body of weapons. When he finished, he handed her the lead rope to the dead youth's horse. "You will ride your pony behind me and tow this one as we go away from here." He put his hand on her shoulder and looked into her eyes. "You will like how I treat you, unless you do not obey me, or try to run from me. Then you will not like it."

Silent, with fear and hate in her heart, she stared at his eyes until he turned away.

"You will see," he muttered, with a brief glance back at her.

They rode in silence. Never far in the lead, Seven Feathers seemed always to be turning and watching her. To simply turn and run was a rash, but tempting idea she mulled over many times, only to conclude in its futility. Although despair soured her stomach and pressed like a weight upon her chest, she wanted to live. She knew Frank would search for her, and she wondered if he would still want her if he knew she'd been raped. If he didn't, she would want to die. But, must he know? Could he tell? What if she were with child? Tortured by her own thoughts, she followed Seven Feathers, numb and insensible to everything but the misery of her dilema.

The sun was still high above the trees when they stopped at the shore of a small lake. She was glad when Seven said they would camp there. She felt tired and, in spite of the coolness of the late afternoon air, wanted to bathe in the placid lake water.

Seven killed a small deer along the way and made her gut the animal. Now, after she gathered kindling under his watchful eye, and built a fire, he showed her how to skin, butcher and prepare some of the venison for their dinner.

"While the meat cooks, I want to wash in the lake," she said. "I feel unclean and my hands smell of the deer's blood. Will you give me privacy?" Her heart seemed to skip a beat as she asked, fearing he would not, for she believed he had watched her as she made her toilet behind bushes as they traveled. Rollo had done this before, laughing and saying crude things that embarrassed her.

The Indian looked at her, unsmiling, and after a few seconds nodded his head. "I will bathe with you," he added.

What she had feared was coming to pass. "I want to be alone when I bathe," she said, her voice shaking. "I will not try to get away."

"Come," he ordered. Taking her by the arm he led her to the water's edge. "Take off clothes and get in water. You think I have not seen woman naked?"

She stood frozen as he took off his moccasins and shirt and began untying the waistband of his breeches.

Robin was shaking now. "I have changed my mind. I don't wish to--"

He grabbed her arm with a grip that made her wince with pain. "Take clothes off or I will do it *for* you." He did not raise his voice, but the way he said it was a threat of violence.

Her whole body shaking, she fumbled at the ties and slowly removed her skirt. Before she could fold it, he grabbed it from her and threw it on the ground.

Turning her back toward him, she removed the shirt and stood tense and shaking, teeth chattering, tears flowing over her cheeks.

"Turn to me," he said, taking the shirt and flinging it to the ground.

228

As she faced him she covered her breasts with her arms. Grabbing the waist-string of her breechcloth, he tore it away; her belly contracted in fear, and she sank to her knees, sobbing, her thoughts swirling in a torrent of fright and confusion.

Kneeling beside her, Seven Feathers placed his hand softly on her back. "Be calm, little bird, and I will take you gently." He pulled her toward him and eased her onto her back. She was shaking violently now, no longer sobbing. Her body seemed out of her control, rigid with fear.

Slowly, firmly, he pulled her folded arms from across her breasts, then licked each nipple. Robin closed her eyes and turned her head away, and shivered as the moistened flesh cooled quickly in the breeze and brought her nipples erect. His hand slid down her belly and again her stomach contracted violently and her knees came up as his fingers searched between her legs. Running his hand along her thigh he pulled her leg toward him, and the other followed. She felt as though her body was resisting on its own, without any conscious effort on her part. It was not the same as when she was raped by Jim, she thought. Somehow, this was more frightening.

She felt his hand again, pushing gently, but with increased impatience, at the soft flesh between her thighs. "Please don't," she managed through clenched teeth, "Please don't do this to me."

"I must," he said, "But it will not be like Jim took you. Or like Rollo would have if Jim not make him stay away from you. To them, all women whores--no good. I like women."

"I treat them good, you will see." He took his hand from between her legs and placed it on her breast, circling the nipple with his finger. "One time I have good woman for wife." He paused and removed his hand from her breast. "Then white man raid village... kill her and many others."

Opening her eyes, she looked at him and he seemed to be staring into the distance. For a moment she felt compassion for him, but his mention of Rollo was seed to an idea that began to grow.

He looked back at her and his hand went back to her leg. As he spoke, she was deep in thought, and his voice seemed far away. "You cannot win against me. I want not to hurt you, but if you fight, you will be hurt and I cannot help that."

She was silent for a moment, then turned her face toward him and looked into his eyes, tears already flooding her own. "All right, I won't fight you. But please be gentle with me. Rollo was rough and hurt me this morning, and I am still in pain."

She did not expect his reaction; red and white bars and splotches flashed in her eyes from the backhand blow he struck her across her face.

"You lie!" he shouted, raising his arm to hit her again.

"No, I'm not lying! It was this morning, after you and Jim left for town."

"Why you not say that when I come back?"

"He said he'd kill me if I told Jim--or anyone--and I didn't think you'd care."

"Rollo have sickness, you know that." She knew it was not a question.

"No!" she lied, "I *didn't* know."

"Jim tell of Rollo getting runny pecker from Chetco whore. Tell him stay away from you. You there when he say that to Rollo."

"I didn't know what he meant. My head was not clear and my body ached. I didn't try to understand words I had not heard before."

Seven Feathers got to his feet and looked down at her, frowning. "Maybe you say what is true; maybe not. We will see. I will take you to shaman I know. He knows white man's medicine and will cure you... *if* you have the sickness." He stared at her briefly, then walked into the water. "Bathe now," he said. "Meat ready soon."

230

Stepping naked into the lake, she no longer felt embarrassed. As she palmed cool water over her body, she began to think of how she might escape. She glanced quickly at her captor who stood nearby, then turned away as he removed his loin cloth, but not before she noticed the sheathed knife that hung from the waistband.

It was nearly dark when they finished eating. Proud of the clever way she had--at least temporarily--deceived Seven Feathers, and cleansed by the fresh waters of the lake, Robin felt better than she had since her ordeal began. But thoughts of her mother and Papa Mac crept into her mind, and suddenly she was overcome with heartfelt pain and a feeling of guilt because she had been so deep in her own misery, she had given little thought to her family and the events that lead to her kidnaping. Crushed by her memories, she called out, Oh, Mama!... Papa Mac!" then buried her face in her hands, and cried. Suddenly revulsed by the fact she was in the hands of one of her parents' killers, she screamed at him, "Filthy killer of my family! Why... why did you do it?" Shaking with uncontrolled sobs, she could scarcely hear his voice.

"Seven Feathers kill no one. White father's death not my doing. Accident of devil sticks... white man caught in own trap."

"It doesn't matter who, or how!" she shouted back at him, her voice hoarse with emotion, "You were there and my parents were killed! My mother... why did--"

"Your mother lives, I think."

Her head snapped up and she tasted her tears as she spoke: "How do you... why do you think?"

"She have gun and shoot one man. I hit her, but not to kill because she is Indian. Seven Feathers never want to kill any woman, Indian or white, especially Indian. Your mother sleep, but breath good when I drag her into small room. I tell Jim she is dead, or he will kill her. Rollo see blood on side of head, and he say she is dead. It is good that he was stupid dog."

She was on her knees praying, now. "Oh God, please let it be true that Mama is alive. *Please.*"

"Come, it is time for sleep." His voice seemed gentle to her now.

He had built a lean-to with a roof of fir boughs, and spread the elkhide and bearskin robes he carried for bedding. Stripping to his loin cloth, he told her to do the same. "Elkhide keep body warm. Feel better when morning come if not sleep in clothes."

"I will sleep in my clothes, as I have for the past three nights."

Angrily, he grabbed her arm. "No! Obey me. Remember, you are my woman."

"I told you, I can never be your woman. I can only be your captive."

He tightened his grip on her arm until she winced, then released her with a push. "You will obey me, or you will be sorry."

As she removed her outer clothing, she though about escaping during the night, while he slept. She knew he would waken at the slightest sound. She would need her clothes, but watched with a feeling of hopelessness as he tucked them under his arm. "What are you going to do with my clothes," she asked.

He looked at her and a smile flickered on his lips. "My head will be on them while I sleep." He pointed to the inside of the shelter. "You sleep there. I will be here," he said, pointing to place alongside hers, toward the open side.

Her thoughts of escape during the night were sinking. She knew it would be near impossible to crawl over him without his knowing. Then came the final blow to her hopes: with a leather thong, he bound her right wrist to his left.

"Why are you doing this?" she asked. I can't sleep being tied to you!"

Again, the flicker of a smile twitched his lips. "I will not sleep unless you are."

When they were down and covered, she lay on her back, watching images of flames from the fire writhe and flitter on the angled roof of their shelter, inhaling the pungently sweet odor of the fir boughs surrounding them. Her thoughts were of Frank. Where was he? Would she ever see him again? Would he want her? Could he still love her?

Seven Feathers was on his side; his breathing was noisy and she felt his breath on her upper arm, then the coarseness of his hand on her ribs. She moved away as much as she could, but the hand followed, moving to her breast. He moved closer and she felt the stiffness of his penis against her hip, and she was frightened.

"I will take you now, little bird... gently, if you do not fight."

Her breathing quickened in panic. "But what of the sickness? You will catch it. Why not wait 'til I'm cured?"

He lifted her breechcloth and ran his fingers through her pubic hair. "I not sure you tell truth. But, if you do, the shaman will cure us both."

Rising to his knees alongside her, his hands moved slowly, lightly, knowingly, pausing as though to absorb the delicate smoothness of her skin and the firmness of her youth. His hand moved between her legs, and down her near thigh, pulling it toward him. Robin lay tense and shivering as he pushed her other leg away, and with her legs so spread, moved between them on his knees.

"Bring knees up," he said quietly, his right hand lifting her left knee.

She knew it was useless to resist, but she seemed unable to respond. With some impatience, and encumbered slightly by the binding on their wrists, he lifted her right knee.

"Relax body, and I will try not to hurt. Better then for you, and me."

Closing her eyes, she tried to blank her mind, to get suddenly to sleep. Nervously, she moved her left arm and her hand touched leather and cold steel. Her brain came alive. His knife! He had removed his loincloth, and there was the knife, within her grasp!

As he moved toward penetration, she seized the knife and pulled it from its sheath. She knew she would have one chance only, and if she failed she would die.

With sudden abandon she squeezed her eyes shut as though to meet her own death, then swung the knife with all her strength into his side. He jerked up, crying out in agony. She plunged it into him again, but this time it struck a rib and glanced away. Lurching forward he reached for her throat with both hands and she felt his warm blood spilling onto her. With fright-given strength, she held away his hand that was tied to hers, but terrified by his gasping and writhing, she dropped the knife. His free hand found her throat, squeezing as he moaned with every breath he took. Frantically she grappled for the fallen weapon, struggling against the choking pressure on her neck. Then she felt the blade, wet and sticky. With her fingers she maneuvered the handle into her palm then stabbed him again. This time the blade slid to its hilt between his ribs.

"*Kopet! Kopet hiyu!* Stop! Enough!" he groaned as he tried to rise, then fell on her. *Chako polaklie*" (Darkness comes), he whispered. They were Seven Feather's last words.

CHAPTER TWENTY-SEVEN

Pushing his body off, she cut the leather thong that bound them at the wrists, and crawled, sobbing, from the lean-to shelter he had built. Smeared with his blood, she sickened at the stickiness and smell of it, and vomited heavily, then lay naked and shaking until forced by the cooling air to return to the shelter and retrieve the buffalo robes, and Rollo's pistol that lay under her clothes that Seven intended for his pillow.

Crawling between the robes, she lay near the dwindling fire, staring at the flames, not thinking, not hearing, only feeling… alone, frightened, betrayed by her Christian God, totally miserable.

From half-sleep she thought she felt movement on the robe that covered her. For a moment she stopped breathing and lay tense and alert, senses straining. Nothing. A rodent perhaps, or her imagination. Readjusting her grip on the revolver, she relaxed and closed her eyes, reassured.

The sound was slight, like a finger being drawn across fine fabric. Then something cold touched her shoulder blade; she jerked away. It touched her again, moving firmly against her as she started to move away, then froze in terror. Snake! It stopped moving, and she held her breath. Every fiber, every muscle of her body was tense, ready and anxious to retreat, but instinct held her still. Was it a rattlesnake, or maybe just a bullsnake or other of the harmless kind, seeking warmth? Near panic, she wanted to scream and her throat was ready, but she knew that a frightened rattler would strike.

Its cold body moved against her back; uncontrollable reflexes instantly arched her spine away and she stifled an outcry as she expected its bite. Motionless, trying not to breath, she waited. Seconds passed, then she felt it slither against her buttocks, and down the backs of her legs. It stopped, its head resting on the calf of her leg.

Terrified, she knew she could not hold still much longer. She had to get out of her bed. The snake was stretched out; if it was a rattler, she knew it must coil some before it could strike--but not much at close range. She would have to move fast. Slowly, she inhaled, then, in one sudden motion kicked her legs forward and out from their cover, then rolled her body away as she flung the robe from her shoulders. She nearly rolled into the smoldering embers of the fire, but she was clear of the snake. Quickly, she threw kindling on the dying fire and as it revived, got into her clothes.

Within minutes Robin could see the robes in the firelight. Setting fire to a large twig, she held it as she flipped the top robe away from the other. Startled, a three foot rattlesnake quickly coiled and buzzed its warning. With the burning stick held toward it, she moved closer. Still rattling, the snake slowly--as though reluctant--uncoiled and glided into the darkness. Gathering a robe around, her, Robin dropped to her knees by the rekindled fire and cried, exhausted.

As dawn drove back the darkness, she stood in the lake and washed the dried blood from her body. Before the earliest bird had uttered its morning twitter, Robin rode out of the camp, towing two horses, Rollo's gunbelt slung loosly around her waist, rifles showing from scabbords on each side of her saddle, a tomahawk slung from the pommel. Heading south, she hoped to find the town she'd been so near the day before.

It was mid-morning when Robin rode into Kerbyville, an awsome and unusual sight for the people bustling about the county seat on this Tuesday morning. Disheveled though she was, she carried herself proudly. Onlookers stood still in apparent stunned silence; all, that is except one young boy who ran ahead toward the jail, shouting: "Sheriff! Sheriff! They's a armed injun on Main Street!"

As she neared a brown, log building, the black and yellow striped door opened and a man walked quickly to the street. A shiver of fear ran through her as she saw the shotgun he pointed at her. "My name is Robin Burns," she announced, finding she had to force her voice above a hoarse whisper, "and I need help."

"Madre de Dios!" the man said, lowering the shotgun, and a look of surprise quickly changed to concern as he reached out to her. Gently, he took her hand, and smiled. "Thank God you are here, *Senorita!*"

Tears of relief burst forth as Robin felt total and sudden release from the torture of the past four days.

She didn't know how long she'd been asleep before Mrs. Reddick wakened her for dinner.

"Good news, child," she said, "Sheriff Howell is back, and Deputy Angeles left an hour ago to catch up with your Frank."

"... *your* Frank," Mrs. Reddick said, and a warm feeling glowed around Robin's heart.

As she brushed her hair, the wonderful odors of home cooking urged her to hurry. It had seemed too good to be true... the news that her mother and Papa Mac were alive. Ephram had arranged passage on the stage, and she would be on her way home to them tomorrow. It worried her that Frank was still searching and might get into trouble. She had visions of him wandering aimlessly, looking here and there forever, not knowing she was safe. Ephram told her Frank left early that morning, and tears came to her eyes when he said they must have passed each other somewhere as they rode in opposite directions. Now she could not really be happy until she was in Frank's arms again. Then the thought began to gnaw at her: Would he really ever be happy with her if he knew what had happened? Even more terrible was the thought that she could be pregnant. There would be only one way she could deal with that. For the moment, she shook it from her mind. There could be no reason, she was certain, for any god to want to punish her that much.

CHAPTER TWENTY-EIGHT

Ephram's map with directions to Jacksonville were well supplied with his personal annotations. Typical, Frank mused, of the care with which his Californio friend seemed to do everything.

The wagon road north out of Kerby, although not yet the route of an established stage line, was the clearest and easiest route linking the Illinois and Rogue River valleys, and the counties of Josephine and Jackson.

The temperature remained cool under the overcast. Rain threatened but fell only in occasional light sprinklings that seemed always to provide MacIver with new energy. They reached Jacksonville while yet thirty minutes of daylight remained.

Frank was amazed at the contrast between Kerby and this community that was bustling with activity, seemingly in defiance of the fading daylight. Lights showed through many store windows, indicating business was still being conducted in the early evening hour.

The Sheriff's office loomed prominent; the door was open and several men standing inside were conversing in obvious good humor. Frank stood in the doorway a minute, looking, trying to determine which of the men, if any, was the sheriff, and hoping to be noticed. It was in vain.

"Pardon me, gentlemen," he said, finally, feeling apologetic for the interruption, "I'm looking for the Sheriff."

"I'm him," came a loud voice from behind where the men were standing. They moved apart, revealing a gray haired oldster in a chair, hands joined behind his head, feet crossed on top of the desk. "What can I do for yuh, young fella?" he asked, smiling.

"My name's Frank Ross; I've a letter for you from Ephram Angeles, Deputy at Kerby." He took an envelope from his coat pocket.

The sheriff's look turned serious and he stood, revealing himself to be a tall man with a huge, trim frame. From behind the desk he reached out a large hand. "Let's have the letter," he said, "an' make yourself t'home."

The men cleared a path to the Sheriff's desk.

"Thanks," he said as he walked through the group. "Sorry to interrupt, Sheriff."

"Business is business," he said, smiling again. "We was just jawin', tellin' lies. They's waitin' fer six o'clock an' we're goin' for some beefsteaks at the Hotel dinin' room."

Opening the letter, he read slowly, silently mouthing each word. Without looking up, he waved his hand at Frank. "Sit down, son," he said, gesturing toward a desk-side chair. "Take the load off." As Frank moved to the chair, he heard one of the men in the room remark in a low voice obviously not meant for his ears: "It's just one a them Navy Colts." He'd noticed when he came in that the three were armed. Now he wondered what caused one to comment about *his* gun.

Finally, the Sheriff finished reading and looked over at Frank, then up at his three friends. "This here says that Marshall Colson's prob'ly dead, since some hombre showed up in Kerbyville wearin' his badge an' flashin' his cree-dents, an' claimin' he got 'em off George's body what had been drowned."

There were mutterings of regret and disbelief from the men, then the Sheriff went on. "That hombre tried to battle it out with the Deputy in Kerbyville and now lies deceased. But at least two critters who was with the dead fella--an Army deserter, by the way--got away, along with a breed girl they kidnaped." The Sheriff looked at Frank and shook his head. He started to speak, stopped, and turned to his friends. "You fella's go on over to the Franco and order me one a them beefsteaks with all the trimmin's. I'll be along directly, but gotta take care of some business here first.

"An' listen to me, gents: don't nobody mention this lad's in town. If word gets out, I'll figure none of yuh's my friend. Don't even mention his name, hear?"

"Sure, Cap." "You got m'word, Cap." "Yeah, Cap, mine too," were the men's promises as they left the office.

Frank was puzzled. "Why did you give that order, Sheriff. What difference does it make if--"

"You said you was Frank Ross, that right?"

"Yes, sir."

"Gold Beach?"

"Yes."

"Last evenin', over at the Table Rock Saloon, there was a guy tellin' us how he saw the fastest, fanciest, most accurate gunshark he'd ever seen, drill some kid that tried to bushwhack him. Then, a few minutes later, he shoots the gun--along with the thumb--outta the hand of the kid's ol' man, *after* the ol' man's got the drop on this Ross fella." He paused and his pale blue eyes bored into Frank's. "Now, you gotta know that story and the name Frank Ross is gonna pass through the ear and mouth of ever' soul in this town before this day is out. Fast gun worship, I calls it. I ain't against good shootin' long as it's law abidin', an' from what we was told, you was defendin' yourself, ain't that right?"

"Yes, I--"

"Well, kid, this here town is full to the brim with hombres that, knowin' you was here, would do anythin' to shoehorn you into a showdown, if not with themselves, with one of the puffed-up turkeys we got hangin' around here that carries his ego on his gunbelt. See what I'm sayin'?"

241

Frank nodded. He certainly didn't want to get involved here in any way that would jeopardize his chances of finding Robin. Archie was right. His reputation would be a force against him. Now he understood the comment by one of the men in the Sheriff's office.

"Now, I get enough trouble without askin' for it. The letter asks me to help yuh. I can't send a deputy with yuh, 'cuz I ain't got none to send. Two's all I got an' one's out sick. The other I need here. Besides, if you're goin' into California, they wouldn't have no jurisdiction there. Best for you is team up with a bounty hunter. Since both them varmits you're after has prices on 'em, you won't have no trouble gettin' one to partner with... ," he paused and stroked his chin thoughtfully, "'ceptin' maybe 'cuz of that Indian, Seven Feathers. He's killed about four bounty men already."

"Doesn't matter. I don't want a bounty hunter with me. "But what about the Army? Ephram said they had a detachment here."

"The small Army detachment we got around here--shame they shut down Fort Lane -- is off ridin' guard on a wagon load of goods--gold, prob'ly--on its way to the damn Union forces. Damn foolish war, I say. How do *you* feel about it?"

The question surprised him. He knew little of it, except that England was generally sympathetic to the southern states. "I really don't know enough about it to have an opinion, Sheriff."

"You're a Brit, ain't yuh? I understand they favor the south."

"Scotch. I haven't been to the British Isles in a long time."

"Well, never mind that. I'll for sure remember to tell the Lieutenant they got a corpse to pick up in Kerbyville. Hope that mortician got plenty ice, or it'll be overripe by the time they get there."

He pulled out his watch and thumbed it open. "It's time I get over to eat. Only help I can give yuh right now is advice, kid. Stay low, out of the crowds tonight. The gent that was singin' your praises last night might still be around and recognize yuh; then we both's got trouble, sure as flies on a shit pile. I can give yuh a bunk here in the jailhouse, an put your horse up in our livery. I'll bring yuh some grub back from the Franco--how 'bout a big steak?"

"That'd be fine. I -- "

"That's it then, an' when I get back, you can tell me about yourself. Meanwhile, think on another name. You'd be smart not to use yours for awhile."

His breakfast was a dried French Roll left over from his dinner, washed down with stale coffee re-heated on the pot-bellied stove in the Sheriff's office. The Deputy, whom he'd met only briefly the night before, lay on the cot in the office. As Frank strapped on his gun, the Deputy propped himself on an elbow. "I like a shotgun, myself," he said.

Frank hadn't really liked him much when they'd met. He seemed to be the Doubting Thomas type. "Oh, why's that? he asked.

"Don't need more'n one shot."

"Neither do I," answered Frank, surprised at his own cockiness.

"Well, you ain't faced the best, I think."

Frank put on his hat and walked to the door. Turning, he looked at the man on the cot and smiled. "Obviously, you *won't*."

The livery boy was up and rolling a cigarette. "Jesus," he exclaimed with disgust, "Seems like the whole damn town's up an' wantin' t'go ridin' before sun-up. Ain't even been able to have me a smoke." He put the cigarette between head and ear like it was a pencil. "Well, whatcher name?"

"Ro... er, Scott," he corrected, "Edward Scott." For a second he forgot he'd given a false name at the advise of the Sheriff.

The kid gave him a sly look. "Yeah, sometimes I can't remember my name this early, either."

He brought up MacIver, then brought the saddle from the tack room. "Saddle him for ten cents," he offered.

"No thanks."

"Five cents? I really need the money, Mister Scott."

"No, I'll do it." He fished ten cents from his pocket and held it out to the boy. "Here, now go have your smoke before someone comes in again."

Looking up at Frank, the lad grinned. "You're okay, for a bounty hunter."

"What makes you think I'm a bounty hunter?"

"Well, your gun rig, mostly. An' they's a lot of 'em works outta here, looking for them army deserters. One of 'em left just 'afore yuh come in. Yuh are one, ain'cha?"

"No."

"Good. Most of 'em's rotten bastards. Well, then you're a range detective or a gunfighter. They's always changin' their names. My guess is range detective. Yuh ain't twitchy enough for a gunfighter--the one's I seen, anyways." Without waiting for a reply, he took the cigarette off his ear, turned and walked toward the door. "Better get my smoke, now."

South of town about four miles, the huge rock formation stood castle-like before the rising sun, casting a long shadow across the road. As Frank approached, a horse with rider moved from behind the rock into the road and stopped, remaining in the shadow. Slowing MacIver from his easy lope, Frank flipped the tie-down from the Colt's hammer, and kept his palm on the butt. Twenty feet away, he stopped. The other man sat smiling, his hands folded across the pommel.

"Mornin', Mister Ross. Beautiful September morn for a ride, don't you agree?"

The man was fortyish, well outfitted. His face--the moustache--even his dapper clothes looked familiar, yet he couldn't place him. "Good morning. You know my name; should I know you?"

"Well, we weren't introduced, but I thought you might recognize me from Cap Will's office."

Then Frank recalled. "Oh, you were in the Sheriff's office when I came in. Right, we weren't introduced."

The corner of his mouth twitched. "Name's Slauson. Harvey Slauson."

To Frank there was something vaguely familiar about the name. "Why were you waiting for me here, Mister Slauson?"

"Well, I heard the hoofbeats getting closer. I always like to know who's coming up behind me, Mister Ross. Now that we've met, perhaps we can ride a ways together?"

"Perhaps. Are you a bounty hunter?"

"Not really, 'though I've been known to claim a reward. I work for the Cattlemen's Association--a range detective." His cheek twitched and pulled up the corner of his mouth into a half grin. "Do you know the time, Mister Ross? I foolishly bet my watch in a poker game last night, and lost."

Frank drew out his watch. "It's twenty past six." As he looked up he saw the revolver pointing at him from Slauson's hand.

"Please get off your horse, Mister Ross." Slauson moved closer as Frank dismounted.

"What do you want with me?"

"I want to kill you."

Frank felt the blood drain from his face. "Why?"

"Because you're worth two-hundred dollars to me, dead."

"That's impossible. I'm not wanted by the law."

"You are by Cyrus Hogan. Word gets around, you know."

"I thought you were on the side of the law."

Slauson smiled. "Oh, I am, I certainly am... when it's profitable. This is just a little business on the side, you might say."

"The business of cold-blooded murder? For some reason I would have put you above that."

245

"Oh, I'm definitely above that, Mister Ross. I will kill you in self defense. You see, when I met you on this road, your horse had come up lame. You were in a hurry to get to Yreka--the Sheriff will testify to that--but since I wouldn't sell you my horse, you tried to gun me down, not knowing that I am--pardon my lack of modesty -- the best gun west of the Rockies."

Slauson dismounted. Moving to a position about five paces from Frank, he slipped his gun lightly into its holster. "I've heard of your amateur exploits with the clod busters, Mister Ross. Now I'm betting my speed and vast experience against your youth and reputed speed, but limited experience." The muscles in his face began to twitch, but his hands were relaxed and steady at his sides.

Frank's heart was pounding, but the scared feeling left him when Slauson holstered his gun and he knew he wasn't to be gunned down without a chance. Slim as it might be against this professional assassin, it was a chance. His eyes focused on Slauson's midsection, his hands clearly visible within the area of Frank's concentration.

"You may draw when ready, Mister Ross. I will draw when you start, or when I reach the count of five, which is the limit of my patience. You, sir, have the advantage of choice." And Harvey Slauson began to count. "One."

If he gives me the advantage, I'll take it, thought Frank.

"Two."

The count never reached three.

"Jesus Christ!" wheezed Slauson, staggering backward, his gun only half out of its holster. As he fell, he pulled the trigger and the last shot of Harvey Slauson's career plowed the dirt at his side, Frank's bullet in his chest, just a little left of center.

By mid-afternoon the sky was black with storm clouds over the Siskiyous. He rode with his head bowed against the gusting wind, while splatters of wind-blown raindrops, big as silver dollars, stung his hands.

Thoughts of how he would deal with the situation in Yreka when he got there, and how he would settle the score with Hogan if he ever got back to Gold Beach, occupied his mind. He wondered if perhaps Adam might not get to Hogan first, when he got well enough. He tried not to imagine what was happening to Robin.

It was dark before he reached the summit of Siskiyou Pass. Lightning and thunder announced a forthcoming deluge. A campfire was impossible, so he picked the thickest boughed tree he could find near the road, and under it, he made his camp. It had been a long day, but he knew the night would seem longer.

CHAPTER TWENTY-NINE

Something had changed. Frank listened, eyes jammed closed in concentration. Water, dripping from the branches above, tapped on his poncho. It was the only sound. He didn't think he had fallen asleep, but he must have. The last he remembered it was raining--raining hard with the sound of a fast flowing river. Now, the flow had stopped. Lifting the poncho off his head he looked around. He could just make out silhouettes of trees against the eastern sky. Time, he decided, to move on.

In the semi-darkness he saddled MacIver, then led him until he found the wagon road. The dawn sky to the south was clear. He was glad the bad weather was behind him.

He reached the summit of Siskiyou Pass at sunrise and rode in awe as shadows peeled from mountains and valleys, revealing the signs of an early autumn. The morning's stillness was broken only by chirping birds and the occasional clatter of MacIver's hooves on granite.

The road narrowed in places where the drop-off was shear and he rode as far from the edge as he could. He thought about the stagecoaches travelling the winding mountain road, and marvelled at the nerve and skill of the drivers, and at the courage--or was it innocence?--of the passengers. He never liked being on the edge of anything from which he couldn't safely jump. His fear of heights had been a problem for him as an apprentice seaman when he went aloft to be "Lookout" in the crow's-nest, or to manhandle canvas from the yardarms. He met the challenge, but never lost his fear.

Down from the summit an hour's ride, the road broadened and

the edge was somewhat less precipitous. Summer-dried grass, trampled and wheel-tracked, carpeted the road to its edge and thinned away in spots too rocky for its growth. He viewed a panorama of straw-colored clearings, slashed by green, wooded valleys.

Approaching a sharp bend, MacIver's head raised abruptly with ears cocked forward. He stopped and Frank felt the animal's breathing quicken. "Easy, boy," he said quietly, hoping it would not be another encounter with a bear. He flipped the hammer loop off the Colt, rested his palm on the butt and listened. He heard nothing. The sun was in his face. To his left, the road's rocky edge sloped steeply into a canyon. A bloody poor place to meet with a problem, he concluded.

A moment passed; MacIver stood motionless, ears rigid and trained ahead. A quiver coursed his body. "Easy, now," Frank whispered, and moved his hand from the gun long enough to stroke the horse's neck.

In a blink--almost without movement--an Indian appeared on the road at the bend. As quickly, the Colt was in Frank's hand. MacIver started, but held steady.

In the Indian's left hand was a bow; his right hand was empty and he raised it in the sign of peace. "Friend," he said, "Modoc white man's friend." He made a twirling motion with his raised hand and two more Indians appeared from around the bend and stood beside their comrade. "Friend," he repeated, "all friend."

They were young braves. A single feather in the hair of the first marked him as the leader and the only one battle-tried. Each was armed with bow, arrows, and a long-knife. They were not a war party--no paint on their faces. He was glad they were Modoc; he'd been told they were friendlier than Klamaths.

For a long interval they stood motionless, then the one with the feather in his hair dropped his bow to the ground, raising both arms. "I am Keintpoos," he said, "No need for gun, we are friend. Hunt for meat to feed family. In Yreka, my friend Judge Steele call me Captain Jack."

Slowly, Frank slipped the Colt back into its holster and raised his hand. "I am Frank," he said, "I am your friend."

A smile spread across Jack's broad face as he lowered his arms. "This is Crazyhair," he said, with a jerk of his head to the right. In the same fashion he announced the one to his left as Big Charlie. "Yreka friends give us white man's names. Modoc name hard for white brothers to say." He laughed and slapped his comrades on the back, then picked up his bow.

The younger braves were well named, Frank noted. Crazyhair with an unruly mane growing straight out from his head in all directions; Big Charlie was just that--a head taller and stones heavier than the others.

Frank nodded as they continued to stand abreast at what was the narrowest section of the road. "I'm pleased to have met you, Captain Jack, Big Charlie, Crazyhair. I hope you have a successful hunt. Now, I've got to be on my way." He walked MacIver about ten feet closer, but the Indians didn't move.

"Why do you come this way, Englishman Frank?" Jack smiled with his mouth as he waited for an answer, but there was no smile in his eyes.

Frank winced at the incorrect reference to his heritage, but only for an instant; he realized they were not ready to let him pass. He thought it best not to reveal his mission. The Modoc's were known to sell their women, and they might be in league with Robin's captor's. "I ride to Yreka to work on the ranch of a friend."

Jack's eyes narrowed. "What is friend's name?"

The question was unexpected, and the only name that came to his mind was "MacLean". As he answered, he knew it really didn't matter what name he gave. He realized he had blundered in telling them he was going to work on a ranch in Yreka. He remembered too late what the Sheriff told him in Jacksonville: Modocs were stealing cattle from the private grazing lands that once had been their territory, and now the ranchers were hiring guns to protect their herds. These Modocs would have noticed his weapons, and he had just confirmed any suspicions they had about him. He had invented a lie that gave these men reason to want him dead.

Big Charlie and Crazyhair looked at Jack, who was staring at Frank. Big Charlie made a grunting sound that may have been a word in the Modoc tongue, but there came no sound from Jack, nor change in expression.

Frank figured they would make no move to attack him while he had the advantage that the distance between them gave him with his guns. Best tell the truth, he decided part of it, anyway, while he had the advantage. As long as they were aware that they were in greater danger of his gun than he was of their weapons, they just might believe him. He tried to keep his voice calm; to avoid misunderstanding, he spoke as though to one just learning the language. "I know what you are thinking and you are wrong. I am not a gunman. I do not kill for other men.

"I search for a young woman, part Indian. We were to be married but she was taken from her home and is now the captive of two men, one white, the other a Tututni. I think they plan to sell her in Yreka. She may be there now. That is the reason I want to go there. Because I do not want them to know I am after them, I thought it best to trust no one, so I lied to you. I must get on to Yreka. I do not want to shoot you, so I must trust you with the truth."

"What you say now, has sound of truth." Jack made a sweeping gesture toward a place at the side of the road, at the same time moving toward Frank. "Sit with us and we will talk more of this."

Frank thought he detected a challenge in the Indian's voice and didn't feel comfortable about the invitation to pow-wow. He thought of the choices he had: shoot them--he must act quickly, for they were now within thirty feet of him; wheel his horse around and make a run for it; or accept the invitation to talk and risk being jumped. Whether they believed him or not, they might want his horse and guns. He didn't want to kill them, so he had to run. Already his left hand had drawn the reins taut. As his legs tensed, the trail horse responded with well trained reflexes and took a step back. As he did so, Frank reined him to the right. As MacIver spun, his right rear hoof slammed hard against a firmly anchored rock. Unable to check his rearward movement, the animal fell heavily backward onto its right side, pinning Frank's leg.

As the horse struggled to regain its feet, Frank reached for his gun. It never cleared the holster. Flashes exploded behind his eyes. Thunder roared in his ears. His head bobbed and jerked in response to muscles he couldn't control. The weight came off his leg and he tried to rise. Another blow to the base of his skull brought searing light, then darkness.

Dragged by his arms, face down, he felt cool and realized he'd been stripped. Drawing his knees up, he tried getting to his feet but couldn't. Things came into focus and what he saw caused him to struggle in terror. Even if, in his panic, he had mustered enough strength to break free, it would have been too late. A swinging motion by his handlers launched him down a steep and barren incline.

Headfirst, he skidded, arms outstretched, palms pressed against the gravelly soil in vain attempt to stop his slide. The incline was steepening; nothing appeared in his path that would keep him from being smashed on the floor of the valley below.

"God help me!" he cried aloud, as if to summon a miracle. Then his right hand struck the exposed part of a well imbedded boulder. The impact crumpled his arm under him and granite edges tore his flesh as he slid over the rock. Slowed by the collision, his body slewed

253

sideways, then began again to gather speed. He felt his friction with the ground lessen as the incline steepened to near vertical. He closed his eyes in preparation for a long fall and for the impact he knew would end forever his search for Robin. An instant later his body slammed onto a hard surface.

A shrill call penetrated the monotone roar in his ears as consciousness returned. It was the Bos'un's Pipe, clear and shrill above the noise of the wind and sea as he lay in his bunk aboard the ill-fated "Charlotte". The pipe was calling all hands on deck. He moved to answer and was caught in the talons of pain and wakened to reality. Opening his eyes, he saw the screaming Red-tailed hawk circle down then disappear from view, behind him.

He was on his back. Right arm flung out, supported on a sharp edge that made it ache. He pulled in his arm then dropped it to his side and slowly sent his hand searching outward. His rapid breathing quickened even more as the hand moved only inches before finding the hard, rock edge. He moved his right leg sideways; his foot went down like it slipped off the edge of a table.

His heart banged in his chest as he realized he was on a ledge scarcely wider than himself. "I'm bloody well alive," he mused, "but now what?" Facing to his right he saw only a panorama of distant mountain greenery, not even the top of a nearby tree. He knew then, he was still high above the valley floor. He wondered how high, but the idea of rising to look did not appeal to him at the moment. Turning his head left, he saw that the mountainside rose almost vertically for seven or eight feet, then sloped sharply away. He could see that a climb back over that ground would be impossible. To fully assess his situation he would have to sit up and look around. He felt nauseous and weak at the thought.

His fear of heights plagued him, and he recalled the time he was first sent aloft to reef sail with his father's crew. "Don't look down, lad, 'tis forbidden, 'specially on yer first climb," the Bos'un said. But at sixteen, curiosity can be an overpowering force. And so it was with him, that day. At only twenty feet above the deck he took a downward glimpse and felt the force of gravity increase tenfold as sweaty hands, on weak and shaky arms, held fast for fear the trembling knees would not support his weight. Then, frozen to the yardarm, he felt the gentle firmness of a sailor's arm across his back. "Keep yer 'ead up, me lad," he said, "Pay no 'eed ter what's below. Mind only what yer doin' wi' yer 'ands. Yer not aboot ter fall." He got along all right after that. Still, he never liked the heights, and he never looked down again.

Worming his body close to the inside of the ledge, he fixed his eyes on the granite wall alongside and sat upright. Pain, lying in wait, attacked as he moved, stabbing the small of his back, bludgeoning his head, scalding the raw, scraped areas from the tops of his feet to the palms of his hands. "Goddammit!" he cried out, more concerned at the moment with pain than with his plight. He looked down at his body, caked with dried blood and dirt. Fresh blood was oozing to the surface in areas disturbed by his movement. "Goddammit! he repeated, "I'm a raw, bloody mess!" Then a proverb of his father's came to mind: "Your pity may be balm to another, but 'tis poison to thyself."

Looking forward over his feet he saw that the rock ledge narrowed and dissolved into the cliff only a few yards away.

With sudden courage he turned his head right and took the forbidden look down. His fears were confirmed as he glimpsed a sparse scattering of large trees on rocky ground too far below to judge the distance. Gripped by fear, he grunted as visceral muscles spasmed and squeezed him violently. He felt like he was falling and sucked air through his teeth. Lungs labored to expand against his rib-cage, now contracted and inflexible, ready for imagined impact with the ground. Taut neck muscles resisted as he faced the mountain and waited for the illusion to pass. His body trembled as shock and fear joined forces.

He tried to clear his head and dismiss the fear; he knew he must if he were to survive. The sun began to warm him as its rays chased the mountain's shadow from the ledge, and he wondered if survival was possible from where he lay. He wondered what was behind him. Excited by the thought that where he had not yet looked, might be the route to survival, he began the painful task of turning over.

Slowly, he rolled his body onto his left side and up against the mountain, then skidded himself over already tortured flesh onto his stomach. He was glad for the pain, for it seemed to diminish his terror. He raised his head just as the hawk, with a fearsome screech, flew at his face. Reflexes turned and ducked his head from the onslaught. The movement saved his eyes as savage talons ripped an ear and gouged his forehead at the temple.

"You bloody feathered bastard!" he yelled, lying flat now, face down, head covered by hands and arms. Blood trickled into the corner of his eye; it gushed from his ear down his forearm, and puddled at his elbow. His body flexed in tension as he waited for another attack. Long minutes later it had not come. He relaxed and lay quietly until the blood stemmed its flow.

Cautiously, he raised his head and studied the area in front of him. His morale surged as the ledge appeared to continue up the face of the canyon wall. Afraid to stand, he moved on raw hands and knees, daring only to look straight ahead.

Slowly, inch by inch he crawled, brushing stones from the path as best he could. Every pebble under the raw flesh of his knees created shocks of pain he tried to ignore. "Keep going," he told himself. "Stop and the pain will be worse when you start again."

The ledge narrowed gradually until his right side began to scrape the rocky wall. A jutting rock struck his shoulder, tipping him slightly toward the edge. His stomach spasmed and he felt as though he was falling. Dropping to his belly, he clutched at the ground, angry at this fear he couldn't overcome. "Jesus, give me strength," he muttered. Defying his fear, he rose again to his hands and knees. His arms felt rubbery. "I can do it," he said aloud. "I *must* do it!" With renewed spirit, he resumed his crawl.

The incline steepened as it approached the top of the cliff. Excitement spurred him now, and he no longer felt the pain. A sharp rise forced him to his belly as he clawed and pulled, and pushed with his feet till he'd reached a small plateau. There, the ledge abruptly ended, still ten feet beneath the rim. Pounding a bloody hand against the ground, he gave in to frustration. "I'm dead! I'm bloody well *dead*!" he shouted to the sky.

He heard nothing more than a squeek before he was struck. It felt like the glancing blow of a rock to the top of his head. He put his hand there and felt warm blood. Glancing up, he saw nothing. A rock, kicked off the rim above him by some animal, he guessed. Then he heard the squeek again; louder, longer, shriller this time. Erect on his knees, he turned toward the sound. The hawk struck him full on the forehead.

He started to fall backward, stiffened and spun his torso in a panic-spurred contortion and fell on his side. His legs slipped over the edge and his body began to follow. Blood ran over his eyes and dripped from his jaw. He felt the edge of the earth grind into his ribs. Desperate fear sped desperate strength to his arms. Slowly, as torn hands clawed and scratched for traction, he pulled himself up, then lay exhausted, his thoughts spinning, flashing by like the numbers on a wheel of chance.

He shook her, though he knew she was dead. "Mum, oh Mum, no, don't be dead!" Scared and crying, he ran from the house toward the apothecary shop at the corner. The chemist there could surely help.

His vision blurred by the cold rain, wind and tears, he didn't see the painter's scaffold hanging at the building's side. It caught him on the cheek beneath the eye and spun him to the ground. For a moment he lay there, stunned, face down and bleeding. Then up, and into the shop he ran and the large, red-bearded man behind the counter quickly moved to meet the bloodied face.

"Good Lord, lad, you've 'ad an accident, I see. Let me just 'ave a look."

"It's not me, sir, it's Mum. She's… she's at home, just lying there. Please help her, Mister Barrett. Hurry, please!"

The voice he heard was not the chemist's, yet for an instant it seemed like a part of a dream. Confused, he opened his eyes and listened, expecting nothing. But there it was again.

"*Hola!* Francisco! On the ledge down there. I will throw a rope to you if you are not too bloody dead to put it aroun' you. An' don' be bashful, eh? There are no *senoritas* up here right now." In a teasing voice, he added, "But one is waiting for you, *amigo*, at Rancho MacLean!"

CHAPTER THIRTY

Gently, Ephram helped Frank sit down, covered him with a blanket, and handed him his canteen. "Robin, she is fine, Francisco, back with her Mama an' Papa, now. So you don't worry no more, eh?"

"Thank God," he croaked, surprised at his hoarseness. "But what happened? How did--?"

"She escape near Kerby, an' come to me. But no more questions, now *amigo*. Drink water firs', then maybe I find some whiskey in my saddle bags to wash it down, eh?"

Looking at the canteen he was reminded of the day Adam brought him up from the beach and revived him on water, a few sips at a time. "Someone's always having to save my bloody ass," he commented. With shaking hands, he tipped the canteen to his lips. He was shivering violently, but the cold water felt good. He could not believe his good luck.

"My God, I thought I was a bloody gonner. How did you ever find me?"

Ephram took a flask from his saddlebag and took a swig.

"I am past here a little when I see this objec' on the road. Now that is something I have seen before, I tol' myself, an' stop to pick it up. Then I hear somebody shout very loud that they are bloody well dead. I cannot believe that someone who is dead can yell so loud. So, as much as I would like to keep what I have foun' for myself, I think I mus' come back to where is this yelling and return it to you, eh?" Reaching into his coat pocket, Ephram took out the Deringer. "I think maybe you lose this little hideaway when you take off your clothes

259

an' try to commit suicide, eh?" Why do you do this, my friend?" Grinning broadly, Ephram sat beside Frank and put his arm around him. "Francisco, I think there is no *Senorita* that is worth jumping from a cliff for, but I mus' say, the *Senorita* Robin come close." He put the Deringer back in his pocket. "I will keep this 'til you have a pocket for it. Now, have a sip of this fine home made whiskey, an' tell me how you get like this, eh? Then we start back, or look for your horse, maybe."

He was still shaking, but he felt warmer now. His spirits lifted, the whiskey even tasted good. He was brief with the telling, and turned toward Ephram when he'd finished. Ephram started to speak when Frank saw them.

"Ephram, look! Jesus, a whole bloody tribe coming up the road!

Dios mio! But wait. They do not attack in this way. See, the leader raises his hand, eh?"

"Don't trust the beggers, or we'll both be over the bloody cliff."

The leader, an elderly man with a broad, leathery face, and wearing a fur hat, spoke: "White brothers, I am called Schonchin, Chief of the Modocs. We come in peace. We come to find the one some of my sons mistook for an enemy of our people. They think he might still live, though he is gone from the place where he fell and was last seen."

Frank spotted MacIver with Crazyhair leading him. The other two were there also. He felt the heat of anger, but sensed that they really were there to try to make amends. Still, he could not restrain himself from blurting out: "I'm the one your bloody sons tried to kill! I would have died on that stinking ledge if my friend here hadn't heard me yell. And that's my horse," he said, pointing.

Schonchin nodded and flexed his bulging jaw muscles. "My sons thought you lie because you try to run from them. We found letter in saddle pockets that show you do not come this way to kill Modocs. We come back now to make right of wrong, too late to bring you up from mountain, but give you back horse and guns and clothes. I am glad you live. I can see you are hurt, and offer you--and friend--safety of our camp, and our shaman, who will put healing salve to your wounds."

Before Frank could answer, the one called Captain Jack handed him his clothes. "I too am glad you live. It would be my shame if you had died. I should have known you were a friend because you did not shoot us like dogs. I will be your friend forever."

Big Charlie came forward with Frank's guns, followed by Crazyhair with MacIver. "You are good," said Big Charlie, a worried look on his face. "We be friends now? Crazyhair too?"

Frank nodded. "Good friends. All of us good friends now," he said, and their faces registered broad grins that left no doubt as to their sincerity.

Frank turned to Ephram with a questioning look. "What do you think, Ephram?"

"There is much daylight left, Francisco, an' I know you are anxious to see the *Senorita*, but I don't think you are in the condition to ride, eh? How do you feel?"

"Like I'd been whipped and keel-hauled, but--"

"Then I think we mus' go to the camp for the medicine, before starting the ride back, *Amigo*. Without something on the raw places, you will have much pain and maybe infection, eh? Besides, the way you are skinned off, if you get back too soon I think you will have to delay the wedding because of whether."

"Weather? What's that go to do with getting married?"

Ephram grinned. "Whether or not you can make love, my frien'."

CHAPTER THIRTY-ONE

Esther Hogan watched from the kitchen window as her husband staggered drunkenly out of the barn and weaved his way to the house. It was hardly noon, and he was drunk already, as he had been frequently since Frank Ross shot Carl, and the thumb from Cy's right hand. She heard him stumble on the steps to the back door, and curse at Billy.

"Lemme alone, dammit. Jus' git outta my way."

"I was jus' tryin' to help yuh, Pa."

"Don't need your help... *kid,*" he snarled.

She couldn't tell which loss Cyrus had taken harder: that of Carl, or of his thumb. He hadn't been the same since that day. He ignored Billy, acting as if he weren't his own, except when there were chores to be done. Cyrus kept the hand heavily bandaged, even though it was healed. "Still hurts," he explained. Protects it case I hit it on somethin'." Well, it sure kept him from doin' any work.

Cyrus stumbled into the kitchen and plopped himself heavily in a chair at the table. "Why ain't my dinner ready, woman?"

"It's about done... another minute or so. You come in early, Cyrus, she drawled. As soon as she said it, she knew she shouldn't have.

"So it's my fault dinner ain't ready, that it?"

He looked at her with a contempt she could not understand. She'd seen it often, and it always scared her.

"No, 'tain't your fault. 'Pears the oven's a bit slow."

"An' who's fault's that, I wonder?"

Ignoring the comment, Esther opened the oven door a crack and peeked at the pork pie. "Crust's a-brownin' now, Cy. Be ready in a minute. It's your favorite." She took corn bread from the warming oven and put it on the table with a crock of whipped honey-butter and a pitcher of milk, then went to the back door and opened it. "Wash up, Billy," she shouted, "Dinner's ready."

With the pork pie served, Esther sat down and mumbled a brief prayer as Cyrus, his mouth full of corn bread, ignored the ritual and served himself some pork pie.

"It's good, Ma," commented Billy.

"Crust ain't done 'nough," said Cyrus with a look at Billy.

"I think it's perfect," the boy said.

Cyrus stopped a forkful of food before it reached his mouth and glowered at his son. "You keep your dumb opinions to yourself, yuh hear?"

"I guess I did hurry it a bit," said Esther, "Your Pa's right, Billy."

"Damn right, I am."

Ashamed for the betrayal of her son's defense of her cooking, she looked quickly away from the hurt in his eyes, satisfied she had appeased her husband enough to ask a favor of him--what *he* would consider a favor, anyway.

"Cy, they's some things I be a-needin' in town. I think a few dollars would cov--"

"No!" he snapped. "I mean, ain't no use discussin' it. The wagon's busted an' I ain't been able to get it fixed on accounta my--yuh know damn well why I cain't work on it!" He glanced at Billy then stared down at the table top. "If Carl was here, he could fix it, by God." he said in a low voice.

"I could fix it, Pa, if you'd tell me what to do. I could be your right hand, Pa."

"Shut up, Billy," ordered Cyrus. "Yuh cain't even saw a board straight."

"I don't need the wagon, Cy. Missus Beeman, uh... Rilla, came by this morning an' offer to ride me in with her, this afternoon."

Cyrus dropped a piece of corn bread on his pork pie and wiped his mouth with the bandage. "Missus Beeman, eh? An' jus' what the hell she come here for in the first place? I ain't friends with him no more."

"Jus" bein' neighborly, Cyrus. She said the MacLean girl escape from the men that raid their place an' made off with her, an' they's all daid now... the men, that is. She's back home with her folks ag'in. Rilla said she was a-goin' in town, an' would like if I could come along. She'll be by about one, Cy, an' I--"

"Shut up! You ain't a-goin' nowheres. Now, did she say anything about that murderin' Ross bastard? What'd she say about him?"

She hadn't wanted to mention Frank Ross to her husband, knowing the wrath it caused whenever Cyrus thought about him. "She jus' said someone was a-tryin' to find him to tell him the girl was found."

Cyruses eyes narrowed and his face took on a sneer. I'll say someone's tryin' t'find him. I bet there ain't a gunman west a' the Cascades that ain't lookin' for the son-of a-bitch."

Esther had an odd feeling about asking, but did anyway, trying not to sound suspicious. "Why? How do you know that, Cy? "

"Cuz I put the word out I'd pay two-hunnert dollars ta the man that kills Ross an' brings me the hunk a' his face with the scar on it, as proof. Whatta yuh think a' that, Missus Hogan?"

Shocked by her husband's admission, she struggled to gather her thoughts enough to say anything. She suddenly felt very frightened. "Cyrus, that's... that's..." Stammering for words, she looked at Billy, staring at his Pa, his mouth open, eyes wide. "Leave the room, Billy, right now. Your Pa's been a-drinkin' an' jus' make that up. Go on now, while I --"

"I ain't makin' nothin' up, yuh stupid bitch." Rising from the table, he grabbed the back of Billy's chair and jerked him away from the table. "Yeah. Get outta the room, Mama's boy. An' don't never tell nobody what I said, or I'll bury you alive, yuh hear?"

Without answering, Billy ran from the room.

"Cyrus Hogan, that's a terrible way a' talkin' to your son." She was shaking, her voice unsteady, and she was frightened. "Cyrus, if you... I cain't believe--"

"Listen, yuh brainless ol' bitch," Steadying himself with Billy's empty chair, Cyrus seemed now to be more under the influence of the whiskey, than when he'd first staggered into the house.

"Stop it, Cyrus! Stop a-usin' that kinda talk on me."

"Shut your mouth an' listen, woman, yuh might as well know I'm gonna wipe the area clean a' them MacLean's, one way, or 'nother. Them sons-a-bitches I hired bungled the job, but I mean to *get* that stinkin' squaw man an' his tribe." He was wild eyed and raving now, his voice rising with each word. "I ain't gonna rest 'til I piss on his grave. Yuh hear me, woman? Not 'til I piss on his grave!"

She was crying now, unable to believe what she was hearing. "Please, Cy, you cain't mean what you're sayin'."

But he went on like he'd never heard her. "I'll find them that took care of the Wiggins' for me. Yeah, they even made it look like injun's done it."

Her hands on her ears, Esther was nearly hyterical with shock and disbelief. Oh, Cyrus, for the sake of God, tell me you jus' make this up, *please*!

"Make it up? How yuh think we got this place after that punk over bid me at the bank sale? Wise up woman, yuh don't get nothin' in this world 'less yuh fight for it."

The reality of the situation had a calming effect on her near hysteria. "Oh my God, Cyrus, that ain't a honest fight for somethin', that's murder." Collapsing into her chair at the table, she laid her head on her arms. "Oh God," she sobbed, "I cain't stay in this house... I cain't stay here. God help us."

She heard the thumping against the floor and looked up. Cyrus, still hanging on to Billy's chair with his good hand, was banging the legs on the floor, staring at her in a frenzied sort of way that scared her.

"You callin' me a murderer?" He slammed the chair hard against the floor. "You callin' me--your own husban'--a murderer cuz I want a good life, away from savages an' other trashy folks? Are you? Speak up, damn you!"

She was shaking so violently she didn't know if the words would come out. "Yes! Yes... you are... a murderer!"

His movement was so sudden she nearly went over backwards in her chair as she drew back from the one he smashed down on the table top. Food, glass and milk splattered in all directions.

Wiping milk from her eyes, she didn't see it coming, and something struck a hard blow on her right cheek. "Bitch!" was all she heard him say.

Stunned, she saw blurred movement of something in Cyruses hand. Covering her face with her hands, she heard Billy's voice.

"Stop hitting Ma! Stop hitting her!"

"Billy," she cried, rising, taking her hands from her face. As she did so, she was hit again, alongside the right eye. Falling back against the chair, she heard a shot as she and the chair went over. Unable to see clearly, she tried to get up, but tangled in the chair legs and fell back. Near panic, she cried out, "Billy! Oh my God, what happen?"

"Ma, are yuh all right Ma?" He was crying.

She felt his hands on her shoulders. Her vision began to clear.

"Ma, are yuh all right?"

She put her hand on his. "Yes, I'm all right." But her cheek throbbed and her eye hurt, and the pit of her stomach was knotted in fear. "Billy, what happen? Where's... ?" Then she saw him. As the smell of

267

gunpowder filled her nostrils she saw him on the floor, the chair leg still in his hand. Smoke drifted upward from the revolver's barrel as Billy laid it on the table.

"I shot him, Ma. He was gonna hit yuh ag'in. I had to shoot him, Ma, I had to."

She stood and held her son close. She was calm now. "It's all right, Billy. It's all right." Cyrus was face down, a powder blackened hole in the middle of his back from a Remington .44; he was very still.

"Is he dead, Ma?"

"I think so, Billy, but it's all right." Tears coursed down her cheeks, but they weren't for Cyrus Hogan.

Robin didn't recognize the woman in the buggy with Carilla Beeman. A new neighbor, perhaps. It was mid afternoon and Lillie, still bothered by headaches since the blow to her head, had just laid down.

"Mama, Missus Beeman just drove up. I don't know the lady with her. Are you feeling well enough to see them?" She knew it was a foolish question. The way Papa Mac put it, her mother would be happy to visit if she were lying pierced by a hundred arrows.

Without waiting for an answer, Robin stepped out to the porch to greet the callers. Smiling, she started to speak, when she noticed the black eye and terribly bruised and swollen cheek on the other woman who, it was obvious from her reddened eyes, had been crying. As Robin stood in shocked silence, Lillie appeared and Rilla, her arm giving her companion support up the steps, introduced Missus Cyrus Hogan.

"Esther has been through a terrible ordeal, but she insisted on coming here to speak to you both, and to Adam, if she may."

Flustered, Robin stammered, "I... I'll see if Papa Mac can... that is, if he's awake."

"I'm awake, I heard," he shouted from the bedroom. "Yuh all come in here."

Adam, his right arm bound to his chest, his right leg and left foot in casts, was trying to scoot himself to a sitting position in the bed when they entered. "Stuff that pillow behind me, Robin, an' I'll be jus' fine. An' hello to you, Missus Hogan... my God! What's happened to you?"

Esther Hogan's chin quivered, and her trembling hands twisted a handkerchief as she spoke, slowly, haltingly. On the raw edge of tearful, emotional releases since her ordeal, Robin swallowed hard to hold back tears, and her own chin quivered with emotion while she watched this distressed woman try to find her words.

"I know what I say... ain't gonna right... no wrong that's been done to y'all. I just find out... Cyrus... my husband... hire them... them renegades that cause y'all a world a' hurt an'... an' misery. I am truly sorry. I knowed for a long time... his ways with other folks... was gonna bring misery back on him an' us. It did. But God finally got in his way, an' he ain't gonna cause nobody else no misery." Her voice broke and she turned away weeping, her hands covering her face.

Adam looked up at Carilla. "What's happened, Rilla?" Carilla's Spanish eyes were black pools of water. "Someone shot Cyrus Hogan. Esther says she did. Billy says he did to protect his mother. Anyway, Cyrus is dead. Billy's with Archie, and our hired hand's gone to fetch the Sheriff."

CHAPTER THIRTY-TWO

They were coming up from south of Gold Beach, along the coast trail. The excitement that had been building in Frank for days made him smile when he saw a familiar landmark that told him he was only about a mile from the MacLean ranch--a mile from Robin, and home! He'd been gone two weeks; it seemed longer.

The boat came into view. High on the beach, its canvas cover rippled gently in the soft breeze. Frank pointed out to Ephram where the boat stranded on the sand bar. Moments later, a large white cross came into view at the edge of the high ground overlooking the beach. As Frank talked about it he was suddenly aware that the boat, and the cross marking his father's grave, were both of the same era, but their histories seemed widely divided in time. Four months ago he was part of another era--another world, it seemed--then suddenly he emerged either by accident or destiny, into this present one. Even more incredible, he thought, was his own metamorphosis. What he had been and what he now was, were indeed eras -- if not worlds--apart.

He breathed deeply, inhaling the mixture of ocean beach smells with the fragrance of the coastal evergreens. A bit of both worlds. "I know now, this is where I belong," he said, thinking aloud.

"*Si*, I can understan' that. The way I look at it, the sea is a place without beauty. No trees, no mountains, no horses, eh? An' wors' of all, no *senoritas*."

"There's the MacLean ranch house, Ephram. On up a ways is a path to the house." He could not subdue his excitement. "I wonder if Robin saw us coming?"

"Hold up a minute, Francisco. I will bid *Adios* until tomorrow, my frien'."

"What do you mean, *Adios*? You're coming on up to the house with me. Let's go, *Amigo*.

"No, I do not wish you to be concern with my presence when you rejoin with your... your family. You have much hugging an' kissing an' talking to do with them. I will ride on to town, where I must visit the Sheriff an' tell him what I hear my prisoner Jim Watson tell you about this Hogan fellow. Maybe he will want me to go with him to arrest this man, eh?"

Frank was disappointed. He had been looking forward to having Adam and Lillie meet his friend. "But why can't you just -- "

"I am sorry, my good frien', but I will come back an' visit you *manana*. You see, it is the truth that I am a crybaby when I see such happiness. It embarrass me, *mucho.*" He put the spurs to his horse, and shouted back, "*Hasta manana,* Francisco. *Adios hasta luego, mi amigo.*"

"Ephram, wait! Archie Beeman's is the next ranchhouse up the road. Stop an' tell them I'm back, *por. favor.*"

Ephram looked back and waved. "Aye aye, sir," he shouted. His teeth flashed in a broad grin.

MacIver seemed to know he was home and needed no urging to gallop up the short hill to the house. He had reached the crest when Frank saw her and was on the ground and running up the steps before the dust cleared from the horses sliding stop.

Enclosed in his arms, she was crying, choking back sobs. "Oh... oh Frank, I'm... I'm so glad you're back."

"Robin," he whispered, "I was afraid I'd lost you." Kissing her, he tasted the salt of her tears, or was it his own? He hugged her tightly, as though to reinforce the feeling that she was again part of his life.

Suddenly she took her arms from around him, and turned her face away. "Mama and Papa Mac are anxious to see you, too."

Puzzled, he wondered why she broke their embrace so quickly. Or was he just imagining things? Maybe it was the odor of the Modoc salve. He could use a bath, too, he decided. Still, he wondered.

The rest of the afternoon and evening was so festive that Frank gave no more thought to the incident. Carefully avoided by everyone, was any mention of Robin's ordeal. Ephram had related to Frank what she'd told him, as to how Seven Feathers had killed Rollo Davis, and that she had managed to get the Indian's knife and escape after stabbing him with it.

Robin seemed happy, but displayed none of her normal exuberance. In a moment alone with Frank, Lillie tried to explain Robin's manner as being "sad-happy"; the result of not quite being over her terrible experience. Frank accepted that and told of some funny experiences he'd had on his search. In most cases he made humorous those which had not seemed funny at the time. He didn't mention his encounter with Harvey Slauson, and saw no reason to after learning what had happened to Cyrus Hogan.

Still, sleep didn't come easily to Frank that night, in spite of the best meal he'd eaten in two weeks, the scotch whisky he'd enjoyed with Adam, and the comfort he felt at being with those he loved. He had once again been disturbed at Robin's evasiveness when he suggested they be married right away. However, there had been comfort in her words to him as they parted at the close of the evening. She kissed him with a fervor that surprised him--and pleased him as well--then as she hugged him, and with her head against his chest she said: "Frank, I love you more than the eagle loves to fly; more than grass loves the dew; and like the spider without her web, without you I will die." Then she ran off to her bedroom.

It was the pounding that woke him, then Lillie's frantic call: "Frank, wake up! Robin not in her room. I hope she with you, Frank.

Please tell me truth, I'm afraid."

"My God!" were the only words he could muster as he sprang to the door and let Lillie in.

It was early daylight, but no lantern was needed to see that Lillie was distraught. "I hope she was here with you, but I see no. Oh Frank, I am afraid she maybe do something bad to herself. You must look for her. Please, put clothes on while I tell you why I am afraid."

As tears rolled down her face, Lillie told him that Robin had been raped and was afraid she was pregnant, and was more worried each day. "Yesterday, before you come back, Robin say she cannot face you if she carry other man's child. Now she is gone and I am afraid what she do. Please hurry to find her, Frank. Look along beach to Lookover Point, a place she like to go. Hurry, she not gone long. Bed not cold when I check."

Frank's mind was racing along with his feet as he ran down the hill to the beach. He knew the place Lillie had called Lookover; it was really Overlook Point. A rocky spit of land half a mile up the beach, it jutted into the surf and rose about a hundred feet above it. Several times they stood there watching the sunset. It was one of her favorite spots.

Her parting words, "… without you I will die," haunted him. Her evasiveness about getting married, her "sad-happy" behavior, all understandable now.

He looked for footprints along the wet sand as he ran, but saw none.

With legs and lungs aching when he reached Overlook Point, he scrambling up the hill, shouting her name again and again. As he approached the point's plateau, he felt a sinking sensation as he saw she wasn't there.

With a terrible, ill feeling in the pit of his stomach, he walked slowly toward the edge. A small, beaded deerskin bag lay at his feet. Picking it up, he smelled the jasmine fragrance and knew it was hers. "Oh Robin, no!" he cried. All his fear of heights and falling was forgotten as he went to the edge and looked down at the surf breaking on the rocks below. "Don't let it be, God," he said, scanning, searching, hoping to find nothing, fearing the worst. "Don't let it be."

Then he saw her. Off to his right, huddled near a rock away from the splashing surf, she seemed to be digging in the sand. He called and his voice broke with emotion. She looked up, and waved.

Running to her, he seemed never to have had so much energy. He seemed to fly down the hill. She ran to him as he approached, and they embraced, kissing as though they had just found each other.

Choked with emotion, it was a moment before he could speak. "Thank God you're all right. Never am I as scared as when I think I've lost you. Your mother's in a panic too. What are you doing here?"

"Getting rid of my fears."

"Your fears? Well, you may have gotten rid of yours, but you surely frightened those who love you. Why were you digging in the sand?"

Robin held out a white, opaque stone. "This is a moonstone. Chinooks believe they are made from the tears of fear and sorrow. For each of their fears, they find a moonstone. And for each fear they overcome, they throw a moonstone into the sea, so the fear will not return."

Resting her head against Frank's chest, she went on in a lowered voice: "Early this morning I awoke and found that something I had feared, I need not fear anymore. Then, as I lay there, thanking God, the other fears I had seemed needless to me. So I came here with my bag of moonstones and, one by one, cast my fears into the ocean."

She paused, and looked up at him, her blue eyes shimmering with tears about to overflow. "I can tell you now why I was so strange last night, especially about getting married. You see, one... of the men..." Her voice wavered and the tears spilled over.

Frank held her tight. "Please don't torture yourself any more. Your mother told me this morning what you were going through. It's over now, and I'll never think of your ordeal as a reason not to love or want you, only as a reason to thank God I have you back."

Kissing her forehead, he stroked her hair as she clung to him a long moment before speaking.

"I'm glad I found this moonstone, for now I have another fear to cast away."

"And what is that?"

"The fear that you wouldn't want me anymore."

Finis

EPILOGUE

STORMS

Dark clouds and rain-filled winds,
Dismal and depressing,
Seem to hide Satan
In their cloak of darkness.
A storm embroils,
Twists and tangles
Limbs and minds.
Then Sunlight throws the cloak aside;
We see not Satan
But behold,
A rainbow lifts our hearts!
And from the storm
Springs hope for life…
A glory renewed.
Wait out the storm;
Look for the rainbow.
For with the storm
God challenges the Soul.

©By Alton M. Barlow
August 4, 1986

ABOUT THE AUTHOR

Alton Murray Barlow was born in California and graduated from North Hollywood High School. As a member of the U.S. Marine Corps Reserve, he was called to active duty in 1941. While on active duty he won appointment to the United States Merchant Marine Academy at King's Point, N.Y. As part of his training, he sailed as a Cadet (midshipman) on a Merchant ship in 1942 delivering war supplies to allied combat forces in the Western Pacific. He graduated from the Academy in 1943 licensed as a Third Mate, and was simultaneously commissioned as Ensign in the Naval Reserve and ordered to active Navy duty. For the next two years he served as a ship's officer with the U.S. Pacific Forces during eight invasions of Japanese held Islands.

Upon acceptance into the regular Navy in 1946, he was sent to the University of Idaho to complete degree studies in mathematics and subsequently was assigned to Navy flight training. Upon completion of training his first assignment as a Naval Aviator was to a carrier based fighter/attack squadron and during the Korean War he flew eighty-five combat missions from USS Essex (CV 9).

After retiring from the Navy in 1966 at the rank of Commander, he was employed by Hughes Aircraft Company as a weapons systems engineer. He left Hughes in 1978 and moved with his family to Grants Pass, Oregon where he studied history of the Pacific Northwest at Rogue Community College and worked part-time as a journalist for the "The Southern Oregon Weekly Review."

As an FAA Certified flight instructor, he taught private flying students in Southern California and served with the Civil Air Patrol in Oregon.

His wife of forty-four years passed away in 1987; he married in 1996 and moved to Virginia. His present interests include writing, skeet shooting and serving as a Docent at the renowned Mariner's Museum in Newport News.

Printed in the United States
76299LV00003B/391-411